The Bard of Souvac

Tony Bishop

ISBN 978-1-64670-297-8 (Paperback)
ISBN 978-1-64670-298-5 (Digital)

First Edition

Covenant Books, Inc.
11661 Hwy 707
Murrells Inlet, SC 29576
www.covenantbooks.com

Dedicated to my dear wife and children for their
support and belief in me through the years.

Acknowledgements

Special thanks to my daughter Brinn for her willingness to help me with art concepts for this adventure.

Chapter 1

The heavy blackness of a moonless night had closed over the town of Souvac, when the man stepped from the cover of the King's Forest. A storm had been building throughout the early evening, threatening to unleash its fury. Suddenly a lightning bolt burst overhead, revealing the man's six-foot-plus frame wrapped in a heavy, travel-worn cloak. His features—except for a neatly trimmed, black beard—were mostly hidden by the hood of his cloak. His piercing gaze fell across the clustered lights of the large town. His deep voice overpowered the rising wind as he spoke, "Now I finish it once and for all."

As he started his descent, a strong wind blew in behind him, bringing with it a spring storm the likes of which hadn't been seen in the land in over a century.

*****

The Traveler's Inn was full that night, entertainers, merchants, and craftsmen were in Souvac for the one hundred years of freedom celebration.

Many of the townsfolk gathered to hear the tales of the visitors and partake of the innkeeper's famous beef stew. Haven was a middle-aged man with short, dark-brown hair, a strong jaw and ready smile. His less-than-average height and recent increase in size around the midsection caused some to think he was a pushover. However, more than one young man had found this to be an inaccurate assumption of the fiery innkeeper.

"Come on, Erick, you've been talking about that barmaid for the last three days. I dare you to smack her on the rump it might get you a date," Eben challenged.

Erick was new to Souvac, but like most young men in town, he was immediately infatuated by the beauty of Haven's daughter, Avalon. The only problem was, he did not know the beautiful barmaid was Haven's daughter or the risk he was about to take. Thus he willingly took Eben's challenge. Avalon passed by the two men, and Erick's hand swung toward Avalon's voluptuous hind end. However, contact was never made as Haven's fist collided with Erick's unprepared nose. The young man dropped to the floor, darkness enveloping his vision. A second later, Haven's left fist, and possibly deadlier, connected with Eben's right eye. He too slumped to the floor consciousness unceremoniously driven from his head.

"Do you think these idiots will ever learn?" Haven asked rubbing his fists.

"Dad, you shouldn't hit them so hard. I swear you're going to kill somebody one of these days."

"Well then, they shouldn't come looking for trouble." Haven reached down, grabbing each man by the tunic. "I'll drag their sorry behinds to the back room."

"Just be a little more careful, you might really kill somebody one day," replied Avalon, who continued serving tables.

Townsfolk were still crowding into the inn's common room, as Haven dragged the unconscious men to the back room. Conversations continued as the town was slowly covered in the blackness of descending night. The crowd was momentarily silenced when powerful winds suddenly rattled the windows and door, while rain thundered against the walls and roof. Those few that came in after the storm settled in had the door blown out of their hands as soon as they lifted the latch and could only close it with the help of other patrons. With the inn filled to capacity, it was as light and merry inside as it was dark and stormy outside.

A young man richly dressed, with dusty-blond hair and crystal blue eyes, was listening to the people of Souvac as they spoke among themselves.

"I'm just saying," whispered a red-bearded man to a small group of locals. "Things haven't been too wonderful lately. These council members are taxing us to the point of death."

"I hear they are going to take up residence in the castle. My boy works as a page running messages for those worthless council members," said a balding man.

"If you ask me, things would be better under the rule of Souvac. At least then we always had gold coming into the kingdom. Now the only time anything happens here is when we celebrate this cursed anniversary," replied a wrinkly-faced man.

"Excuse me," the young blond man said. "I couldn't help overhearing your conversation about the council. I am new in town and…"

"See!" The red bearded man slammed his half full mug of ale on the wooden table. "I'm new in town," he stated in a mocking tone. "This used to be a kingdom, not just a town."

"I am sorry, I did not mean to insult anyone." The young man raised his palms in a gesture of conciliation.

"Oh, never mind, Red. Ask what you like," stated a large, burly man joining the group.

"Yes, I just wondered what is happening here. I was told that Souvac was ruled by a council who worked with the people to improve the living conditions for all here."

"I'll tell you what is happening," stated the oldest man in Souvac, joining the growing group. "Many years ago, King Bowen left for some reason, leaving the rule of the kingdom in the hands of nine families. They were meant to hear the voice of the people and work to make Souvac better than it had been under the true kings. However, their children and children's children became corrupt, loving the position, power, and gold above the people. So they have done what Souvac did and ruined us all once more."

"I wish we had a king like Bowen and Tean," said the burly man.

"Hear, hear," replied the group in unison.

The group continued to discuss the plight of the kingdom, and the young man listened intently.

Several minutes later, one of the older men in the group spoke out, "Alas, they have complete power now, and there is nothing that can change it." At this he raised his mug, draining it of the remaining ale.

"Aye," said the group, raising their individual mugs and, following the old man's lead, drained their own. After this, the group slowly dissipated into smaller clusters.

The evening carried on, and many of the craftsmen, merchants, and entertainers went up to their rooms. With their departure, the common room grew quiet as those not sleeping at the inn knew they would soon have to venture into the still-raging storm to go home. The door had remained closed for nearly three hours since the last group entered. So as a blast of cold wind and rain blew in, everyone looked up wondering who this could be.

A man walked in and closed the door with ease, in spite of the still-howling wind. Lightning flashed outside the windows, and muffled whispers around the inn were heard as new conversations about this strange man began. All eyes were on him as he surveyed the room. When his eyes fell on Haven, the stranger's powerful voice sliced through the whispers.

"A table by the fire if you please?"

Seeing a man not to be trifled with, Haven quickly began clearing a small table by the fire that had recently emptied.

When the man was seated a few moments later, the innkeeper looked under the cloak's hood at the man's face and was drawn into his ageless, forest-green eyes. A twinge of recognition tugged at Haven's memory. He had heard of or met someone with eyes like this before.

"Have I met you before, sir?"

"I have not been in Souvac for many years," replied the stranger. "The last time I was here, your father was just a child."

Haven's eyes widened in shock as memory came rushing back to his aging brain. He stepped back as if he had been punched in the face. "You are him—or he. You are the Bard of Souvac!"

The silence in the inn deepened further, as those still present watched the exchange between the two men.

"Yes, and I am here to finish the story of Souvac once and for all." Power and trepidation filled his words.

"What is it you will finish exactly?" asked a blond-haired young warrior two tables away. He was dressed in polished armor and wore a large sword on his left hip. A bright-blue cloak rested casually on his shoulders buckled with ornamental clasps of a white bear to his armor. He was known as the greatest swordsman and warrior in Souvac, often adventuring to other lands.

The Bard looked at the man, taking in his appearance and sizing him up. "I will tell you once I have eaten. Until then, continue as you were," said the Bard with a quiet force that demanded obedience. The whispered conversations from before the Bard spoke resumed, this time as excited chatter about this new guest's mysterious words.

Haven was quick about bringing the stew, along with his finest house ale, to the Bard. "Begging your pardon, sir. I was told by my grandfather and father about the Bard of Souvac, but they never gave me a name to go with the face."

"There is no name for the face. I am merely the Bard of Souvac. Now leave me in peace for a time."

The blond-haired warrior who had spoken earlier was talking to Avalon. The two had known each other from childhood and spent many years as best friends.

"He doesn't look old enough to have known your grandfather as a child. He can't be more than forty years old."

"If the stories are as true as Haven says they are, then that man did know my grandfather and great-grandfather," replied Avalon, unconsciously sweeping her auburn hair from her face.

"You really want me to believe this man was not only alive at the time Souvac and his knights disappeared but is alive today, looking no older than Egin the blacksmith?"

"Yes," replied Avalon as she cleared the table. "My grandfather told me stories about him. He came here frequently in the years following King Souvac's disappearance. He would tell the tale of what happened and of great treasure kept at the very heart of the King's Forest. He also said there would come a day when a rightful king would return and bring prosperity back to the land. Then we would truly have freedom again, like that which was had when the great King Elam ruled." She finished wiping the table with a rag.

"If there is great treasure at the heart of the forest, then why hasn't anyone ever claimed it?" asked the blond warrior. He stood just over six feet tall, with his hand resting casually on the decorated pommel of his great sword. His well-muscled shoulders flexed under his tunic, and he carried a look of disbelief on his handsome face. Those who lived in Souvac knew this man and knew he was a great swordsman and adventurer despite his mere twenty-four years.

"Because it is already claimed," replied the Bard, his deep voice cutting into the young man's moment.

"Perhaps it needs to be reclaimed." The young warrior was obviously trying to regain his position in this fight of words.

"Perhaps, and what is your name, boy?" The Bard ate as he waited for the answer.

"I am Koyne Dale, the greatest warrior in all of Souvac."

A few cheers and whistles came from the depleted crowd.

"Well, Koyne Dale, boy warrior, how will you claim this treasure?"

This remark from the Bard sent an angry flush of red across Koyne's scowling face.

"Before you do something regretful, listen to me. I have traveled the world for one hundred long years and have finally found an answer I have sought. You, Koyne, are actually one piece of that answer."

The Bard's wry smile and unexpected words had Koyne's jaw falling slightly, even as he tried to keep a stoic expression on his face.

"I seek three men to go with me into the heart of the King's Forest. For it is nearly time for the treasure to be, as you say, claimed. Of course, there is the simple matter of destroying its immortal guardians. I rejoice that a strong young lad like you will be with me on this potentially perilous endeavor. However, before anyone else volunteers," he looked straight into Koyne's eyes, "I must tell you what awaits us."

Koyne shifted slightly, as did all still gathered at the inn, awaiting to hear the Bard's tale.

"This tale begins with the childhood of King Souvac, then known as Coran Cavous. Coran's parents were wealthy landowners and friends of the great King Elam. Elam's son, Prince Tean, became friends with Coran, and as a friend to the prince, Coran would spend weeks at a time at the castle learning with Tean everything that a king would need to know in order to rule. As they grew older, they were as close as any two brothers ever had been, and King Elam was like a second father to Coran.

"When the boys reached the age of twenty, problems began. You see, Coran fell in love with Tean's betrothed, a beautiful maiden named Aislyn. She had hair as yellow and soft as corn silk, eyes as blue as the sky, and the face of an angel. She was one of the finest women I had ever seen, for even in death she retained her beauty. She loved Tean as deeply as a woman can love a man and cared for Coran as though he was her brother. Months passed as Tean and Aislyn followed the royal courting rituals. All the while, Coran fell deeper and deeper in love with Aislyn. During this time, jealousy and hatred found their way into his heart. He started to resent Tean and the king. He felt that in some way, both men had wronged him. King Elam had witnessed this change from a distance and warned Tean, but always the loyal friend, he told his father that Coran was as a brother and all would be well. King Elam remained skeptical.

"The week of the wedding feast, Tean found his friend alone with Aislyn in the castle gardens. He hid in the shadows and overheard Coran express his love for Aislyn. She replied that her heart belonged to Tean, and Tean alone. She told Coran that she considered him her dear friend. Tean stepped out of the shadows upon hearing Aislyn's reply. Coran looked at him for a brief second, loathing burning in his eyes, before running away.

"However, Coran was not ready to give up on his obsession and snuck into Aislyn's room in the castle the night before the wedding. He again professed his love for her, begging her to run away with him. He promised that he would make her happier than she could ever be with Tean. She again refused, emphatically stating, she did not love him. Disregarding her rejection, he grabbed her in his arms and began to forcefully drag her away. Aislyn, gripped with fear, began screaming for help.

"Unable to sleep, King Elam was walking the halls that night, as he often did. He was just down the hall from Aislyn's room when he heard the screaming. Rushing down the hall, he burst into her room where he saw Coran dragging Aislyn toward the door. Angered, he called for the guards. Coran became enraged, released Aislyn, drew his sword and charged the king, stabbing him through the heart. As the rage drained away and the realization of what he had done entered his mind, Coran looked once at Aislyn, fear and anger visible in his eyes, before fleeing.

"Shortly after Coran had fled, three guards arrived with Tean at their lead. He told them to wait in the hall as he surveyed the scene. Anger and sorrow gripped his heart as he looked upon the face of his murdered father lying just inside the door. Bending down, he gently closed his father's sightless eyes. Aislyn staggered across the room to Tean as soon as she saw him, falling into his arms she told him between sobs what had occurred. Tean gently separated himself from Aislyn and stepped back into the hallway overwhelmed with grief.

"Find Coran, catch him, and execute him for his crimes. Then return his body to me." Anger resonated through Tean's words, in a tone the guards had never before heard from their prince. In his state of sorrow, Tean didn't realize those guards were Coran's loyal friends. They had trained with him, had been knighted together, and he had been their captain.

"They had grown close to Coran over the last several months especially, for he had confided in them as he had fallen into the deep spell of anger, hatred, and jealousy. They had heard the lies he told about the wrongs Elam and Tean had done to him and all those that lived in the kingdom. They had even begun to sympathize with Coran's pain at not being allowed to love Aislyn, just because the king said she was to marry the prince. With all this now racing through their minds, they followed after the fugitive.

"They tracked Coran for hours, finally finding him in a clearing at the very heart of the King's Forest. Seeing their friend scared and alone caused them to hesitate in following the drastic orders of the prince. Their failure to act immediately on Tean's orders started their path of betrayal.

"Coran used his silver-tongue as his friends hesitated, saying he had gone to say farewell to Aislyn, and as he was preparing to depart, the king came in and attacked him. He had merely defended himself, and that was why King Elam lay dead in the bedchamber. He then told them about the evils that Elam and Tean were engaged in. These lies were so convincing that the knights started to question further the goodness of their king and prince. After all, Coran was close to both men and had been deeply involved in their councils. Coran continued weaving lies and planning how they together could make the kingdom even better than it now was. He created pictures of greatness in their minds of how wonderful the kingdom would be with him as king and they as the loyal captains of his armies. The knights started to share their ideas, and the plot to overthrow the kingdom continued in earnest. They plotted through the length of the day, and slowly as the evening shadows fell over the clearing, another shadow fell over their hearts.

"The Evil One had watched as jealousy entered Coran's heart. He then fanned the growing embers of anger to a raging fire of pure hate. He delighted as this pathetic human murdered his king. Watching from his underground lair, reveling in this man's fall, he saw an opportunity to further his work of death and destruction in the mortal world.

"Once the sun had set and a fire had been built, this being of immense power emerged from the trees cloaked in blackness so that his features could not be distinguished. 'Coran, your plotting is in vain, for you do not have the power to complete your plans. However, if you swear fealty to me and an oath of perfect loyalty to each other, I will grant you all that you desire,' the voice, barely a whisper, resounded with death and deception.

"Yet Coran, blinded by his own lies and ambition, was enthralled by the being and asked, 'If we so swear to thee and each other, what will my knights and I be granted?

"'You, Coran, will have Aislyn and the crown, as well as your knights' undying loyalty. Your knights will be known as the greatest warriors and captains of men wherever they go in your service. Not even a full army will stand before the might they will wield.'

"Only after visions of grandeur were fed to their corrupted minds, blinding them further to what they were about to do, did they kneel before the Evil One and swear allegiance to each other and him by his unholy power.

"'Know this, if any of you break the oath of loyalty you have sworn to one another, you will be cursed and imprisoned in this forest clearing for eternity. If you break your oath of fealty to me, you will be destroyed,' said the Evil One as he vanished back into the trees.

"Once he had gone, Coran turned to his three companions. 'Jerec, you have been my faithful friend, you are the strongest and most skilled fighter of us all, therefore I name you my chief captain. Oaran, you have skills with training animals the like of which I have never seen before, and so you will train all the horses for my armies and lead my cavalry. Kell, you are eloquent of speech and keen-minded, therefore I name you my adviser in all things.' Each of the knights bowed their heads and gave thanks to their new king.

"The four men left the forest then, traveling into the southern kingdom where King Garion ruled. They knew they needed a safe place to hide while spying and finalizing their evil designs. Not only would this friendly and prosperous kingdom be their hideout, it would become the first victim of King Souvac's rule.

"Months had passed, King Elam's funeral had taken place, and Prince Tean and Aislyn were married. Tean often wondered during that time what had become of Coran and the knights he had sent after him. He had sent out other search parties, but no one had any information concerning the four men. He worried that he had been too harsh in judgment of Coran and feared all four men might be dead.

"As the months passed, Tean grew into a king much like his father. He even continued the practice of giving audience to the citizens of the kingdom in order to have their grievances heard.

"Coran and his knights knew all the activities of King Tean during this time through underhanded means. With all their plans laid out, the day they had looked forward to finally came.

"Coran went to the castle disguised as a commoner seeking audience with the king. He followed others past the guards stationed throughout the audience chamber. Once in view of Tean, he ran to the dais, upon which the throne stood, and prostrated himself before the king. Guards jumped to the king's side, weapons drawn. Coran sobbed and apologized for what he had done, begging for forgiveness. Realizing his childhood friend and brother was before him, Tean's heart softened. Waving his guards away, he stood and walked down the three steps to his father's murderer.

"'Coran, you were a brother to me, and as such I release you from the death that awaits you. However, justice must be served. I cannot imprison you as law dictates because I love you. However, you must leave my kingdom and never return.' He bent down and took Coran's hand, giving him his life.

"Coran came up on his knees, looking in Tean's face. A wicked smile and look of victory shone in his eyes as he pulled Tean toward him, stabbing him through the heart with a dagger he had concealed in his tunic.

"As Tean fell, Coran took the crown from his fallen body and placed it on his head then turned to face the people gathered in the hall. Several of the king's guards rushed at Coran, but his three loyal knights stood around him, seemingly appearing out of thin air to cut down the charging guards. 'My subjects, I am your king, and any that defy me will find themselves like this man, his father, and their pathetic guards.' Coran looked down at Tean, who was still gasping for breath. 'I am King Souvac now. Your friend and brother Coran is no more.'

"'You will suffer death and eternal damnation worthy of your treacherous actions. My blood will see to that,' said Tean with his dying breath.

"Coran took Aislyn as his wife and prisoner that same night. This kingdom, along with two surrounding kingdoms, fell into eighteen years of sorrow and fear. Eight and a half months following the marriage of Coran, who was now known only as King Souvac, Aislyn had a baby boy. He looked just like his mother and seemed to have none of King Souvac in his countenance. Aislyn named him Bowen and kept him to herself as much as she could, teaching him to be strong and moral, loyal to the ways of King Elam and Tean. The only thing she did not teach him was that he was Tean's son, knowing he would be in mortal peril if this knowledge was shared with him.

"King Souvac taught Bowen all about warfare and how to use all weapons of combat. The knights of Souvac, as they were now called, assisted in teaching Bowen the use of weapons, strategies, and manipulation as well as assassination techniques. King Souvac could see his son had goodness in his heart and might not be corruptible. He often wondered if he could trust his son as he trusted his knights. However, as wicked as Souvac was, he still held some semblance of love for Bowen.

"As the years passed, the knights of Souvac attacked neighboring villages and kingdoms, killing thousands with the king's army. They delighted in murder and plunder. These campaigns made their king wealthy and powerful and allowed them to use the skills enhanced by the Evil One's magic. As Souvac gained greater power, he watched all things that went on around him. He noticed his son Bowen going out among the peasants (for peasants they had become under Souvac's rule) from time to time. They loved and respected Bowen in ways they never had the king. Souvac could see that he did not have the peasants' loyalty. Only fear of him and his knights kept his subjects in place.

"As Bowen neared the age of eighteen, King Souvac began feeling anxious and fearful. His fear and anxiety were so great that he did something he had not done in twelve years. He went to the heart of the King's Forest and called upon the Evil One. That dark creature did not come but sent his witch in his stead. She crept from the trees with ragged breath, clothed in tattered, dirty robes, a crone as ancient as the forest itself perhaps. Her face was white as though it had not seen the sun in centuries. Purple scars stood out on that stark face in horrifying contrast to her skin. Her black eyes gleamed with an unholy light. King Souvac was so repulsed by her that he tried to leave but could not and found himself frozen in place. As she continued forward, the smell of rotting flesh emanated from her bloodstained robes.

"'What do you seek, my king?' she hissed through missing teeth.

Souvac, leaning away, replied, "My son is becoming a man, and I fear him. He is nothing like me and desires not my ways. What shall I do with him?"

"'Your son he is most definitely not. The prince is the son of Tean, whom you murdered. The queen was already with child when you wed her that night.' A smile played at her lips.

"'Why did no one tell me years ago, that I could have had a son of my own?' He looked at the witch, clenching his fists and teeth. 'I will kill Bowen and make Aislyn give me a son of my flesh.'

"'This course of action is ill-advised, my king. Besides, your loving queen saw to it after Bowen's birth that she would never again bear a child,' the hag sneered. 'You have known all along in your heart that he was not yours. You merely tricked yourself into believing you had fathered the child. Now depart from here with your trivial matters, the Dark Master has no time for you, unless…'

"'Unless what?' asked the king, desperate.

"'Unless you desire a child by me. Master would smile on a child between us, since your queen will not carry a child ever again.'

"It was well after midnight when Souvac returned to his castle. He called his dreaded knights to him and began setting forth his plans as he sat in his throne. 'Bowen must die tonight mysteriously. The queen cannot know I had a hand in this,' he said, shaking with anxiety.

"'How should we proceed, my lord?' Jerec hissed, moving closer to the throne, a gleam of anticipation in his hateful eyes.

"'He must die tonight,' Souvac repeated, his voice shaking even more. 'It must look like an accident.'

"'We could take him up to the tower walk. He is always up there. We will throw him off the edge. Make it look like he was up there alone and fell. I will place a bottle of your strongest wine on the wall to enhance the effect/' Kell's black eyes held cold calculation.

"'The bottle must be mostly empty,' replied the king.

"'As you wish,' the knights replied, bowing in unison.

"Aislyn, having become accustomed to spying on the king's councils with his knights, crept quietly to her son's room and slipped inside. It was unusually cool that night, and Bowen was curled up under several blankets.

"Aislyn rushed to his bedside and shook him awake. 'Bowen, wake up! Hurry, my love, your life is in danger!'

"Bowen sat up bleary-eyed and looked at his mother. 'What is it?'

"'There is no time to explain, they are going to kill you.' Her voice was shaking with fear as she looked at her son.

"Bowen came to his feet, grasping his mother's shoulders gently, guiding her to sit on the edge of the bed, 'Calm down, what is happening? You're white as a ghost.'

"'There is no time now. I should have told you years ago.' She looked him in the eyes and softly touched his face. 'Bowen, Souvac is not your father.' Bowen's eyes widened, but he didn't speak. 'You are the son of Tean, son of Elam, the true kings of this land. Souvac killed your father and grandfather. Bowen, I beg you, leave tonight that you may live. They are coming, and I fear I am too late.'

"'Mother, I have suspected for some time now that he was not my father.' As he spoke, an idea came to his mind, and he quickly began putting on his armor. 'Through the years I have listened to the knights' conversations while they trained me, especially when I was young, they were less careful about their words. On one rare occasion, I heard them speak of a powerful oath that they were subject to. This information may protect us both, but you need to go back to your bedchamber before Souvac returns to find you missing.' Pausing, he helped his mother to her feet. 'I will not leave you here to live out your life in misery.'

"That was the last time young Bowen saw his mother in life. As she rushed away, he continued to dress in his armor and weapons. Strapping them in place, he prepared to face the knights. Moments later, the knights opened the door and silently rushed at the sleeping form of Bowen. Pulling back the covers, they grabbed pillows and wadded up blankets.

"'Looking for something?' sneered a voice from a darkened corner. A lamp flared to life, temporarily blinding the knights as they looked for the speaker. Bowen was standing, sword in hand, prepared to meet his attackers.

"'So you were warned of our coming. It is painfully clear who alerted you. I am sure our king will take care of your meddlesome mother once and for all,' said Jerec.

"'You will die tonight, Jerec, unless the curse takes you first,' replied Bowen.

"'You know nothing of the curse.' Fear showed in Kell's black eyes.

"'I asked my father for a birthday gift, didn't he tell you? I asked him if I could replace you three and become his general. He seemed quite pleased with the idea and came up with this plan to be rid of you all.'

"'Liar!' the knights yelled together and rushed at him.

"Bowen was able to defend himself with some difficulty. After all these were the men who had taught him to use a sword. A dagger from his blind side came around in a wide arc and cut his cheek. Bowen beat back his attackers and touched his face.

"'I do know of the curse that will befall you if you betray the oath sworn to the Evil One. You have until sunrise to reach your prison in the forest. By spilling my blood, even this much,' he said, holding up his left hand, blood glinting on his gauntlet, 'you have brought the curse down upon yourselves. I am the son and blood of Souvac, the blood that you swore to protect. Now begone, unless you wish to die by the curse here and now.'

"As these words left Bowen's lips, an ear-piercing scream ripped through the cold interior of the castle. The knights looked at each other, eyes suddenly glowing red. They rushed from the room toward the king's bedchamber. When they burst through the door, they found their king standing near the fireplace covered in blood, eyes staring at nothing, his sword lying on the floor next to Aislyn's body. The fire had burned low, and the morning sunrise was only a few hours away.

"'Aislyn has spied on us for the last time,' said the king, his voice hollow. 'Is your part complete?'

"'It is done,' said Jerec venomously. 'But we will not go alone to the hell that awaits us. You will accompany us. First, however, you will die for your betrayal.' The knights raised their swords.

"'What do you mean by this?' Souvac's attention came screaming back to his knights. 'I am your king, you swore to protect me!' yelled the king.

"'You tricked us and brought the curse down upon us!' yelled the knights as one. In their anger, they rushed the king, each stabbing and slashing at the defenseless man. 'Your son carries your blood, which we spilled, the blood we swore to protect,' Jerec hissed into Souvac's ear as he lay dying.

"Souvac's eyelids rose slightly as he spoke his final words. 'Bowen is no son of mine. He is Tean's.'

"His eyes closed forever as understanding entered the evil minds of Souvac's knights. They looked as one toward the window. It was still dark, but they knew they had much to do before they must be to the King's Forest. They howled in rage at being tricked. They wanted revenge on Bowen, but did not have time to seek it.

"After the knights fled, Bowen found his mother on the floor of her bedchamber. The words 'I am finally free, my son' were written on the stone floor in the queen's blood. It was Aislyn's last message to her son.

"The knights took Souvac's bloody corpse, his crown, and as much of the dead king's riches as they could fit into carts. They then fled toward the forest with as much speed as they could, for the skies over the eastern mountains had begun to lighten. The hooves of their horses thundered; the wheels of the carts sounded like a mighty wind as they raced along behind them. The sun, which chases away all shadows and dark things, had nearly crested the top of the mountains when they entered the forest. Those three foul beings looked back once, cursing the false son of Souvac.

"'Someday we will be free again, and when we are, we will find and destroy your bloodline, Bowen,' vowed the leader Jerec.

"They then traveled to the heart of the forest, taking with them an unlucky young man they had captured moments before on the road. The poor sot tried with all his power to run away, but alas, he was unsuccessful and remains their prisoner to this day. They entered the cursed clearing where they made their oath at the same moment the sun completely cleared the mountains.

"Souvac's knights built a makeshift throne from dead branches to place their king on. Once his body was seated in his high place, they piled all the riches they had brought around his feet and throne. They sang a song of lament for themselves in an evil language forbidden by the world as darkness closed over them. As they finished, the teachers of that song separated from the nearby trees and stepped forward. The witch in her rasping voice approached Souvac's corpse, 'I told you it was folly to go after that child.'

"'Cursed forever are you, knights, unless you use your prisoner wisely,' said the Evil One, pointing at the young man who had lain tied up at the edge of the clearing, paralyzed with fear throughout the day.

"The Evil One and his witch then left, and to my knowledge have never returned to the King's Forest," finished the Bard. Leaning back in his chair, he sipped at his ale.

"How does the tale end?" asked Avalon.

"What do you mean?" replied the Bard.

"You old fool, she means what happened to the knights, and the treasure," said Koyne.

"They remain just as they were, in the clearing in the middle of the King's Forest, waiting for someone to release them," said the Bard matter-of-factly.

Deep silence fell over the room as the crowd pondered the Bard's last statement.

Chapter 2

The silence following the Bard's tale was broken, again by Koyne Dale, "Now, that is a great story. One of the best I have heard in years."

"Thank you," replied the Bard with a smile. "Are you trying to tell us that this is the true story of what happened to Souvac and his knights?"

"Yes."

Koyne sat there open-mouthed for a brief moment. "I have heard different versions, all of which sounded less fantastic and more truthful. For instance, Souvac and his knights were killed in a fight against an invading army. The invading army freed the lands from his rule and reestablished peace. However, Queen Aislyn and her son, Bowen, disappeared from the kingdom shortly after the invasion."

"Really, and who were these great liberators? Where did they go, and why did they leave this land free?"

"Maybe it was King Bareth. Everyone knows Souvac was never able to take Bareth's kingdom," stated Koyne smugly.

"Except, King Souvac never wanted Bareth's kingdom. He saw it as a cold, desolate place not worth the time and effort it would take to overthrow it." Koyne had no response to this last comment. "Perhaps I should tell my own story now and bring you all up to date on the remaining truths of what transpired so many years ago."

"I was nineteen when I left the shallow vale where I grew up in the deep south. Before King Souvac's attacks began, it was a prosperous farming community. You see, even though Souvac had already overtaken and destroyed Garion's kingdom, of which our vale was a part, we in the deep south had not experienced the full evil of King Souvac and his knights. To us what they had done was mostly rumor and stories from travelers, for they never attacked our vale directly. I wanted to know the truth of these tales.

"So I began my journey with a few coins and the ability to tell fascinating stories that entertained the villagers. My parents were humble goat farmers, and I thought I could travel the lands telling tales, earning money with which I could help support them. My father told me it was not necessary to go, but I really wanted to know the truth about Souvac. I wanted to include it all in the tales that I would tell. Oh, how I have come to regret that idea. With these youthful, ignorant thoughts and dreams bouncing around inside my head, I left my home.

"I traveled toward the great north kingdom of King Bareth to tell my tales. Like Koyne mentioned, Bareth's was the only kingdom near Souvac that had not been overthrown. I had hoped to pass close to the kingdom of Souvac in order to learn all I could about it. I believed, as I said before, that information would liven up the tales I would tell as I traveled. As I went from town to town, I asked about King Souvac and his knights. I had become completely mesmerized by the idea of them. With each new tale I heard, I was more desirous to learn the truth. With each town and village I went to, I heard the same things. They were protected by black magic; they had power from the Evil One himself. The horses they rode were as black as darkest night. Souvac and his knights would live and rule forever, for they could not die. The stories became more dire and awful as I found myself in lands that had been fully conquered by King Souvac. However, I maintained youthful skepticism about much of what I had heard, probably more so than you, young Koyne. From all these stories, I created my own story to tell. I believed I had a perfected tale I could tell King Bareth when I left a broken-down inn just south of the original border of the kingdom of Souvac.

"I was in the barren lands, traveling on the Great North Road, the very night the curse came upon the knights of Souvac. I was just a few miles from the crossroads, close to the center of King Souvac's power.

"I had ended my day's journey at the edge of the trees where the road entered the King's Forest, just after sunset. I did not know how deep into the forest the road traveled, but I did not dare enter it at night. I could sense something malicious in the forest. It was bitter-cold, so I built a fire in the middle of the road and found myself unable to sleep. It was as if something was watching me from the depths of the trees. I sat huddled by my fire, praying the light and heat would keep me safe. My firewood ran out a couple of hours before sunrise; suddenly fear gripped my heart. I felt a sudden sense of urgency and knew I had to leave, to get beyond the crossroads. I still feared the forest and could feel something powerful and menacing inside waiting. What it could possibly be waiting for, I couldn't imagine. However, the urgency to get to the crossroads was greater than my fear, so I packed and left before the sun cleared the mountains to the east.

"I was in the northernmost edge of the forest when I heard the first wail, it sounded like a mixture of human and animal, throaty and high-pitched. It echoed all around me, as if it was streaming out of the ground itself, roiling in the air all around, freezing the blood in my veins. The wailing continued rising and falling like the wind; I quickened my pace. I thought I could only be a couple of miles from the crossroads at this point, so I hurried on. I had cleared the forest's edge and could finally see the hedgerow that marked the crossroads a short way off when I heard the thundering of hoofbeats and the rattling of wagon wheels. The wailing and hoofbeats grew louder, and I started running as fast as my legs could carry me. It was then that an intense feeling of pending doom seeped through my body, spurring me on. If I could get to the crossroads I would be safe. I started running harder and faster than I had ever run before. Suddenly there they were directly before me, when I was only feet from safety. I looked directly into the lead knight's eyes and saw my own doom. I ran harder, and he spurred his horse and cart to a frenzied, breakneck pace. As I tried to dive over the hedgerow for safety, a grip like iron pulled me from the air and into a wagon loaded with fantastic treasure. Fear covered me like a blanket, flowing into my very bones, and I passed out.

"When I came to, it took me awhile to realize I was even awake, the surrounding darkness was so thick I couldn't see anything. I heard voices close by, harsh, skeletal-like voices singing. It was a horrible song. I did not understand the words, but I could feel the hate and despair emanating from them.

"It wasn't long before my vision started to adjust to the darkness and I could faintly make out the shadowy forms of three men clad in black plate mail. Before them was a throne made of dead wood. The treasure from the wagons was piled all about the throne, upon which sat the corpse of King Souvac. He sat tall in his gold chain mail with a golden crown on his head, his sightless eyes open and staring. When their song ended, an even blacker shadow detached itself from the trees to my left and approached them. It spoke with a quiet voice that reverberated through my whole body and reminded me of the vilest of things. I tried to press my body into the ground to hide from whatever it was. I lay there hoping that it was all just a horrible nightmare. Then I heard words that caused me to look up at the four evil creatures before me.

"'You pathetic fools! I gave you all you could ever ask for, and yet here you are trapped in this clearing forever," said the vile being, evil flowing from him, filling the clearing, as he stood before the knights. It seemed as if I could see dark, wispy lines of power emanating from him into the ground and into the knights.'

"'We were tricked by Bowen, the royal spawn of Tean and Aislyn,' replied Jerec.

"'I know what happened, worm. Do you think I do not see what occurs around me?' whispered the evil one. Despite the quietness of his voice, the words tore through me like the freezing winds that blew through the White Mountains. He gestured my way, as though he could feel my inner turmoil. 'Why did you take this boy from his journey to Bareth?' asked the dark being.

"'I don't know, Lord Kish. I saw him running, fear burning in his eyes, and a feeling of inevitability washed through me. Here was a distraction from my pain. I saw him the way a cat views a mouse, a victim to be tortured, toyed with, and discarded,' replied Jerec.

"'Do not be as stupid as you have proven up till now. Use him to your advantage,' said Lord Kish.

"'How do we do that, and to what purpose?' asked Oaran.

"'Quiet, Oaran, I am the only one that speaks to Lord Kish. Now that King Souvac is dead, I am the chief captain,"' said Jerec.

"'I would actually like to hear from Oaran as well as Kell, Lord Jerec, for you are not the only one who is cursed here, and it looks as if you might be here awhile due to your treachery,' said the vile Lord Kish, with a silent laugh.

"That was when I noticed the witch. She had been completely hidden in his shadow, but she now stepped forward to speak to the dead king. 'I told you it was folly to go after that child.'

"'Yes, witch, he sees that now,' replied Lord Kish. Turning, he spoke again, 'Lord Jerec, I am not without compassion. I will give you, Kell, and Oaran a way that you may lift the curse that binds you here for eternity. Then you can fulfill that pathetic vow you made upon entering this prison. If three men will swear loyalty to our good king on his throne, they will take your place, and you will all be free. Know this, when three take your place, you will lose all the powers I have granted you. You will be mortal, once again you will be subject to age and death. You are fortunate, indeed, that you captured this young bard, since you need someone to tell the world that you all exist here with that vast fortune.' As Lord Kish said this, he looked over at me. I could see nothing of his face hidden deep within the cowl of his black cloak, but I felt his power wash over me like a raging river. 'Stand, bard, and come here.'

"I rose without wanting to, the bindings falling from my wrists and legs. Under his power I moved to stand before those five evil beings. It felt as though fear itself ran in my veins, yet I didn't—nay, couldn't—shiver or quake with the feeling of it. Instead I spoke, 'What is it you want of me?' It was as if the words were painfully ripped from my throat.

"Lord Kish seemed to smile, though it could not be seen. 'See, knights of Souvac, a willing servant to help you find freedom. I give you power and authority from my realm to create an oath between yourselves and this bard as you see fit. I caution you, choose your oath words well, and use this prisoner wisely. Once your oath is set, I give permission that one of you may escort your prisoner to the edge of this forest. That individual may not step beyond the trees and must return immediately to this clearing upon completion of the task. The witch and I will return when you knights of Souvac are set free.'

"The witch cackled at this statement, high and piercing. I closed my eyes as that cold, harsh sound penetrated my very core. When I opened my eyes, the witch and her master were gone.

"After they had gone, Lord Jerec and his fellow knights spoke together about my fate. I would have fled if my legs would have allowed it; instead I overheard these words.

"'What is it we should do with this bard? How can we cause him to do our bidding?' asked Jerec.

"'Perhaps, my lord, we can endow him with the immortality that we possess until we are set free,' said Oaran.

"'What do you think, Kell?' asked Jerec.

"'My lord, the Evil One told us we must use this bard to find freedom. However, we must use the right wording to trap him in our power and not be tricked again. If you will allow me, my lord, I will make the oath between him and us,' replied Kell. Jerec simply nodded his assent.

"I could hear their plans for me and guessed at what my life might be like after the next few minutes. They turned toward me, and I could see that the one named Kell had taken a place in front of the others, a look of satisfaction on his grim face.

"As Kell drew close enough to me, that I could smell his fetid breath, he asked, 'Do you wish to live, bard?'

"By this time, my fear was spent. I was ready to die if that was their plan. 'I have no wish to die,' I replied. The men before me seemed to enjoy that answer, their mouths twisted into hideous grins.

"'Then we offer you a deal, your life for our lives,' said Kell. 'We will swear an oath between you and us. Our part is that by using the authority given by Lord Kish, the Evil One of the underworld, we will grant you immortality. You will not have to suffer death or sickness while we reside here in this forest. All you have to do for us is travel the lands and tell the tale of which you are now a part. This and no other will be your story. You must tell the story in its truth, as we will rehearse it to you.'

"They then rehearsed for me the tale about Souvac and themselves, their lies, murders, deceits, and conquering. I knew there was something wrong with their version of events, but while they spoke, it seemed that a small ray of light pierced my mind, bringing with it an idea that would give me some measure of advantage over these men, for suddenly, I had a way to get the full truth.

"'When we are freed from our cursed life here in the King's Forest, you will be free of this oath. We are free when three men agree to take our place, standing watch over the corpse of our king and his treasure. You must tell these men that if they travel to the heart of this forest and swear allegiance to King Souvac, they will gain the great treasure that lies here,' said Kell.

"'Is that all I must do? Tell the true tale of the knights of Souvac? I need not force anyone to this fate?' I asked.

"'Oh no, those who swear to us must come of their own free will. For we are all bound by that law, even the great Lord Kish cannot force anything upon anyone,' said Jerec. 'Should this feat take you longer than expected, you must return once every five years to report your progress. What is your answer?'

"'It seems I have little choice in this matter.'

"'Of course you have a choice. Swear your service to us or die. It may not be much of a choice, but it is your free will to choose your fate,' Oaran said with malicious glee.

"'Then I swear an oath that I will do as you have asked of me. I will tell the true tale of King Souvac and his knights, for my life. I will return every five years and report my progress. If any chooses this fate I, and only I, can bring them into this clearing that you may be set free.'

"'And we swear to you, Bard of Souvac, that you will taste no physical illness or death while you are on our errand, until the day that we are set free. However, pain we will allow you to feel, so you do not forget our power over you,' replied Kell.

"'I have one question before I leave on my errand. When you are freed, what will you do?'

"Oaran, who had not said much, spoke up before he could be silenced, 'We will destroy Bowen and rule the kingdom until our lives expire.'

"Jerec quickly backhanded him. 'What we will do is no concern of yours. Now, Oaran, lead the Bard of Souvac out of the King's Forest and start him on his errand.' Jerec looked at me and smiled. 'Now that you are in our service, your name will carry with it a taint of evil and fear.'

"I turned toward Oaran, a feeling of despair creeping into my heart and mind. 'What had I just done?' I thought. A gauntlet-covered hand then grabbed me by the tunic and began forcefully dragging me out of the clearing. The Bard of Souvac. 'Oaran, show him some of our powers as you go so he will understand the position he has just placed himself in.'

"'Yes, Lord Jerec,' he replied.

"I did not know what direction we traveled, but Oaran talked the whole way telling me of the powers they possessed by the grace of the Evil One. He showed me in my mind's eye torturous things they had already done and could yet do, inflicting on me mental anguish. This became their way of controlling me from inside the forest, a way to hurt me far more than any physical pain I would ever suffer. It seemed as though we walked for hours before we came to the edge of the King's Forest. When we arrived, I could see no roads or familiar landmarks.

"'I thought it would be good for you to learn of your powers as well as experience some despair and fear before you get anywhere,' said Oaran.

"'I looked at him and smiled. 'I have stood before the Evil One of darkness, an empty field doesn't frighten me.'

"'You are learning quickly the strength that comes from the powers of Lord Kish.'

"'There is no strength in it, only knowledge that I will be temporarily safe from harm. There is no eternal salvation in darkness, only temporary power, Oaran. You would do well to remember that.

Shouldn't you be getting back to your clearing?' It was not a smart thing to say but somehow it felt right.

"'And you, Bard, would do well not to threaten me.' As his anger swelled, so did that power which he held. His eyes burned with fire, and the next thing I knew, I was waking up at the edge of the forest, the midday sun shining down in my eyes, my head nearly exploding with pain.

"I wandered for several days in a state of awful despair. I would have avoided all people had there been any around. You see, Oaran had set me adrift at the southwest portion of the forest, where there was nothing but empty grassland. As time passed, I began to recognize an innate knowledge of where I was at all times. I learned this was part of my dark gift, bestowed through my oath. I often felt hungry during my first few days of wandering but had no food or cause to eat.

"Six days passed from the time I was left at the edge of the forest, and the time I found my way back to myself. I wandered the empty lands in a despair that I could not shake, but as the days passed, I realized I would never be lost or hungry again. I now held powers from the Evil One, and no matter how temporary they are, they gave me strength. I made a decision to follow the plan that had come to my mind when I made the oath with the knights. I decided to go to the kingdom of Souvac and speak with King Bowen.

"When I arrived, I went straight to the castle to find the new king. He was in the throne room meeting with all the landowners whom he had restored. When I finally got through the questions of the guards, I was allowed to wait for a meeting with the king in the castle atrium. It was surprisingly sunny and warm, considering it was early spring.

"I was brought some refreshment about midday by a servant of the castle. This was the first time in two weeks I had seen food or water. Part of me wanted to tear into it like a wild animal, but the other part of me was hesitant. I wondered if my ability to eat and enjoy food had ended. Hesitantly I sipped at the water. It felt like a cold renewal flowing through my body. I ate the refreshments and found the taste to be more spectacular than anything I had ever eaten. It was like a blessing from some otherworldly being, a feeling came to me: just because I was cursed didn't mean I was forsaken. For the first time in over two weeks, hope entered my heart, as I waited for the king.

"Two hours later, King Bowen entered the atrium. He was very courteous as he addressed me. 'I am sorry, sir, I had an urgent meeting with the landowners. I was told it was important that you see me at my earliest convenience.'

"'Yes, Your Majesty, it is quite important. You see, I am the Bard of Souvac.' The king looked at me a bit confused. 'I have met the knights of your father, King Souvac. They are trapped in the heart of the King's Forest with the corpse of the late king.'

"At that, he interrupted me. "Souvac was not my father, Tean was.'

"'I am sorry, my lord, I did not mean to offend you.'

"'Please don't call me lord, or king, for I am no longer such.' He immediately understood the strange look I gave him. "It is bitterly clear that man cannot rule alone without the possibility of corruption. So I am creating a new ruling government, one of the people that will far outlast any king.' He spoke about this subject for several minutes before seeing my disinterest. 'I apologize. I am passionate about what I am doing. Let us get back to your tale before I get really long-winded. You say these knights are trapped at the heart of the King's Forest?'

"'Yes, but I believe you already knew that.'

"'Then they can do no harm to the people of this world any longer, we shall do nothing and let them remain trapped for eternity.'

"'I am afraid that won't work, my lord, for they made me swear an oath to them. They were given authority from the Evil One, Lord Kish himself, to instate this oath. I must travel from land to land telling the true tale of King Souvac and his knights. Until I bring three men to take the place of those knights, I cannot die. They have powers with which they can summon, and to some degree watch and control me. Please, tell me what transpired here, and I will add it to the tale they told me. From both sides I will find the truth.'

"'Very well,' he said and rehearsed to me all he knew of Souvac and the three knights. He also gave me access to all the records he had kept, as well as those of his mother.

"The tale you all have just heard about Souvac was the combined version of all these parts, as well as a few things I have picked up over the last one hundred years. You now know, most of what I know concerning that king and his knights. So are there three, make that two, more brave souls willing to risk life and limb on this foolish quest, as Koyne is already coming?"

Koyne spoke up immediately, "Why would we go if our reward is only to be trapped in place of these knights while they are set free to wreak havoc?"

"That is a fine question, Koyne. I do not seek men to take their place; instead, I seek individuals that would, if possible, help me to destroy them once and for all. I believe I said that earlier. I know there is a way to end their existence in this world, while keeping those free that would otherwise take their place, and now I know where to find it."

"Where exactly do we find this mystical way to destroy immortal beings?" asked Koyne.

"I have been told of a man who lives northwest of here in the White Mountains. He knows things about the workings of the Evil One's powers that no other living person knows. It is said that he communicates with the God of the Living. That is where we will go. Now, is there anyone here brave enough to join me?"

"I will come. I could use a good adventure," said Koyne.

"I wasn't asking you, boy, you are already coming. That sword might be sharp, but you are a bit dull," stated the Bard.

Again Koyne's face flushed with anger. He would have made a threat then if not for Avalon's calming hand on his arm.

"I will also come," said Avalon.

"Avalon, you're a girl. You can't come with us."

"Your concern is flattering, Koyne, but I feel in my heart that I am meant to come."

A man sitting one table away stood up. He had a build similar to the Bard, tall and strong. He had black hair and coal-black eyes set deep in a well-traveled face. "I would like to join your group, Bard, as I have been trying to meet up with you for some time now."

"Indeed, and what is your name, sir?"

"My name is Jason Lye. Most people know me as Jace."

"It will be good to have you with us on this dangerous journey, Jason Lye," said the Bard, eyeing him curiously.

"Can anyone come, or is it just limited to you good Bard and three others?" said a richly dressed young blond man with blue eyes from a table near the door. He was the young man that had been listening to the grumblings of the people of Souvac. He looked to be twenty at the most and nearly six feet tall, but slight in build.

"I did not set a limit to how many people can travel with us, only how many must go before the knights when we reach the heart of the King's Forest."

"I will come with you. You may call me Graham." He then got up and with some difficulty opened and closed the tavern door, walking out into the dark and stormy night.

"I guess we won't be seeing him again," said Koyne with a wry smile.

"Don't be so quick to judge others you don't know, Koyne. In fact, all of you should put that bit of advice in your heads and cherish it. I rarely give advice to anyone, but this you can count on as truth—people will always surprise you for good or ill. Besides, I know that boy's family. They are as dependable as any. He may look slight of build, but he will be as valuable to this journey as any of you. To those joining me, come sit at my table. The rest of you not scurrying for safety, mind your own business."

Koyne, Jace, and Avalon joined the Bard at his table. Many of the remaining guests left at that point, struggling with the door as Graham had. The few patrons that remained were gently sent away a few minutes later by Haven.

Jace spoke up as soon as the four companions were alone. "What about Graham? Should I go find him to join us?"

"No, I will speak with him tomorrow. As you all know, tomorrow is the one-hundred-year anniversary of the freeing of this kingdom from that evil king and his knights who gave it its infamous name. I must travel tomorrow, alone, into the heart of the King's Forest and report to the knights of Souvac my progress. You will enjoy the celebration, and the following day, try to find out about the way north and west. Discover if you can the best passes that will take us into the depths of the White Mountains. Also, begin making preparations for a long journey. I should be back in less than three days."

"If you have been planning all this for a hundred years, shouldn't you have the preparations and travel routes figured out?" Belligerence sounded in Koyne's words.

"Koyne, I have spent most of the last hundred years traveling the length and breadth of this world. Do you know how much a place can change in one hundred years?"

Koyne sat speechless.

"I have no doubt you are a fine young warrior, Koyne, however you must learn to listen, trust, and follow direction. I cannot do all the preparation for this journey, therefore, I call on all of you to assist me."

"Why has it taken so long to get a group to follow you?" asked Avalon.

"I could have had any number of people accept a proposal and follow me to the King's Forest over the last hundred years, but that is not what I have been searching for. I have been searching for a way to destroy the knights once and for all," replied the Bard.

"Why let us be the ones to follow you, you have especially seemed to choose Koyne," stated Jace.

"For now let's just say I am playing the odds. Koyne has been hailed by people of this town as a warrior. I need a warrior. As for you, Avalon, and Graham, I need at least three, and you all volunteered, which begs the question, Why are you willing to come with a complete stranger on a perilous journey?"

Jace looked at Avalon for a moment. "I'm looking for answers that I believe only you hold."

The men looked at Avalon next. "I don't want Koyne to leave without me," she said, looking at a blushing Koyne.

"It seems we all want something out of this journey," said the Bard. Standing, he called to Haven. "I would take a room now, sir, if you don't mind."

"I am sorry, Bard, I have no rooms open tonight."

"Take the room top of the stairs fourth door on the left-hand side," said Koyne. "I will find another place to sleep." He winked at Avalon, a move Haven didn't fail to miss.

The Bard nodded and left the common room of the inn. *Such brave souls have volunteered to come with me. I hope they are not disappointed by what will happen to them during this journey*, he thought to himself as he climbed the stairs.

Later that night, after the inn was quiet and empty, Haven approached his adopted daughter as she washed down the final table. At a little over five feet tall, she was very beautiful with shoulder-length auburn hair and a well-muscled build. Haven and Avalon's relationship had become strained slightly over the last year due to his protective nature. Reaching out a trembling hand, he touched Avalon's shoulder.

She turned to face him, waiting for him to tell her he wouldn't allow her to go.

"Avalon, I know that you are in love with that impetuous young man Koyne, you probably have been since he walked in here as a muddy faced child, but I fear for you going on this journey with the Bard of Souvac."

Avalon looked away and took a breath as if she would say something.

"My darling, before you say anything, please just listen to my words. I know I am only the fat innkeeper that took in a young orphan girl, I am not your true father. However, I consider you my true daughter, and I love you as much as any man could love his daughter. You are a woman now and quite capable of making your own decisions about your life, so I will not try to stop you. I will only ask that you think long about the dangers that might exist on this expedition." Haven pulled Avalon into his strong yet gentle embrace and held her for a few moments.

When he let go of her, she looked at him with tears in her eyes and mouthed the words "I love you" before hurrying off to bed.

The Bard having watched this private conversation from the shadows at the top of the stairs turned and made his way back to his room.

Haven stood for a few moments in the middle of the empty common room where Avalon had left him. "I knew her adventurous spirit would take her away one day, but I had hoped it would not have come so soon." Tears began rolling down his cheeks as he departed for his own bed.

Chapter 3

Morning dawned bright, sunny, and warm despite the terrific storm that had raged throughout the night. Cleanup of debris started before the sun cleared the mountains, and by early afternoon, venders were setting up their wares for sale. It seemed as though everyone from the surrounding lands was in Souvac for the celebration that was expected to last days. All of Souvac was decorated with colorful ribbons and signs. People filled the main thoroughfares and parks buying and selling, eating, drinking, and talking merrily. The smells of freshly roasted meats and vegetables wafted through the streets. Everyone was there enjoying themselves—everyone, that is, but the Bard of Souvac.

The Bard left the Travelers' Inn as soon as the storm died out. The eastern sky was beginning to lighten as he made his way through the debris-ridden streets of Souvac. He was surprised when he got to the edge of town to be met by a young man with crystal-blue eyes. "May I come with you now, Bard?"

"No, Graham. It is not time for you to confront the men that killed your family."

"How do you know they killed my family?"

"These men have been the cause of many deaths. They are full of power from the Evil One. The only reason anyone would seek them out is revenge, and you, my boy, are seeking them out. That storm that blew in with me was caused by them. They are angry with me and my lack of success over the past hundred years. They have waited all this time in a smallish clearing in that forest, waiting for me to deliver them from their prison." He pointed vaguely at the distant trees. "If I were to take you with me now, they would torture you to death just for the sake of using their powers again. More importantly, I recognized you, it is a safe bet they would recognize you also. Their hatred for your family is as powerful as can be."

"So you do know who I am."

"You were just a baby when I last saw you, but there can be no mistake, you have your parents in you."

"May I at least travel with you to the edge of the forest?"

"You may come with me to that point, but then you must return to Souvac and join the others in the preparations and festivities. As I said, I will be in the forest for more than just today."

"I will do as you tell me, sir."

They traveled the rest of the way in silence, each of the men deep in thought about what was coming. Graham worried about the journey they would soon endure, and whether anyone would emerge alive from the mission they had chosen to embark upon. Would he ever face the men who had been the cause of so much death and pain to his family? Would he be able to make them pay for his father's suffering? These thoughts swam through his head as they had done since he learned the truth about his origins.

The Bard worried about far different issues. He would be facing the full wrath of the knights he was going to see. The one-hundred-year anniversary being celebrated in Souvac was a slap in the face to those who were trapped in the forest, away from the kingdom they had controlled for so many years. They were close enough to know what was taking place but far enough away to be unable to do anything about it. He knew he would endure intense pain this visit, of body, mind, and soul.

The Bard took his time as he made his way up the small incline to the edge of the forest. It was still early as the two men found themselves standing under the trees that were turning green with new spring buds. Graham had on a couple of occasions opened his mouth to speak but closed it quickly as he looked at the Bard's face. The Bard started when he looked at Graham.

"I am sorry, Graham, I got so caught up in my thoughts I forgot you were with me."

"It's all right, but I wonder if you could answer a question I have about something you said to me earlier."

"Perhaps when I have returned from the task at hand, you may ask me your questions. For now, you must go back to the village. Find the others and assist them in their preparations."

Without another word, the Bard turned and strode into the forest. Graham sat in the shade of those trees for almost an hour before making up his mind to follow the Bard. He took five steps into the forest when a powerful force hit him in the chest, stopping his progress. Initially it felt like a hand gently pushing him back. He tried several more times to enter, but the force got stronger and stronger until a feeling of malice and hate began gripping at his heart. Frustrated with the situation and a bit fearful, he gave up and turned his back on the trees that would not let him pass. He made his way back to Souvac but did not join in the celebration. Instead he went to the old castle and toured the building that had been home to great kings.

That night, after all the merchants closed their shops and booths, Koyne, Avalon, Jace, and Graham gathered at a table in the Travelers' Inn. They sat for a time in silence eating and drinking their fill.

Jace's deep voice broke the silence, "Has anyone seen the Bard return from his meeting in the forest?"

Koyne and Avalon looked at each other and mumbled they had not.

Graham surprised them by answering, "I traveled with him early this morning up to the edge of the forest. He went in alone and said he might be in the forest for more than just today. I tried to follow him, but something prevented me from entering the forest."

"Are we sure he will return at all? Perhaps he is just a bard trying to scare us with his stories, or it's a farce to get us all excited, prepare for a journey and then he takes off having a good laugh," said Koyne, his voice filling with agitation.

"No," replied Jace. "He is the Bard of Souvac. He has been searching for a way to destroy the knights. I have followed him for years, trying to get close enough to have a conversation, but until yesterday, he has eluded me. Now he is assembling a group to end the knights once and for all. I believe the Bard has finally learned something that will afford him a way of destroying the knights. Always in the past, he tells the same tale, never varying, and leaves that night so nobody can follow him. This time he has called individuals to come with him. Koyne, you were chosen by the Bard, and, Graham, he spoke in your favor, which indicates you each have a specific role in this adventure. I do not know what role Avalon and myself will play in this, but the Bard has never gathered together a group to go after the knights. This is the first time I have ever heard him mention a journey into the White Mountains, or anything connected to the God of the Living.

"As far as why he chose us, who knows? We all have secrets, things we are hiding from each other, and perhaps things that have been hidden from us. Yet it appears that somehow the Bard knows or is at least guessing what these secrets are."

They all looked at one another, quiet suspicion dancing in their eyes.

"He didn't choose us, we chose to go with him," replied Koyne.

"You keep telling yourself that, if it makes you feel better," said Jace.

"Well, I don't have any secrets. I was orphaned when I was very little. Haven found me and took me in. I have lived here in Souvac since that time," stated Avalon.

"Perhaps the manner in which you became an orphan is the secret, Avalon," replied Jace.

"So what do you suggest we do while we wait?" asked Koyne, trying to change the subject.

"I thought it was obvious. We continue preparing for a journey, we speak to anyone we can to learn as much as possible about the northwest, particularly the White Mountains. We should seek information about a man that speaks to the God of the Living, since they were supposedly all killed when Souvac ruled. We must buy pack animals, tools, weapons, and armor for those who don't have any. Then when the Bard arrives, we leave," Jace said all this as though it cost him nothing.

"That sounds expensive, and I have just a few bronze and silver coins. How do you suggest we pay for all these things?" asked Koyne.

Avalon shrugged her shoulders but didn't say anything.

"Perhaps the Bard left money for us to use," said Jace without conviction.

"I will cover the expense. We can start purchasing what we need in the morning," said Graham. "Now if you will excuse me, I will be going." Graham stood and again left the inn.

"Where do you suppose he goes at night? He is definitely a stranger here, and no other inn is reputable enough to even enter, especially if he has as much money as he claims," Koyne said with a slight edge to his voice.

"I told you, we all have secrets. Perhaps he is like me and prefers to sleep under the stars. I will see you both at dawn," Jace said then also left the inn.

"Avalon, I fear we have thrown our lot in with a group of crazy people," said Koyne once he felt sure Jace was far enough away not to hear him.

"I think they are sweet. I just want to get going. I feel strange, an urgency that I have never felt before. Plus, it is so hard with my father right now."

"What, is Haven trying to keep you from going?"

"No. He...well, he is really sad about it, and I hate seeing him in any kind of pain. He is trying to be supportive, but I know he wants me to stay," she said with her head down. After a moment of silence, she looked at Koyne, whose facial expression indicated he was trying to understand but not coming close. "Oh, forget it. I will see you in the morning." Shoving her chair back, she stood and stomped away.

Koyne sat at the table alone trying to figure out what he had done to get in trouble with Avalon. He remained there late into the night until Haven approached.

"Koyne, I have never asked you for anything. I know you are interested in my daughter, and you know what I have done to others that have shown similar interest."

"Are you threatening me?"

"Yes, so shut up and listen. I expect that if you love her, you will protect her in every way possible. Do you understand the meaning of every way possible?"

"I think so."

"I hope you do, because if you don't protect her in every way possible, nobody living, dead, or undead will be able to protect you from me. Are we clear?"

"I believe so."

"Good, now get out," said Haven, with more force than kindness.

"Do you really think you could best me?"

"I only became an innkeeper after I found Avalon. Before that, I lived a much different life, so yes, I could easily destroy you."

Raising his hands, Koyne stood and promptly left the inn.

*****

It was very cold inside the King's Forest, even for early spring. The Bard reached the heart of the forest minutes before Graham decided to follow him.

"Who is the whelp that came with thee, great Bard?" Jerec mocked. "There is something familiar about him."

"He is a young lad from Souvac. He came with me to hear my stories, as he called them."

"Yes, but there is something familiar about him," said Jerec. "Shall we let him enter our kingdom?"

"Do what you will with yourselves and your prey. I have no interest in him," said the Bard without emotion.

"Oaran, keep him out while we talk with our potential savior," said Jerec. "I suppose, you again have nothing to report to us."

"Actually, I have much to report. I entered Souvac last night and went to the Travelers' Inn. Thanks to your amazing storm, many people were there. I finally found three that will come with me to see you and take the oath."

"Why, if you found them, did you not just bring them with you today? Bring them and release us, that we can join their one-hundred-year celebration of our disappearance. We could really entertain them," Jerec said, grinning maliciously.

"They won't come if they think there is no hope for their lives. I have convinced them to take a journey to the White Mountains with me. There, a man will be waiting for us to give false hope to those who travel with me. Then I will bring them here, where you can do with them whatever you please."

"Are you trying to deceive us, Bard? Who is this man that is waiting for you and your travelers?" asked Kell.

"I told them there is a man who talks with the God of the Living in the White Mountains. This man will supposedly be able to tell us how you can be defeated. That will give them the hope they need to follow me wherever I lead them."

"I don't like the sound of that, Bard. I think you are trying to find a way to destroy us. Is that why it took you so long to find three men to come with you?" asked Kell.

The Bard's voice and anger rose as he lashed back at the knights. "Do you believe there is a man who speaks with the God of the Living? You know better than anyone, Kell, the last speaker vanished from these lands one hundred and ten years ago. I, like you, have suffered for this past hundred years. At first I tried to forget what I was a part of, but when I found happiness, you destroyed it. My wife and child were killed when I came to you after the first five years, remember? Somehow you used your powers to bring them here ahead of me and kill them!" The Bard's eyes filled with tears. "I want to be free of this curse as much as you, only I want to find peace in death, not distribute it throughout the land."

"How long will it take you to make this journey and return to us?" asked Jerec, his eyes cold and unfeeling.

"I do not know for sure, my lord," said the Bard, his voice quivering. "If all goes well, we should return in several weeks."

"Very well, but I warn you, Bard, if you try to trick us, I will see that anyone you have ever loved will be dealt with. You are right, by the way, it was us who had your wife and child killed. Let me show you how." Jerec touched the Bard's forehead.

For hours horrifying images flashed through the Bard's mind. He saw his wife running with his son folded in her arms. Black, hairy creatures chased after her; he could hear her screams echoing in his mind, tearing at his sanity. When they caught her, claws slashed and ripped at her body. He felt the horrifying fear, the physical anguish that his beloved wife and infant son felt as they died. These scenes repeated over and over in his mind's eye. Then, just as suddenly as they had begun, the images were gone. The Bard sat alone in the darkness of the forest, great sobs racking his body. The moonless night was hiding him from mortal eyes; only the stars saw the Bard curled up on the earth, crying throughout the remainder of the night.

"What did you show him?" asked Kell after the Bard ran screaming from the clearing.

"I showed him his wife and child being killed by Oaran's pets. He will not dare betray us. Physical pain is easy to forget over time, but pain of the heart and soul lingers. It is much more poignant in the end, and so much more satisfying to watch. Oaran, just in case he feels he truly has nothing to live for, I want you to send one of your boarhounds to follow him. If he is up to something, I want to know about it. Plus, there is something about that boy that came to the edge of our forest. His presence stirred a great focused hatred inside that I haven't felt for many years."

The Bard jerked awake from unsettling dreams of the past. He remembered life after he left Bowen's presence in Souvac. Flashes of the past flickered through his mind like lightning. He had met a beautiful maid in the lands to the north, where King Bareth ruled. They quickly fell in love and were married. Four years later, she had become pregnant with their son. The Bard had, at that time, convinced himself that what had happened in the King's Forest was not real and settled down to live out his life in happiness. One month before he was to return to the forest, he could feel himself being called. He tried to refuse those calls, but in the end, the knights summoned him in the one way he couldn't refuse.

One morning he awoke and found his wife and son missing. He searched for them near their cottage, until a nagging feeling gripped his heart. A feeling of doom began pulling him, drawing him south toward the King's Forest. Once inside the forest, he found a fresh trail. Following the trail, he found his wife's torn cloak and his son's blanket covered in dried blood. With no trace of the bodies, he automatically assumed the worst. Since that time, a part of him had died.

Thoughts continued to race through his head. He wondered if what Jerec had shown him was true. It was such a long time ago, and Jerec was prone to twisting the truth. He desperately hoped the horror he had seen wasn't the truth. Standing up, he began walking to a place he felt he had to visit. The morning passed away. Finally, the Bard took in his surroundings with bloodshot eyes. Noting the sun was straight above his head, he wondered how long he had been walking.

He heard trumpets sounding in the town below, which helped his mind come back to the present. *I still have at least a day and a half before I must return to the inn*, he thought. Once again he reflected on the nightmarish images he had seen. *I knew Jerec would be angry and try to torture me in some way, but my wife and child?*

Try as he might, he could not push the images away. As the day waned toward night, he continued to torture himself over the deaths of his wife and son as he continued walking. "If I had gone to the knights on my own, perhaps I could have returned to Caiti and Sam afterward. I could have taken them with me as I traveled," he said to himself. It was no use dwelling in the past, but there he finally stood, looking down on the small shrine he had built. It was on the exact spot where he had found his Caiti's bloodied torn cloak so long ago. He sat there for hours talking to his wife and son as though they were present. As night settled in, he lay down by the shrine and fell into another restless sleep.

He woke before the sun and built a small fire. He warmed some salted meats from his pack and cleaned his face with warm water. After eating, he sat in meditation to get his strength up even more. When the sun had risen above the mountains, he took out the maps he had both made and acquired throughout his journeys. He poured over those maps through the morning and into the afternoon. When he felt he had found the safest and fastest route to the mountains in the northwest, he packed his things and made his way back to the traveler's inn.

Once again, the four that would travel with the Bard were gathered in the tavern eating dinner. They discussed what they had learned about the passages to the northwest together and tried to formulate their plans for departure.

"Did everyone get weapons and armor?" asked Jace after everything else had been discussed.

"I have my father's things," said Graham.

"Who is your father?" asked Jace.

"That is none of your concern," responded Graham, looking at Jace coldly.

"We found some things for Avalon," said Koyne, speaking for himself and Avalon, trying to alleviate the tension coming from Graham.

"It was difficult to find anything that fit me, and most of the blacksmiths laughed at me when I asked for armor, especially Egin, that filthy, no-good son of a crow," declared Avalon.

"Very well, now if the Bard would show up, we could get started on our journey immediately." said Jace with a cautious smile on his face.

As if on cue, the door opened and the Bard stepped inside. He looked around the room and. seeing his four companions, moved over to join them; once seated he called for stew and ale. "Are you ready to start this adventure on the morrow?" he asked.

"We could go immediately, if it would suit you better," Jace said.

"No, I will need time to rest tonight, and it will be better if we travel by day. I feel that the knights do not trust me, as well they shouldn't. It is a good bet that Oaran will send one of his creatures to follow us."

"What kind of creature?" asked Koyne

"They are twisted animals, created by Oaran through torture using the powers of the Evil One. From my understanding, they can only travel at night. The knights will know where we are starting from but should have trouble tracking us if we travel by day. Have you learned anything about our destination?" he asked. His food arrived, and he ate while listening to the reports of his companions.

"We did not find much. To get to the White Mountains, we have to follow the Great North Road past the Kraggs that mark the southern border of Bareth's kingdom," stated Jace.

"From there, a road leads west for nearly fifty miles before you get to a pass that leads into the mountains. That is all anyone could tell us," stated Koyne.

"We asked for more information about the pass, but all we heard was stay away. There are rumors that it is haunted or cursed," said Graham.

"One old man that I talked to said anyone that tries to use the pass disappears forever," Avalon quietly stated.

"It appears we have disappointed you, for I venture to guess that you already know all that we have told you," said Jace to the Bard.

"I wouldn't say everything. I have not been in that area for nearly five decades." He laid his maps out on the table, and they discussed the route they would follow. "I believe the pass you all are referring to is Windy Pass." He pointed to a spot on the map. "I have never gone through that pass or into the mountains beyond the foothills here." He again pointed at the map, indicating a place called Watcher's Hill. "This is right along the path that I thought we should travel, so your information has been helpful. I am curious about the warnings related to Windy Pass. I will ponder on this. We will leave just after sunrise, traveling out of town with any merchants headed up the Great North Road. We will turn off the main road just beyond Kragg's Pass and travel west through Berkley's Forest. After that, I believe our course is set based on your added information, but we may have to take it day by day. Now we should all get a good night's sleep. We will have a long day of travel tomorrow."

They looked at the map as the Bard described the places they would be going.

"How long do you think this will take?" asked Avalon.

Getting up from the table, the Bard replied, "It could be several weeks. We should plan on a longer rather than shorter time frame, to be safe." He left the table then, going up to his room.

The companions looked around the table at each other.

"What kind of creature do you think will be following us?" asked Avalon, her voice tinged with fear.

"The kind that is dark, full of evil, and malice like its master, I suppose," said Jace. "Koyne may be right, Avalon, this trip could be more dangerous than we thought. Perhaps you should consider staying behind."

"But I already have my sword and armor," said Avalon, trying to sound brave.

"And absolutely no idea how to use them," interjected Koyne. "What if we find ourselves in a dangerous spot? You could be hurt or killed," said Koyne sternly.

"So could you!" Avalon protested. Standing up, she ran from the table, tears falling as she went.

Haven stood behind the bar washing glasses. He watched and heard everything that was happening with his daughter, especially since she had decided to go on this adventure. As she ran by the bar and into the back of the inn where her room was located, a look of anger crossed his normally jovial face. His powerful hands tensed, and the tin mug he held gave way to his grip. Looking down, he inspected the crushed mug, tossed it in the rubbish bin, and tried to decide if he should go to his daughter. He just started to turn when he heard Jace speak.

"You better go after her, mate."

"Sometimes I don't know what to make of women. Show concern and she yells insults at you, then cries and runs away," said Koyne in exasperation.

"Avalon is as afraid for you as you are for her. She's scared about this journey but trying to be brave," replied Jace.

"You're probably right. I'll go get her." He left and followed Avalon's path toward her room. As he passed Haven, he received a look from the innkeeper that made him flinch slightly.

Jace and Graham stayed at the table for a while more. They talked over various points of the Bard's tale concerning the storyteller and the knights, trying to speculate about methods they could use to destroy the knights of Souvac. After an hour of discussion, they came to the conclusion that they had no definite answer to that question. They agreed to pursue the matter with the Bard as they traveled.

The rest of the time they spent on more personal information.

"I first heard about the Bard when I was very young. I remember seeing him for the first time when I was ten. He was telling his tale at a carnival in Tarshish. I was there with my mother, it was the only trip we ever went on together. I listened to his entire tale and was greatly intrigued. My mother often told me about the Bard after we returned to Bareth's kingdom. I think she fancied him, but so did many of the maids and women where I came from. I was eighteen when I left home again. I was trying to find him.

"My mother had been killed by a great white wolf while gathering berries in the woods near Bareth's castle. I was a short way off gathering wood and heard her scream, but by the time I got there…" Jace stopped and cleared his throat of rising emotions. "There was nothing I could do for her. With her last strength, she pulled a piece of paper from her skirt pocket and handed it to me. It simply read, 'Find the Bard of Souvac.' I had no other connection there in Bareth's lands without her, so shortly after putting her body to rest, I left, traveling from place to place, trying to locate the Bard. I felt like I had a destiny connected to him, but circumstances prevented me from getting closer than hearing his tale, until now. That is basically how I came to be here, Graham. How did you wind up on this crazy adventure?"

"I came from the southeast, from Tarshish actually. I traveled for months to reach this place. The Bard told his tale in Tarshish several years ago, but I suppose that traveling a hundred years alone, he has been nearly everywhere on this great continent, and possibly beyond. Anyway, I came here to follow the Bard also." Graham looked Jace in the eye for a few moments, as though trying to find some hidden secret before looking away. "That is all anyone needs to know about me for now."

"You don't give out much information about yourself, do you, Graham?"

"No, I do not," he said defensively.

"Very well. Good evening, Graham." Draining his ale, Jace got up and walked to the bar, where he began speaking to Haven.

I keep very much to myself, unless I find I can trust the person I am talking to. I don't know if I can trust anyone here yet, Graham thought to himself.

Just as he was getting up to leave, he saw something move outside the window. He ran to the inn door, opened it, and stepped into the dark and empty street. Looking right and left, he couldn't see or hear anyone. Above him, hidden in the shadows on the wall, perched Oaran's boarhound. Completely black, it walked on four muscular legs covered in bristly hair. Its tongue, long and thin, wriggled back and forth as it prepared to attack the young man. Only Oaran controlling its mind kept it in check. Graham, feeling a sense of foreboding, left the inn then traveled to his secluded campsite in a thick grove of trees behind the castle. Once there, he decided to use his father's information and entered the castle. It only took a few minutes to find the hidden entrance and enter the labyrinth under the castle.

"What do you make of our Bard, Oaran?" asked Jerec. "He is up to something. I don't trust him and never will. In fact, once we are free, I should like to kill him myself."

"Are you sure you still know how to wield your sword? After all, it has done nothing but sit in its scabbard for the last fifty years or so," scoffed Jerec.

Oaran turned, fire dancing in his eyes, as he drew his sword and advanced on his captain. In the blink of an eye, Jerec's sword was in his hand, dancing before Oaran's face. Oaran attacked, his strokes appearing clumsy next to those of Jerec.

"You have been playing with your little animals so much that you have lost your ability with a sword. I might just have to kill you when we are free, no sense in keeping a useless warrior for my army."

Oaran attacked again, his strokes coming harder and harder, his eyes aflame with murder. His assault was powerful but had no control. Jerec easily deflected the poorly guided blows before burying his sword in Oaran's throat. Oaran staggered backward, trying to maintain his footing. A dark blur flew out of the dark trees, smashing into Jerec's back, knocking him to the ground. The beast tore and scratched at Jerec's neck and head.

Oaran pulled the sword from his throat, the wound healing instantly; his maniacal laughter then danced around the clearing as his boarhound continued its vicious attack. "Maybe I don't need a sword to defeat you, Captain." Jerec threw himself to his back, smashing his armored body into his attacker, which loosened its grip. Reaching back, he grabbed the creature by the scruff. Rising to his feet he spun, launching the boarhound away. When it renewed its attack, Jerec pulled a dagger from his belt and buried it in the creature's skull. Despite the searing pain of the poison from the beast's claws, Jerec stood before Oaran.

"Get on your knees!" Jerec commanded with such force that Oaran had to obey. "If you attack me ever again, Oaran, you will be the first to taste my blade when we are free. I will not stop cutting until your limbs are no longer attached to your worthless body."

"Yes, Lord Jerec," mumbled Oaran.

Kell watched this exchange as he usually did, from the shadows of Souvac's throne. He saw Oaran stand and turn away while Jerec stood erect, not letting any weakness show, despite the pain he knew was coursing through his captain's body. He watched as both men entered their makeshift shelters on opposite sides of the clearing. Then he turned to the corpse of Souvac.

"I regret ever having listened to you. Your lies destroyed all of us and anything we might have ever cared for." While he spoke, he absently rubbed a bright-blue stone that he wore on a silver chain around his neck. "I will be free, and I will do what I can to prevent Jerec from completing his plans," he said to the lifeless king.

In his shelter, Oaran was also plotting against his captain. He had been commanded to keep his boarhound from attacking the members of the Bard's company, until Jerec knew what plans had been laid. However, that didn't mean he couldn't have a little fun. With a thought, he sent his pet into a frenzy, destroying what it could in Souvac, sending horses and other animals fleeing in all directions. As a final thought, he sent his boarhound after the boy that had caught a glimpse of his beautiful creature. It would be best if there were no witnesses.

Graham exited the secret door he had used to enter the labyrinth of the castle. He held in his hand what he had searched for. It was right where his father had said it would be, including the document which he would use at a later date. He now felt truly ready to proceed with the quest. Suddenly, sensing he was in danger, he drew the ancient sword that his father had given him, blindly swinging it in a great arc. He felt the sword bite through flesh and bone. Then the weight of something heavy crashed into him, knocking him backward into the still-open passage. Graham rolled the dead creature from him. Lighting a torch, he examined his attacker. The squat powerful legs with clawed feet were frightening, to be sure, but paled in comparison to the vicious-looking maw that held two rows of teeth. As he studied the creature, he felt an added measure of strength and confidence enter his body and mind. He then sealed the passage with the creature's body inside.

In the forest clearing, Oaran growled with anger. A second of his precious creations was now dead. He knew he could not let Jerec know of this failure, but now was not the time to worry. The Bard would not be leaving anytime soon or unnoticed.

Chapter 4

The next morning came and went without anyone leaving Souvac. Horses were stolen, or run off, merchant wagons were damaged, and property went missing. It was a grand-scale mess.

"Who would have done this?" asked Avalon, as the group of travelers stood in the road in front of the travelers' inn, packs on their backs. They had been looking around town at the mess that had been caused during the night.

"I saw something move outside the window of the inn just after Jace left the table. I was practically alone in the common room, and as I stood up, I saw someone, or something, dart away from the window," said Graham, concern showing in his eyes.

"There are people here from nearly every corner of these lands. I daresay anyone could have done it." The Bard scanned the damage. "It could easily have been caused by drunken youth trying to be humorous," he continued, as though he really believed this explanation.

Koyne walked up, joining the rest of the group. "I have spoken with the merchants and the city guard, it seems nothing was stolen, just misplaced and scattered from one end of the town to the other. The missing horses are being rounded up on the plains to the west. The biggest problem is the damage to merchant wagons which, truth be told, isn't that substantial. This seems like a delaying action. Maybe the knights didn't want us to leave unnoticed," said Koyne with a wry smile.

"It is possible," said the Bard, smiling in turn. "It seems Lord Jerec wants to know our every move. Perhaps he doesn't trust me. Graham, it seems you have had the first glimpse of the creature that will be tailing us into the northwest, and possibly back." The Bard sighed. "I will not be a pawn in Jerec's game anymore. Gather anything you may have forgotten, and say your goodbyes, if you must. We are leaving without delay."

Without argument, everybody followed the orders. Avalon and Koyne went to see Haven. Graham and Jace, not having anyone to say farewell to, stayed with the Bard and helped him procure horses. They met in front of the Travelers' Inn an hour later in order to depart.

"Will we still be following the route we discussed last night?" asked Jace.

"No, we will go straight up the Great North Road several miles, turn slightly to the west, crossing the plains in order to go through Kragg's Pass. With Bishop's Marsh on one side and the Kraggs on the other, we will be hard to spot or follow. Not to mention, Jerec doesn't know about that pass," said the Bard, smiling again.

"Isn't Kragg's Pass where the North Road enters Bareth's kingdom?" asked Jace, a puzzled look on his face.

"I will lead you to the Kragg's Pass of ancient time and use. It is known only to a few, as its use ended after an earthquake hit nearly three hundred years ago. That earthquake formed Bishop's Marsh and tore the narrow portion of the Kraggs open, through which the Great North Road was built and put into use."

"I have heard of the marshes, but not the pass. As I understand it, there is nothing but the sheer face of the Kraggs on the far side of the marshes," Koyne said.

"Koyne, you have much to learn, but I will leave it a mystery for now and let your own eyes behold the truth. I know a safe passage through the swamps that will completely obscure our trail and give us some time to work with."

"You are sure we won't die in the swamps?" asked Avalon, who had just returned, her eyes red and puffy.

"Of course, I have passed through many times unscathed."

"Yeah, but you're immortal," Mumbled Koyne.

The Bard pretended not to hear this last comment. "I want you all to begin. Just ride casually up the Great North Road. I will catch up to you shortly."

Mounting their horses, they started on their way, no one taking notice of their departure as most people were still trying to sort out the mess that Souvac was in. They traveled at an even pace, looking back frequently until the Bard had rejoined them with three pack horses in his wake.

"All right, here we are, let us pick up the pace a bit," he said as soon as he rode up to them.

They pushed their horses into a steady gallop. Within an hour, they were jumping the hedge that lined the Great North Road and moving freely through the open plains. A little past midday, they stopped to rest themselves and the horses. Each member of the group dismounted, saddle sore, except for the Bard and Jace. They were accustomed to long rides on horseback. After an hour of rest, the Bard insisted they get moving again. This leg of the journey went even faster as they pushed the horses to even greater speed. The Bard did not want to be on the plains when night came. They reached the first sign of Bishop's Marsh two hours before sundown and dismounted.

After a brief inspection of the area, the Bard spoke, "We are a bit south of where I had wanted to come. We will have to go north along the edge of the swamp a short distance and turn west again to enter the safest way through the marsh."

"How deep does the mud get the way we are going?" asked Jace.

"Not much more than ankle-deep, if we walk and lead the horses. If we try to ride, the horses could bog down enough to break a leg."

"Let's get our boots dirty then," said Koyne in a black mood.

Continuing in single file, the Bard led them to a spot where they could enter the marsh. Loosening the ropes, he set his three pack horses running north and east, away from the marsh.

"Why did you do that?" asked Avalon as the horses were running away.

"Well, my dear, we are going to be tracked tonight. I don't want the creature that tracks us to know we went into the swamp. Those horses are our diversion," he said patiently.

"What about the supplies in the packs? I imagine those would have been useful," said Koyne sarcastically.

"Koyne," the Bard said with the patience one used when talking to a child. "The packs were filled with rocks."

He then turned as if that simple explanation said everything and led the way into Bishop's Marsh.

At first it was just soggy grass that sprang back, leaving no trace of passage. After a mile, they began to encounter thick, slimy, black mud that reeked of decomposition. Initially, the Bard was right, the mud rarely crept up past their ankles,; but after another hour, the mud was more often than not knee-deep. This might not have been so bad, if the smell had been a little less awful and the bugs had not been the size of dinner rolls. Each traveler, except the Bard, stopped more than once to retch as the rotting smell of decomposing plants and animals filled their nostrils.

They stopped early on and put cloaks around the horse's heads to keep the bugs from getting at their eyes and ears. Time passed ever more slowly, and every step became an arduous task. Just as Koyne was about to complain, after retching a third time, mists sprang up, wrapping cloaklike arms around them, souring his mood even further. As the sun lowered on the horizon, the tendrils of mist began creeping like worms through their clothing, saturating each layer before moving ever closer to the tender flesh of the travelers. Before long, the sunlight that could still penetrate the mists was turning everything around them gold and pink as the sun descended behind the distant hills to the west. Finally, the visible sunlight dropped below the horizon. The temperature immediately dropped, and the weary travelers began to shiver with cold.

"If we get caught in this marsh after dark, we will be as good as frozen, Bard," Koyne said with distaste.

"I didn't spend a hundred years finding the necessary people to take on this journey just to see you freeze or give up on the first day of the journey, young friend."

As he finished talking, he seemed to rise ghostlike out of the mud that was trying to hold him down. The others stopped momentarily, frightened by what they were seeing. Suddenly, as if conjured, a warm breeze blew across their faces, clearing the mists before them, showing the Bard standing on a solid stone slab protruding into the marsh.

"You see, just where it is supposed to be. Now if you will all come out of the mud, we will set up camp." The Bard smiled. "Perhaps, Koyne, you will learn to trust me before the end of this journey."

Needing no further invitation, the others scrambled from the marsh. On the solid stone of the Kraggs, the mist seemed unable to gain a hold. Looking around them, they found the broad shelf they were on was as flat as a tabletop. The cliff face, which wrapped around them in a great arc, seemed to have door and windowlike openings cut into it. Some of these did, in fact, have doors just inside the openings, closing off whatever lay beyond. Where the stone of the Kraggs ended, the mists of the marsh took over, swirling around them, blocking out sight and sound. The air near the edge of the marsh continued to be rank with the smell of rot and decay, but stepping away from the edge of the marsh four to five feet found clean, cool air filling the nostrils and lifting the spirits. The Bard's charges looked around, dumbfounded at this remarkable place.

The Bard's voice brought everyone out of their revelry. "We will camp inside one of the larger rooms here where a fire can be built. There is a fresh water spring through the middlemost opening. Do not go far, for that is Kragg's Pass. There is a door left of the pass opening. Do not attempt to open it. In the morning, we will rise at first light, find lamps, and make our way through the pass."

Leading them to the first and largest opening to their right, the Bard gave instructions for the three men to stable the horses in the chamber directly to the left, then go into Kragg's Pass, find the spring, and refresh the water bottles. Avalon followed the Bard.

"What is carved into the stone?" Avalon asked.

The Bard drew a long sword that had been hidden beneath his cloak. "These are runes carved by the people who once lived here." He stretched his arm as high as he could and pointed with his sword at the runes that curved in an elegant arch over the entry. On either side of the opening facing them were the images of two men with long beards. Their arms were stretched above as if holding the archway up.

"What do the runes say?"

The Bard looked at Avalon. He opened his mouth to speak, closed his mouth, and finally replied, "It doesn't matter."

Passing through the ornately carved opening, and moving to the center of the room, they found a large firepit with stacks of dried wood nearby. The firepit was also stacked with wood ready for lighting. In a matter of seconds, the Bard had a fire burning. Avalon could feel the cold being chased from her very core by the orange and red flames.

"Avalon, dear, you are showing great courage in coming on this journey. I want to be sure you are doing well. There are many things that can occur on a quest like this. Some of them are good, and some are bad. Are you truly ready for what could happen?"

Avalon looked away from him and into the fire. "I know you all think that because I am only eighteen I don't know about the world. Haven, bless him, told me almost the exact same thing when I said goodbye." She stopped then, as if gathering courage to speak again. "I saw both of my parents die when I was very young. Every night in my nightmares, I see that moment when the light left their eyes. It has taken me years and all the love my adopted father had to help me find some semblance of peace. Somehow I know I will find something on this journey. Ever since you told your tale, I have felt a pull. It's like having a glimpse of the future, feeling like I finally belong somewhere. I dreamed last night a strange dream about my parents. For the first time that I can remember, I saw my parents alive in a dream. They told me to follow you, to never look back, for I am a key to the success of this mission. I believe this quest will bring new meaning to my life."

"Very well, I must ask one more thing. How old is Koyne?"

"He is twenty, his birthday was just last month. Why do you ask?"

"Has he always been so disagreeable?"

"No, but he is under a lot of stress. He worries about me," said Avalon, a smile playing at her lips. "He is quite prideful, and I know the way you have been teasing him has gotten him out of sorts. He has been in more than one fight defending his honor and mine through the years."

"I see. Let me know if you notice any further change in his behavior."

Before Avalon could respond, the three men returned with their bedding, having stabled the horses in the chamber appointed by the Bard. Upon entering the large chamber carved from the living stone, Jace let out a loud whistle that reverberated against the polished stone walls. "How big is this place?"

"This chamber is easily forty feet wide and two hundred feet deep, extending thirty feet straight up. It was the grand council room as well as the king's audience chamber," answered the Bard.

"What king?" Graham asked.

"I don't exactly know, but I believe his name was King Kragg. That is why these mountains were named the Kraggs, though I am sure only a few remember that fact. Last time I was here, I did some exploring in order to learn about the people that built all this. I learned that a large group of people came here from the White Mountains through the passage we will use tomorrow. They were a very hardy people, shorter in stature than men, but with great skill in stone—and metalwork as we see by the figures and carvings at the front of this throne room. They carved or improved the natural openings and passages you saw when we arrived. Each opening leads to abandoned houses, shops, storage areas, and the like, all of which have carvings and runes indicating what they are. Others lead to mines, dead ends, or worse. At the very end of this hall, there is a dais with a throne. The throne has the same runes carved into it that are above this chambers opening. In all my world travels, I had never seen anything like them, before encountering them here. With time and study, I was able to translate portions of it. One day it seems something very strange occurred, and they all vanished. I don't know how or by what means. It was shortly after the great earthquake that caused Bishop's Marsh to appear that they disappeared," the Bard said.

"What else did you find as you searched the openings and passages?" asked Jace.

"There are stores of food for man and horse, weapons, armor, various other things. Amazingly, the food is still fresh, the weapons are still sharp, and the armor still bright. Again I don't know how or why, but it is. You might say there is a magical quality to this place."

While they laid out the bedding and prepared to sleep, the Bard told them more about what he had found.

"Do we really need to leave at first light? I would like to look around some more," said Graham. Avalon and Koyne nodded in agreement.

The Bard shook his head side to side. "We can gather food water and anything we are short on supply of but then we go. It is best not to linger long in any one place. I do not want Oaran's boarhound finding us."

"I thought you said we would throw off his trail by coming this way," said Jace.

"Oh, that I did, I expect that the boarhound Oaran has sent to track us will have some difficulty finding our path. However, there is always a chance it could find us if we stay in one place too long, especially since Oaran is determined to have us tracked. More importantly, the faster we complete our mission, the faster we can be free of the knights of Souvac. When this is all over and the knights of Souvac are defeated, I could bring you all here and show you around, if you like." The group nodded their agreement. "Now it is the time we get some sleep." Without further word, the Bard lay down, rolled into his bedding, and fell into a deep sleep.

"I guess there is no point arguing," Avalon said, a little downcast.

Minutes later the others, excluding Jace, had rolled into their bedding to sleep. Shortly thereafter, the soft, deep breathing of the sleeping travelers could be heard, interrupted occasionally by light snores. When it seemed all were asleep, Jace rose from his place by the fire and started walking toward the doorway.

"What are you doing?" asked Koyne.

Jace started a little, not realizing anyone was still awake. "I feel uneasy in this place. I can feel something here, a presence of something or someone watching us. I was going to go stand guard by the entryway. I will wake you up to take a turn. After your watch, wake Graham to take the last watch. About three hours apiece should suffice." Then like a whisper, he vanished into the darkness of the hall.

Koyne grunted and started thinking his curiosity about this place had been growing ever since he had stepped out of the marsh. Dwarves were supposed to be the best at finding and creating treasure along with swords, armor, and all other weapons. Looking over at the form of Graham, he decided to act. He quietly moved to Graham's side and shook him.

"What is it?"

"I'm feeling like we should do some investigating of this place."

Graham sat up quickly, looking over at the Bard. "I don't think he wants us to go rummaging about."

"We don't need to go far, this hall is big enough that we could just explore a little. We can't go outside the doors anyway as Jace is keeping watch. What do you say we just look around the throne room? We might even find a bit of shine."

"What's shine?"

"Graham, shine means treasure, silver, gold, weapons, maybe even some platinum or jewels."

"We can't take anything, that would be wrong."

"It's only wrong if you take it from somebody. The Bard said this is a dead city, the people have been gone for over a hundred years. If we find anything, it has no owner."

Graham looked at the Bard and Avalon sleeping in their blankets. "What if they wake up and find us gone?"

"We will only go for a few minutes, just look around the throne room here."

Graham's own curiosity about this place and what it had to offer had also been peeked by what they had seen already. "All right, just for a few minutes."

The two quietly moved deeper into the chamber. They saw the throne on its raised dais and searched all around the empty space.

Koyne was getting bored and disappointed when he heard Graham whispering loudly.

"Koyne, come here, I have found a secret door."

Graham stood at the far left of the throne, holding open a narrow door made of stone that was only four feet tall. Koyne smiled as he slipped past Graham. Once through the door, the passage opened up slightly to allow the two men to walk through comfortably. As they walked through the pass, the door behind them closed silently. After just a few minutes, they stood outside in the fresh air, having pushed open another stone door. Looking around, they got their bearings and realized they were right in front of the stables. The Kraggs curved around in a great arc past the stables. Looking at each other, they smiled and headed for more adventure.

When they had originally stepped out of the marshes and seen the walls of the Kraggs, it appeared to be one smooth surface curving in a great arc, but as they searched, they realized the smooth appearance was an illusion created by the skilled craftsmen who had once lived here. There were many large crevices that when you walked into them revealed what might have been shops and homes. Doors made of stone and wood were plentiful; some were locked, but most were unlocked.

The two men searched everything they could, entering any doorway that was not locked. Throughout their travels they found a few coins, mostly brass with a couple of silver and gold ones. Graham especially enjoyed exploring the empty shops; he wondered what items may have adorned the shelves when this city was alive and vibrant. Koyne was a bit more aggressive in his search of what seemed to be homes, but it was as the Bard had said—the place was completely deserted.

*****

Jace finished his watch and walked back to the bundles of blankets he thought was Koyne.

"Your watch," said Jace reaching out and grabbing empty blankets.

He looked around quickly and moved to Graham's bedding, which he also found empty. Anger boiled in his mind as he thought of the trouble these two might be getting into. Not wanting to alert the Bard, he made his way back to the entry of the hall where he sat on a stone bench. His mind raced, and his anger fumed at Koyne and Graham. Just minutes later, he jumped as a strong hand grabbed his shoulder from behind. Unable to move or call out, he sat frozen for a split second until the Bard's voice broke the silence.

"Setting a watch is a good idea. I will take over for the rest of the night. Go back and get some sleep, you will need your full strength tomorrow."

Nodding his head in acknowledgement, Jace stood, his heart still racing, and made his way back to his bedroll. The Bard waited only a few minutes before stepping out into the mists. He didn't have to go far before he saw the creature squatting low to the ground, its thick arms and legs supporting it. A mass of black hair fell from its head and face.

*****

"Koyne, we should be getting back. We have been out here a long time."

"You're probably right," said Koyne as he rummaged through cupboards of another empty dwelling. Disappointed by the lack of treasure to be found, the two quietly headed toward the throne room. They were skirting the edge of the Kraggs when they saw the squat creature sitting on its haunches in the middle of what would be the main square. Crouching down to crawl along the base of the Kraggs, they were even more shocked when they saw the Bard emerge from the throne room and walk out to talk with the creature.

It immediately started talking to the bard in its deep, guttural language. "What are you doing here, Bard?"

"I felt this would be the safest way to bring my charges to the northwest," answered the Bard in the language of the creature.

"Have you told them about me?" It asked.

"No, I told them little about this place and its people, but I told them nothing about you or why you are here," he answered.

"What about the two who are searching every house and shop, I have nearly killed them both several times."

"I will deal with them. I watched them explore the throne room but did not think they would find the secret passage out."

"Very well, but I want every last coin they found returned to me. Why do you travel this way? There is nothing here for anyone."

"I travel to the White Mountains to speak with Odin," replied the Bard.

The creature's eyes opened wide. "Why seek the speaker to the God of the Living?"

"I go to find answers and give hope to those who follow me, and we do not know if he is a speaker. The last speaker we know of was killed by one of Souvac's knights over a hundred years ago."

The Bard and creature spoke for a time back and forth, question for answer. As they spoke, Jace watched from the shadows of the great hall. After listening for several moments, he slipped out of the hall in an attempt to find Koyne and Graham.

He found them hiding in the shadows of two pillars standing on either side of the door they had been warned about by the Bard when they first arrived. Koyne was holding his wrist and trying not to make any noise as he writhed in pain.

"What are you two doing?" whispered Jace.

Graham spoke, "We were just looking around a bit. We were sneaking back because of the creature when the Bard showed up, we tried to get in the first door we saw in order to hide, unfortunately it was this one that the Bard warned us of."

"Why does Koyne appear to be in so much pain?"

"He tried to pick the lock, and something like lightning shot out of the lock and into his hand and wrist."

"We need to get back to the great hall without the Bard or that creature spotting us, follow me."

Graham looked at Koyne, and the two men quietly followed Jace. Staying to the shadows and crouching low, they quickly made their way back to the throne room. The Bard and the creature with him watched their progress all the way back to the entrance.

Jace pressed the two men back to the bedding where Avalon had just awakened. "What do you two think you were doing? Sneaking off like that could have put your lives and our lives in danger," he said, motioning at Avalon. "Now the Bard is speaking with, at least I think he is speaking with, whatever that creature is out there."

"We are sorry, we did not mean to cause any harm, it's just this place is so amazing and we wanted to see what was here. We knew it would be our only chance since the Bard had mentioned leaving at first light," said Graham apologetically. Koyne was still holding his wrist and looking miserable as he shook his head in agreement.

Jace shook his head and sighed loudly. "Let's go take a look and see what the Bard is up to."

The group approached the doorway quietly and looked out. At first they could see nothing. Then the cool mists of the marsh that had finally made purchase against the Kraggs swirled, and there in the distance was the Bard still speaking in that harsh, guttural language with the thick, squat creature.

"Do you think that is Oaran's boarhound?" Avalon asked, fear shaking her voice.

"I don't know, but that must be the reason I have felt so uneasy since we arrived," said Jace. "But if it is a boarhound, how could it have gotten here before us if it didn't know where we were going?" he asked in almost the same breath.

"The Bard must have told it to meet him here. I don't think he is working against the knights but for them," said Koyne, wincing with pain. "After all, he is free from the curse once they are."

Graham promptly came to the Bard's defense. "He is not in league with the knights. He has traveled the length and breadth of these lands trying to discover a way to destroy them. He is not bound to the curse, he is bound to an oath. Don't you pay attention? We don't even know if that is Oaran's creature."

"Look, we may be a little uneasy about this place, but Graham is right. This doesn't mean the Bard is working with the knights," said Jace, waving his hand in the direction of the Bard. "That creature could be something that lives in the caves around here. We know the Bard spent time here, maybe they crossed paths. He could be placating it so it doesn't bother us. There are a million scenarios we could play out in our frightened minds. In the morning we will just ask him about it. I'm sorry if I gave any indication the Bard is less than trustworthy," he said to Graham.

"Don't apologize, I know we are all on edge," replied Graham.

Koyne looked skeptical. "Let's wait until we get into the pass. If we find the Bard sneaking off for secret meetings with this thing, then we bring it up."

"Very well. Let's just go back to sleep," said Jace.

As they started to turn away, they froze. Taking one last look out at the Bard and the creature, they saw a strange blue light dance in the creature's eyes as it looked over at them. Reaching out a thick hand, it touched the Bard's leg and pointed to the opening. The Bard turned, and they could see the same blue light in his eyes. He turned back to the creature, spoke a word in that strange guttural language, and started toward the great hall. The creature turned away and vanished into the mists.

"It looks as though we will talk about it tonight. We've been caught spying," said Jace in his deep voice.

"Shall we talk here or by the fire?" asked the Bard, stepping through the opening.

"By the fire," they mumbled together like naughty children.

Once seated around the fire, the Bard spoke. "I was hoping none of you would see me talking to him. I had planned to keep his existence a secret from all of you unless it could not be avoided."

"Is it Oaran's creature? Will it kill us as we sleep? Is our mission compromised?" asked three different voices.

"Will anyone know if we die here tonight?" asked Avalon, shaking with fear again.

The Bard put a calming hand on her shoulder.

The three men were staring at the Bard, full of anticipation about his coming answers. "That was not Oaran's pet," began the Bard. "That was a man, or dwarf, as they were better known. He is the last of his people in this world that anyone knows of. They built this place hundreds of years ago when they left their homes in the White Mountains. This was the last city of the dwarves, they called it Kragg's Golden Valley. Kragg was their greatest king. He found ways to create peace with other nations, especially in the northwest where they originally lived. Eventually there was a great war between men, dwarves, and dragons. Kragg and his people fled in secret from their ancient mountain home to get away from the fighting and death of the war. Kragg had found the secret pass we will travel through and used it to bring his people here. They worked many years, turning this place from nondescript stone into the beautiful kingdom it is. When it was finished, he sent men back to the lands north and west to see if the wars had finally ended. Those he sent returned and reported everything west of them was destroyed. Kingdoms had burned, dead and decayed bodies covered the land. They found no living soul of man or beast, save the wild animals that roamed freely. For two hundred more years, they lived in this place against hope that other clans of their people from the White Mountains, Blue Mountains, Slate Hills, and Jewel Mountains would find them. They left markers that only dwarves would recognize to guide them here. It became unsafe for any dwarf to travel from this kingdom, if found alone or in small groups they were captured, tortured, and killed. Finally, one day Kragg and all his people disappeared. Everyone, that is, except McKray. He lives here taking care of everything until the day his people return."

"Who did those awful things to the dwarves?" asked Avalon.

"Men that wanted to know the location of the ancient dwarf kingdom, hidden in the vastness of the White Mountains. It was called Odin's Hall and supposedly had great treasuries of precious jewels, gold, silver, and the finest weapons and armor ever made. McKray says that it is a rumor and Odin's Hall never actually existed. He said the home they fled from in the White Mountains was called Garon's Hall. It was completely destroyed and all the wealth stolen during the wars."

"I thought you could only tell the tale of Souvac," said Jace.

"That is true to a point. What I told you was a brief history. Honestly I don't always know what I can say. So I give it a try. If my tongue is bound, I know not to speak anymore," replied the Bard.

"So what is this McKray's story? Why did he stay or get left or whatever happened to him?" asked Koyne suspiciously.

"If you want to know that, ask him yourself. That is his story and his life to share, not mine. Now, if everyone is satisfied that I am not a traitor, go back to sleep. We have a long road ahead of us tomorrow. Don't bother with a watch for the rest of the night, McKray said he would watch over us. Oh yes, before I forget, I need you and Graham to hand over everything you found while snooping about," said the Bard, looking pointedly at Koyne. The two men emptied their pockets of what they had found and handed it to the Bard. "What did you think of this place as you explored it?" he asked as he put the coins in a pouch and tucked it away under his blankets.

"The architecture is quite different from anything I have ever seen," replied Graham. "It has a heaviness to it with strong lines and runes carved into so many places."

"It is deceiving in appearance, what appears to be a smooth arc around a courtyard is actually full of…I don't even know what you could say other than more crags. There are stairs that lead up many levels with shops mainly on the first and second levels and what appeared to be homes above. Each was so unique in layout and design that it was exciting to search," stated Koyne, still holding his right wrist.

"I do wish we had time to show all of you more of this place, as it is truly a sight to behold, but we are pressed for time and must be going at daybreak. I implore all of you to get what sleep you can with the remaining hours before the sun rises." Again the Bard stopped speaking and rolled into his blankets before anyone could respond.

I still don't trust you, Koyne thought as he rolled into his blankets, his eyes on the Bard's back. Suddenly the words *I know* sounded in his mind. Slightly confused and a little shaken, he fell into a restless sleep.

The next morning, when the four companions awoke, sunlight was streaming into the hall from various sources. Looking around, they could see the immense size of this once-kingly hall. Standing, Jace noticed the ashes from the night's fire were gone and fresh wood was piled in the fire pit. Looking toward the entryway, he noticed bundles on the ground.

The Bard's voice came booming into the hall. "Pack your bedding and come outside."

This time there was a small amount of hesitation as they packed their bedding and made their way toward the opening. As they neared the bundles, they found it was armor, each bundle marked with one of their names.

"Pick up your new things and come out here," instructed the Bard.

Each shouldered a pack, leaving two, and stepped out into the early-morning sunlight. Mist still hung over the valley, giving a slightly gloomy start to the day.

"McKray took the liberty of preparing armor for us while we slept. He says we may need it as we make our way through the pass. We will be leaving in a couple of hours, so put your armor on and get the feel of it."

"I have my father's armor, I don't need these things," said Graham.

"Graham, take the armor McKray made. It is better than anything any man has ever made or used," said the Bard flatly.

"But these are my father's things. I can't just leave them behind."

"I understand your attachment to your father's armor and sword. Carry the extra weight, if you desire, but I tell you, dwarven armor and weapons are far superior for the fight ahead," the Bard said, indicating the armor and weapons forged by McKray.

Resistance glittered in Graham's eyes and stalwart posture.

"I know your father's armor is precious to you. You could leave it here. McKray will look after it for you."

"No, I won't," boomed the deep, rough voice of McKray from one of the many openings. "The boy is welcome to leave his father's things here in my vault, don't worry, they'll be safe, lad. But I will be joining you for a time on your little adventure, Bard." McKray had stepped from a door near the stables, sunlight dancing off his polished silver mail lined with gold. A jeweled belt around his waist held several weapons. Gold and silver were also braided into his dark-black beard. A helm of the same make covered his head. His jet-black hair fell from under the helm reaching the middle of his back. His black eyes danced with fire as he advanced on them. They stood in awe at the sight of this man, thick as a well-grown tree and full of purpose.

"It will be good to have you along, my lord," said the Bard.

"Enough of that lord business, you hear me, I know I can't kill you, but I can put a dent in that scruffy head of yours."

"What are the other two packs and armor for?" asked Avalon shyly.

"More importantly, how could McKray have made all this armor in one night and have it fit so perfectly?" asked Koyne as he easily swung his great sword in his new armor.

"Don't be a ninny, I can do things with metal that you can't even dream. Now throw that pile-of-dung sword away and pick a real weapon from that rack over there," he said, waving his hand.

Koyne, about to launch into a tirade, was quieted by a hand from Jace. "These are dwarven weapons, don't be a fool."

Koyne's anger abated. He shrugged and walked to the weapons rack.

"To answer your question, Avalon, McKray tells me we might find some company on the other side of the pass, so he prepared these just in case," replied the Bard.

Graham shook his head and sighed. "I will use the armor, but I am bringing my father's sword."

"Bring it here, lad," said McKray.

Hesitantly, Graham handed the sword to the dwarf and prepared himself for the harsh words that were sure to come.

"By Odin's beard, where did you get this?"

Graham looked at the dwarf. "It was my father's," he mumbled. McKray, holding the blade below the hilt, turned it toward the Bard.

"Interesting, very interesting," was all the Bard said as the two exchanged a knowing look.

Graham opened his mouth to speak, but McKray interceded, "You, lad, have been carrying around a dwarven weapon all your life, it appears. You're lucky to still be alive," he said as he handed over the sword. "Right, the rest of you, get your armor on and choose your weapons. Graham and Avalon, I suggest you each take a short bow as well as whatever else you choose. Jace and Koyne, you each take a long bow as well."

Before long, they were all dressed in the new armor and practicing with their weapons. Graham returned from putting his father's armor in the vault led by McKray.

"You all seem to be getting the feel of your new weapons. Now learn to trust each other. We are going into the pass, and the dangers present in there are real," stated the dwarf.

Gathering their belongings and packing the horses with the supplies, extra armor, and weapons, they moved over to stand in front of the opening that was Kragg's Pass. Nearby, a passage blocked by a heavy-looking wooden door with large pillars on either side seemed to hum deeply.

"You all start. I will make it look as though nobody has ever been here," said McKray.

After they had entered the pass McKray did as he said he would, then walked over to stand in front of the humming door. "When I return, Father, I pray you will forgive me and let me come home." He reached out and touched the door with his gauntlet-covered hand. As he touched the door, the morning mists cleared, and the bright sunlight reflected off the walls of Kragg's Golden Valley, causing it to shine like a precious jewel. "A more beautiful sight never has been seen as your kingdom, Father," said McKray, his eyes burning with the sight.

Chapter 5

McKray caught up to the others just a few hundred feet inside the pass. The carved stone walls, floor, and ceiling were perfectly flat. While leading the horses, they occasionally felt drafts of cool and warm air, which kept the cavern from getting stagnant and musty.

"Did your people build this pass?" Avalon asked.

"The pass was already here, we just made it smooth and created the airflow holes which keep the air circulating along the length of the pass."

"What sort of danger might we find in the pass? What is it we need to be aware of?" asked Graham.

"You're a wee bit jumpy, aren't ya, lad? There is danger inherent in everything. There are no real dangers here, a few harmless bats that might scare the weaker of ye, but the only thing I can think of that I would consider dangerous are the crystal spiders." Seeing the furtive glances of his companions, McKray continued, "I wouldn't worry too much about them, they only come out of their deep nests to find food. Since the pass is full of bats, especially down past the airflow holes where the spiders live and hunt, they hardly ever come out to play."

"Then why did you tell us the pass is dangerous?" asked Koyne.

"I already told ye danger is inherent in everything, 'tis better to be prepared than surprised," responded the dwarf.

"Tell us what the crystal spiders look like just in case," urged the Bard.

"Oh, they're wee little things about the size of a dog. They are crystal-like, blending in with the stone, as if ye see right through em, for the most part. It's true they can be hard to spot, so you just look for their eyes. The eyes flash in light like red fire. That's the best thing to keep 'em away too. Always keep one or two of the lamps burning. Their eyes are real sensitive, so these lamps just plain burn, the same way the sun burns our eyes. They are a bit venomous and can kill you with two or three good stings." Avalon turned to look at McKray; seeing the look of terror in her eyes, he quickly continued on. "But it's like I said, they rarely come out to play. Plus, we have the lamps. So no worries, eh," he finished.

Koyne put his arm around Avalon. "Come on, we are going to be fine," he reassured her.

"How long will it take us to reach the other side, Bard?"

"We left fairly early, so we should be through in three, four days at the longest. We will take several breaks a day to keep ourselves from getting exhausted. When we feel the need to sleep, we will sleep posting a watch, just to be safe."

Thus, they continued throughout the first day, leading their horses at an even walking pace, talking as they went about various unimportant things. They stopped periodically to eat and rest. Having no indication of what time, it was outside this underground passage, they began to be irritable—except for the Bard and dwarf who seemed to know exactly what time it was no matter where they were.

After an exhausting march, the Bard called them to a stop. "We will picket the horses to the iron rings in the walls, place our bedrolls, and set watch."

Holding the lamps above their heads, they found they were in a larger, rounded section of tunnel. To their left were iron rings anchored to the passage walls. To the right, the passage extended to allow for a large group of people to camp.

"Have we passed other places like this?" asked Jace.

"Just one smaller one a couple of hours in. You probably missed it as McKray was telling us about some of his run-ins with the crystal spiders," answered the Bard. "Koyne, you and Avalon build the fire and make dinner. Graham, you and Jace tether the horses and bring water for us all. McKray and I are going a little further down the pass. We will be back before too long. You do not need to worry about setting a watch, nothing will come from behind us, and we will be guarding you from the front. After you have eaten, get what rest you can."

"Save some of that meat for me, will ya, lass," McKray said to Avalon with a wink. "I am not like the Bard, I need food to sustain me."

"Come, McKray, quit flirting. She's much too young for you," the Bard said with a smile that vanished as soon as he turned away. Starting down the passage, he stopped and waited for the dwarf.

McKray joined him moments later. "You don't have to wait for me. I would have caught up."

They moved down the passage in silence. After a half hour of walking, the Bard stopped and looked at McKray.

"You are sure the brothers will be at the end of the pass?"

"Yes, Bard. They will be there. You may not appreciate it, but I am quite a bit older and fairly more experienced than you are. I have the gift of my father and would appreciate it if you would stop questioning me. Do we really have to do this?"

"If they aren't ready, they won't survive the final confrontation. They must be tested and strengthened like the steel you temper for weapons and armor." The Bard sighing, continued, "It is not a lack of trust in your abilities, McKray, it's me. "This could be the most important thing I have ever done. I want to make sure it is done right. I need to know as much about these three men as possible. I know Koyne's history, I suspect some things about Graham, he is related to Bowen. Jace is a complete enigma."

"I will get close to Graham and get him talking. You need to find out the truth about the other one. What about the girl, why is she here? Mind ye, I'm not complaining. She is beautiful."

"I don't know why she is here, other than she wanted to come. Now focus and let's get this sorted."

They laid the rest of their plans over the course of an hour. When satisfied that everything would work according to their plans, they made their way back to the others in silence, both thinking about the next few days.

"McKray, I saved some dinner for you," Avalon said when she saw them enter the lamplight.

"Oh, thank you, lass, but shouldn't you all be asleep?"

"It took longer than expected to get the horses tethered, the fire started, and dinner cooked," replied Avalon.

McKray sat down next to the young woman and tasted the food she had prepared. "This is delicious. If you're still free after this journey, I may ask you to come live with me for a while. It is so nice having the company of a beautiful young woman such as yourself." McKray winked at her.

Koyne flinched slightly at the dwarf's words before standing up from the fire. "I'll take first watch, even though you don't find it necessary." He looked at the Bard. "That is, if it's all right with everyone."

Everyone nodded their agreement as he looked around at them. Then he stalked off into the darkness of the passage. The Bard watched him go, his eyes glowing that strange bluish color. He saw Koyne sit down against the wall, well outside the lamp light, and start talking quietly to himself.

Jace came over and sat by the Bard. "Where have you traveled these many years of your life?"

"Why do you ask, Jace?"

"Just curious, I guess. I know from your stories that you were born in a small town in the south. You have been in Souvac a few times. You even spent time in Bareth's kingdom to the north. I was just curious about what other places you have seen and traveled to. I admit, on occasion I have wanted to travel with you, but you seem to vanish if anyone tries to follow without your consent." Jace looked at the Bard and smiled.

"I don't usually like company, ever since..." The Bard trailed off, and his eyes changed as if they were looking deep into the past. After a moment of silence, he shook his head and continued, "I have traveled the width and breadth of this continent. I have also traveled across the great seas to distant lands. Even though I was sworn to tell the tale of the knights of Souvac, I learned many incredible new tales about great men and women during my travels. When this is all over and the knights are destroyed, I will travel the rest of my life and tell these other tales. For they deserve to be heard."

Jace's voice changed slightly as he asked, "Do you really think we can destroy the knights?"

"I suppose that is what we will find out for sure when we reach the White Mountains and speak with Odin. Do you mind if I ask you a question, Jace?"

"You are, of course, feel free to ask me anything."

The Bard turned his body, looking into Jace's eyes as if looking deep into his soul. "Why did you volunteer to come? I know some of the reasons for Graham, and I chose Koyne, but I honestly don't know what role you will play in this quest."

"I said earlier that I wanted to follow you, the truth is, I have tried many times to follow you. I hoped you might help me. When you started asking for volunteers, I could not pass up the opportunity. You see, my mother was killed when I was eighteen. My father died when I was just a baby. I have been alone for many years. My mother, with her last living strength, gave me this note." Jace produced the note he had carried for so many years; the yellow color and frayed edges showed something of its age. "When I was still a child, my mother told me you knew my grandfather. Knowing who he was is the key to understanding everything about my family. Since her death, I have been traveling, trying to find out about my grandfather and my heritage. I don't know why, but I have always searched for the truth about where I come from. Perhaps it lies in one of those other tales you have learned." Pausing, he added, "I am different than most men. I can literally feel myself dying, like watching the sands of an hourglass fall. I want to learn the truth of my origins before my life runs out. I hope you will be able to help me find out who my grandfather was."

"I am not sure how I can help you, but I will do what I can." He was about to speak more when he heard McKray's rugged voice break through his thoughts.

"We need to get some sleep now if we plan on completing tomorrow's leg of the journey!"

"McKray is right, we have a long day ahead of us. I will think about what you have said. If I remember anything specific, I will let you know."

Nodding, Jace stood up to walk away.

"Wait, what were your parents' names?"

"My mother was Catherine Byrne. My father was called Doran Byrne."

"What were your grandfathers' names?"

"On my father's side, Ryan Byrne. I don't know on my mother's side, I was told that his name had to remain a secret for the safety of my family." Sadness was evident in his voice. He looked at the Bard a moment longer before going to his bedroll.

The Bard, with thoughts flowing through his mind, stood and walked over to where Koyne was keeping watch. "Is everything all right, Koyne? You seem a bit worked up."

"I'm fine," he said, subdued.

"When you get tired, come and wake me for the next watch," said the Bard.

Koyne merely nodded and continued staring down the empty passage.

The Bard walked back to where the others were bedding down and sat by McKray. "I am a little concerned about Koyne, I will stay awake and watch him tonight. He may be slipping a bit too far into himself. I want you to stop flirting with Avalon."

McKray's eyes practically stabbed the Bard through the heart.

"I know it's all in good fun, but it seems to be having a negative effect on Koyne. Besides, I thought you were going to work on getting to Graham." The words carried only as far as McKray's ears.

"Oh, I'll get Graham to trust me all right, but tell me why you are so concerned about Koyne over there," McKray whispered back.

"I will tell you when I can. I need to watch him a while longer. For now, just stick to the agreement and trust me."

As the night wore on, the Bard stayed awake watching Koyne. He did not get up or offer to take the watch, even as the night waned and morning came.

Eventually, Koyne stood up and walked over to where the Bard was now pretending to be asleep. Gently nudging him awake, Koyne spoke, "Bard, I think I kept watch through the night."

The Bard sat up, blinking away false sleep. He looked off into the distance and after a moment responded, "So it seems you have. We have a long road ahead of us today. Do you need rest?"

"No, I am ready to go. Let's wake the others and be on our way," he answered, again subdued.

"Very well, we'll eat before we go. I'll get the food if you'll wake the others."

Koyne proceeded to wake their companions, going to Avalon last.

The group ate a quick meal of toasted bread and boiled oats, before starting down the passage again. An hour later, McKray dropped back from beside the Bard to walk with Graham at the back of the line.

"The Bard tells me you are interested in my past, particularly why I stayed when the rest of my people disappeared from the land."

"Yes, I am curious about you. In the city I come from, there are stories about dwarves. I was wondering if your people all left, why would you stay hundreds of years after they had gone? Are you angry at your people? And how have you lived for hundreds of years? The stories I have heard about dwarves told me they had longer life spans than humans, but…"

McKray put his hand on Graham's shoulder. "Easy, lad, I'll answer your questions, if you promise to answer some of mine, with the agreement that we talk a wee bit slower."

"Agreed," replied Graham with contained excitement.

"To be perfectly honest, I didn't choose to stay behind," started the dwarf. "I am the son of King Kragg. I was quite young when we arrived in the Golden Valley. My people worked very hard to make a home there, since we fled our homes in the White Mountains. The Bard probably told you how great my father was for keeping us out of war. The truth is, he did keep us from war, by running away from humans. I was angry at my father for giving up all we had to avoid battle. We could have easily destroyed the humans and stayed in our mountain home.

"I have since come to learn, my father was right. However, at that time, I became lazy, I would not do or learn anything my father tried to teach. I allowed my belief that I was smarter than my father, and his counsel blind me. One day, some of the men who were mining came across an unusual chamber with an intense energy source. My father studied it for years, finally learning what it was and what it did. By this time, however, he did not view me as his son. He refused to tell me anything about the chamber, its energy source, or what it did. He kept it guarded night and day, keeping me and only me from going near it. My persistent attempts and outright disregard for his authority caused him to take drastic measures. One day, he built a door and endowed it with power to seal completely and forever without the key.

"At last, he gathered our people together in a great council in the very hall where you slept the first night. He told them to pack as many of their possessions as they could carry and meet at the door by nightfall. That night as the sun was setting, my people approached the door, one by one he gave them instructions and sent them into the passage where the energy source was located. I stood by his side and heard his every command. I wish I could say it was because my father wanted me there, but alas, I was there for my mother.

"Finally, after everyone else had gone, he sent my mother through. Only he and I remained. When he looked at me, tears were falling from his eyes. He told me I was not allowed to come, for I had lost what it is to be a dwarf. I tried to retaliate, but he grabbed me with his powerful hands and spoke, 'When you have gained all the knowledge this valley has to offer, when you learn what it is to be a dwarf, then you will be allowed to follow. Until that time, I give you life and the ability to see into the near future for the benefit of others. Help those who seek help in your presence and come to us when you are ready. I love you, McKray, you have been and always will be my son. The things I have kept from you, you are not ready for, I pray that one day soon that will change.'

"After that, he left, sealing the door as he went. I thought I heard him crying as he retreated down the passage. Since that time, I have learned all the lore of my people. I also learned it was never my father pushing me away but me pushing him away. I have yet to find the key that will allow me entrance to the chamber and my people beyond. So I am helping you folks on your way. You are all going to see the speaker of the God of the Living, so I will come as well. Perhaps he will know how I can get through the door."

McKray stopped talking and looked up at Graham. "So that is my secret. That is everything important to know about me."

Graham looked at the dwarf for a moment before responding, "You and I are similar then. I am Graham, son of Bowen, son of Tean, the true king of what is now called Souvac. My father turned the kingdom of Souvac into a town run by a group of wealthy landowners and left to avoid conflict. I am a prince as you are. Like you, I intend to get back to my people and regain the throne."

"We no longer have thrones to sit on or people to rule over, Graham. We are as noble as our works, and that is all. Trust me, lad, there is nothing grand about ruling over people. It is best to let them rule over themselves. Give them some guidelines, help them with laws, and they will do well enough for themselves if they are taught properly. Wait a moment. How is it that you are Bowen's son? You seem a bit young to be who you claim."

"I will tell you, if you tell me about your ability to see the future," replied Graham. McKray nodded his acceptance of the terms, so Graham continued, "Like I said, my father left Souvac and traveled to Tarshish where he worked for a merchant, sailing ships. He told me that one of the islands he did business with had tonics to keep their people younger much longer than normal. That is where he met my mother. She joined him, and they started their own business of keeping merchant ships safe. In other words, they destroyed the pirate ships. This made them very wealthy, and when they were in their nineties, they retired. My father was ninety-eight when I was born. Last year he got sick, and before he died, he told me all about his past. He gave me his sword and armor and asked me to find the Bard. He said he had, since my birth, begun to reflect on every aspect of his life. His only regrets were leaving Souvac without a rightful king and doing nothing to help destroy the knights of Souvac. So I plan to erase both of his regrets."

"Did he ask you to erase his regrets?"

"No, but why else would he ask me to find the Bard?"

"Now you are asking the right question. Your tale is very interesting, and it actually gives this old dwarf a bit to think about." He looked at Graham, who was staring at him with a look of expectation in his eyes. "Auugh. I get visions of the future, usually not very helpful. However, between you and me, that's how I had all the armor ready. I've been seeing your whole group in my dreams every night for two months. Don't tell Koyne. I prefer he thinks me capable of what I implied," said McKray with a wink.

Graham and McKray talked the rest of the day, even when the group stopped to rest or engage in weapons practice. Before nightfall they were as good of friends as were ever found in the land.

"What about elves, are they real? Did they ever exist in this world?" Graham asked the dwarf as they sat eating that night.

"Why ask me?" muttered McKray over some salted pork.

"All the books I have ever read about dwarves also included stories and pictures of elves," answered Graham.

"Look, lad, if you want to stay on my good side, you'll have to stop asking questions about that race of idiot beings. My people have been here since before the mountains were formed. We formed them after all. We don't like to associate ourselves with elves, even from a mythical standpoint. Now get away from me before I split your head," the dwarf grunted, rubbing Graham's head, roughly teasing.

Graham went over to sit by Jace. "Be careful not to mention elves around McKray. It seems he isn't a fan," Graham said with a chuckle.

The Bard watched and listened to everything that had happened that day. Jace had walked alone, seemingly deep in thought. He was proficient with weapons and had been helping Avalon master the use of her light mace and scimitar. Koyne was slipping further and further into himself, despite Avalon's best efforts to keep him close to her. The only time he seemed to come alive at all was during sparring practice with Jace. The Bard realized it would take all of Avalon's strength and will to keep him from slipping away. All these thoughts swirled through the Bard's mind, distracting him as the group settled down for the night. He did not notice Jace approach until he spoke.

"Who will keep the watch tonight, Bard? We know Koyne stayed awake all last night. Graham and I can split it tonight."

"No, I need you all rested for tomorrow, for we will try and finish the last leg of the pass. I will take the watch tonight. I do not need sleep," replied the Bard.

"You seem more distracted than usual. Is there anything I can do to ease your burden?" asked Jace.

"Just be ready for tomorrow, I want to get out of this pass before sunset tomorrow."

"I thought this was a three—to four-day journey."

"It is, but we are riding more than walking, and I pushed us a bit longer and further than previously planned today. We will be pushing even faster tomorrow. I feel we need to reach the end before sundown, if possible."

Jace shrugged his shoulders and rejoined the others.

Everyone turned in for the night as the Bard sat awake. When the deep, soft sound of sleeping bodies was all that could be heard, McKray got up and silently crept to the Bard's side.

"You knew that Graham was Bowen's son, did you?"

"Yes, I suspected as much," replied the Bard distantly.

"He has grand plans to help destroy the knights, then return triumphant to Souvac to take his place in the castle and fix everything. I tried to talk some sense into him, but I don't know if it did any good."

"I think he may give up his plans when we reach the heart of the King's Forest. There he will see what becomes of overambitious men." Changing the subject, he continued, "Koyne is falling quickly in the blackness of this place. We need to get him out of here as soon as we can. Avalon is holding tightly to him, but he has started pushing even her away. I did not realize being in the darkness of this pass would affect him so negatively."

"I don't suppose you are going to tell me what you mean by that."

"Normally I would let you get the truth from Koyne, of course, but it seems I miscalculated his condition, and he doesn't know himself. Koyne is the great-grandson of Oaran of the three knights of Souvac. About a year before the knights were cursed and sent to the King's Forest, Oaran met a beautiful young woman by chance. She was traveling and came from one of the smaller towns in the south. Her skin was almond brown, her hair was as black as a moonless night, her eyes crystal blue. She was average height with a slender grace and hidden strength. Her beauty was so complete that when Oaran came upon her outside the castle walls, even his black heart was softened. She was attracted to him but scared at the same time. As time passed, they drew together more and more. Finally, a month before he was cursed to the forest, he and that beautiful woman wed in secret. That night as they consummated their marriage, Oaran's posterity was established in her womb. To this day, Oaran has no idea what became of his young bride. He also has no knowledge that he had a child. It's possible that he has completely forgotten that he was ever married or in love.

"I found this same woman several years later. She had given birth to Oaran's son, Christean. He grew into a strong, good-looking man with a dark secret. When he reached adulthood, his mother told him who his father was. This information nearly destroyed him. He fell into darkness, slipping further and further toward what his father was. Finally, he met a woman that had power enough over him to dispel the darkness. They wed, and she had a son. His joy was complete for a few years, until sickness took his beloved wife. He left his five-year-old son, Boren, with an old maid and left. Christean returned when Boren was twenty and told him about his grandfather, Oaran. The dark secret continued in Boren, who also fell into darkness. He followed the same pattern as his father and, after many years, met a woman who bore Koyne. Boren left before Koyne was even born. He finally tried to find his son but was unsuccessful. Koyne knows nothing of his heritage. This is his secret. I share it with you since Koyne is unable to reveal it himself. He has had Avalon in his life since childhood, she has kept him in the light, if you will, but being here in the dark for days is not helping him. It seems even without the knowledge of his heritage, the curse is passed on, we need to get him out of here as quickly as possible," said the Bard. "And that is also why I need you to stop flirting with Avalon. Her innocent attentions on you are driving him into a dark place."

"All right, I will stop with Avalon, even though I think I was making some progress." McKray gave a sly wink. Then more seriously, he asked, "Does this mean our plans are changing?"

"Yes, old friend, it does. Tomorrow we pick up the pace a bit, no more practice breaks. We make for the end of the pass as fast as we can."

When morning finally came, which wasn't quick enough for the Bard, they packed up and ate as they walked. McKray led the way with Graham, who was asking endless questions of the old dwarf. Koyne and Avalon rode together behind McKray and Graham while the Bard and Jace brought up the rear. For the most part, the Bard watched Koyne like a protective father, lines of worry creasing his face. Occasionally, Jace would try to make conversation but soon gave up the attempt. After several hours of hard riding, and only one short break, McKray stopped the line, dismounted, and went ahead into the pass alone. The rest of the group dismounted as well. The Bard was just beginning to wonder what the dwarf was doing when the sound of booted feet came speeding back toward them. They could see the dwarf's eyes glowing that strange bluish color as he came running into view.

"Prepare for battle!" he yelled as he ran. "Crystal spiders up ahead and probably from behind!"

They quickly pulled their weapons from the packs on their horses and placed their lamps in a ring around them. The sound of the approaching spiders spooked the horses, which bolted forward down the pass from where McKray had returned. The first assault came from behind, almost immediately after the horses took flight. Large, crystal-like bodies scurried along the floor, walls, and ceiling toward the small group of travelers. The Bard was shouting orders for combat as the spiders closed on them. The Bard and Jace stood together against their attackers coming from behind. Graham had moved to the middle of the line with Avalon while Koyne had moved to stand with McKray at the front of the line. Graham and Avalon fired arrows into those creatures, advancing along the ceiling and walls, as Jace and the Bard cut down any creature that ventured near their swords. The spiders died easily and quickly, falling at each stroke, and with each arrow, their bodies were piling up, making it difficult to fight or even see the spiders that were still attacking. The group was slowly moving closer together as the spiders attacked. The six adventurers were tiring from the constant assault. Finally the spiders began to fall back, but just when it seemed they might be able to start a retreat, a second group of crystal spiders came at them from the side McKray and Koyne were defending.

"To the front, attack, attack!" yelled McKray.

Graham quickly turned and started firing at the second group of advancing enemies. The combatants were slowly pressed into a tighter and tighter knot. Suddenly the lamps that were giving off light and helping slightly to hold off the advance were knocked over and dowsed.

"McKray, have Koyne move behind you, Jace, get behind me!" yelled the Bard.

However, neither man moved away from the battle. Taking a quick look to the side, the Bard realized Jace could see in the pitch-black of the pass and from the sounds of the battle behind him, apparently so could Koyne. The fight continued to rage on both sides despite the impenetrable blackness of the pass.

Several more minutes of vicious fighting ensued, then just as suddenly as the crystal spiders attacked, they withdrew. The Bard found the knocked over lamps and quickly lit them. In the renewed light, Avalon and Graham could see the piles of dead spiders strewn around the cavern floor.

"Why did they attack?" the Bard asked, looking at McKray.

"It may be that they have been aware of us from the first night and have been craving the sweet smell of our flesh. We are very near the end of the pass, and it is most likely they chose to attack us when we were most at ease. However, this is where the pass narrows most. We are lucky they attacked here, in a place easy to defend," replied the dwarf.

"How much further to the end?" asked Koyne, still breathing heavily.

"No more than a mile. Now let's get moving. Everyone, grab what arrows are easy to retrieve, Graham and Avalon are nearly out of them." McKray pulled an arrow from a fallen spider as he spoke.

Without delay, the group followed the orders. Soon they were jogging down the last stretch of Kragg's Pass, Graham and Avalon with full quivers. After just a few minutes, they could see daylight at the end of the tunnel. They all broke into a run as they could taste truly fresh air and see sunlight. Avalon fell behind as the others made for the opening. Suddenly a thick, sticky rope wrapped around her ankle, tripping her to the ground. Her brief scream startled the others. Koyne turned midstride and saw her hit the ground. A large crystal spider sitting in an air hole in the cavern wall had tripped her with a web. Koyne dropped his swords and pulled his bow from his shoulder, knocking an arrow. He could see something changing inside the spider as it crept out of its hole and stood over Avalon. The crystalline insides shifted, and an obsidian black pointed stinger became visible. He shuddered as the six-inch stinger descended to the tip of its body. Without further delay, he took aim and let the arrow fly. The arrow struck the spider just as it started to inject Avalon with its venom. Dropping the bow, Koyne ran to Avalon's side, pushing the spider's body away. He frantically cut the web from her ankle with a knife, picked her up, and ran past his companions into the sunlight visible at the end of the pass. Graham retrieved both Avalon's and Koyne's dropped weapons, while the Bard shouted at the others to follow. Soon they were all breaking free of the darkness of the pass, into the fresh air of a spring evening.

Chapter 6

As the Bard and those that followed him exited the pass, they stopped short to see Koyne kneeling on the ground, Avalon's limp form lying on lush green grass before him. Standing in front of them were two men, pointing loaded crossbows at them. Having no energy left, the group raised their arms in surrender.

McKray, bringing up the rear, pushed his way forward. "All right now, what's going on here?" He looked at the two armed men, then down at Avalon. "Well, don't just stand there. Damien, round up the horses and picket them in the pines. Sterling, gather wood to build a fire. We'll need to boil some water and get this young woman taken care of." McKray knelt in the soft green grass, putting his hand on Koyne's shoulder.

As Jace opened his mouth to reply to the dwarf, the two men lowered their weapons and hurried to follow the orders.

"Don't mind those two. They are acquaintances of mine and mean us no harm," said McKray.

"How bad is Avalon hurt?" asked Koyne, his eyes red from crying.

"She isn't hurt bad at all, Koyne. You killed that creature before it could really sting her. Chances are she will be a little nauseated and tired for a day or two, but she will be fine. We should draw out the poison here and make camp close by," replied the dwarf.

With the excitement presumably over, the rest of the group looked around, taking in their surroundings. They stood in a large grassy area that was circular in design. Other than the opening to Kragg's Pass they had just come through, it appeared they were surrounded by towering cliffs that extended thirty feet in the air. Vibrant green mosses were affixed to the stone walls, giving the place splashes of earthy color. The unknown men had disappeared around an outcropping of rock to their left that shielded the mouth of the pass from whatever lay beyond.

The two mystery men returned a short time later. "Build the fire inside the pass. Boil water and bring it here," he told the men on their return. Silently they obeyed.

By now the group was seated on the grass. "Who are those men?" asked Graham.

"That is Sterling and Damien Cro. They are twin brothers who live in a small village east of here. I met them several years ago right here. They are some of the only people who have ever found the opening to Kragg's Pass on their own. They were as adventurous in their childhood as they are now."

Everyone settled into silence, waiting and watching, while McKray worked on Avalon, assisted by Sterling and Damien. After what seemed like an eternity, Avalon stirred and opened her eyes.

"How do you feel, lass?" asked McKray.

"Tired and weak, but a little better. What happened?" she asked.

"I'll let Koyne tell you, after all he's the one that really saved your life. Koyne, if you will follow Sterling and Damien, they will lead you to a safe camp area. Avalon will need you to carry her, so, Graham, if you'll be a good lad and get Koyne's pack for him. Jace, carry Avalon's pack. The Bard and I will be along shortly with their weapons."

"Look. If you and the Bard need to talk, just say so and we'll go," replied Jace, acting exasperated.

"Aye. You're smarter than you look, boy," teased the dwarf.

"I'm also older than I look, so don't call me boy."

"Don't get sassy. As old as I am, you will always be a boy to me."

Smiling, Jace picked up Avalon's pack and followed the path the others had taken. After he was gone, the Bard came out of his silent revelry.

"What happened back there, old friend? Those spiders should never have attacked us. We hadn't done anything to make them aware of us."

"Those confounded creatures are aware of everything that passes through their domain, Bard. However, why they attacked is simple, I, uh, encouraged it."

The Bard, about to respond, was cut off by a look from the stout dwarf.

"It's like you said—that kid, Koyne, was slipping fast into the darkness. He needed something to pull him out. A battle for the woman he obviously loves was the best way to do it. I never intended for anyone to get hurt, but that girl will be fine. She has the blessing of Odin on her. Plus, we learned some valuable information. Both Koyne and Jace have the ability to see in the blackest dark imaginable. I don't know about you, but I wonder more and more about Jace. Maybe he is also a missing great-grandchild of one of the knights."

"All I know about him is, he has tried to follow me from time to time. He says he is looking for information about his grandfather, or at least information regarding his heritage. Just before his mother died, she told him that I knew his grandfather, so he has come along hoping to find out the truth."

"Well, do you know who his grandfather is?"

"To be honest, I have no idea. I have tried to gain all knowledge of the knights of Souvac that I can, but nothing seems to track with Jace. I have searched every memory I have and still can find no connection to him and the knights."

"Perhaps he is lying to you, he could have made up his story to use you. Is it possible he is working with the knights? He did say he has followed you and heard their tale, perhaps he has already entered the forest, spoken with the knights, and is reporting back to them somehow."

The Bard's eyes darkened slightly as he poured over this possible scenario.

"Mind ye, I'm not pointing fingers, just giving possibilities."

"I hadn't thought of these things. I think I will watch Jace a bit closer. In the meantime, we will see if you were right about Koyne."

"Just wait," McKray said, shouldering his pack. "Koyne will be thinking only of her for the next several days. You see, I know a few things about the working mind of a man in love."

"Really? You have never told me that tale before."

"What's the point. You wouldn't be able to share it anyway, and this is a story to be shared," said McKray, winking at the Bard.

As night settled in, the dwarf and Bard stepped through a curtain of thick, down-hanging pine boughs and entered the hidden campsite where their companions were waiting. Jace, Graham, Sterling, and Damien were sitting together around a small fire talking. The Bard and dwarf sat down with the four men and joined their conversation. The Bard looked over at Koyne and Avalon. They were a short distance away. Avalon was wrapped in a blanket, and Koyne was holding her protectively in his arms. They were speaking in whispers to each other, but the Bard could hear them clearly.

"Avalon, you really scared me back there. Your skin was so cold, you weren't moving, I thought you were dead," said Koyne, lines of care creasing his dirt smudged brow.

"I'm sorry, Koyne. Maybe I shouldn't have come with you." Reaching up, she gently caressed his face.

"No, I'm glad you're here. I didn't realize how much I cared about you until I thought you were gone. I don't want you to be afraid of what lies ahead for any of us. I will always protect you and keep you safe."

Looking into his eyes, she saw them glittering with moisture. "I love you, Koyne. I have since the day I met you." Kissing him softly, she smiled, her hand still resting on his face. "I remember the first time I saw you. You were all covered in dirt then too."

Blushing with the memory, he smiled. "It was the first time I had traveled anywhere. My father left before I was born. Mother had to work all the time to take care of us. One day she said, 'We are leaving this wretched place and going to Souvac.' I didn't think there could be so much difference from one place to another. We traveled for days and arrived just in time for my seventh birthday. She took me out for stew at your father's inn that night. I had always wanted to feel like a man. When you came over, took my hand, and sang to me, I did."

"It was your beautiful eyes that made me fall for you." Koyne flinched slightly as she giggled, reliving the memory. "Is something wrong, my love?"

"No. I just…there is something… I think there is something wrong with me."

Shifting position, she sat facing him, looking into his eyes, searching for what he was hiding. "Koyne, please stop hiding from me. I love you, if there is something bothering you, please tell me. Trust me."

"Avalon, I do love you. There is something about me that you should probably know, but I just don't quite understand, or even know what it is myself." Avalon's eyes lost some of their sparkle at his words. "Please don't be upset with me. I can't tell you, because I am still trying to figure it out in my own mind. I have been living life one moment at a time, but now I am starting to truly search for answers about, my life, my father, and my future. I believe I will find those answers on this journey. It's possible the Bard knows exactly what I am looking for, and that is why he called me to this quest." Taking her hands, he drew her into his arms once more. "Avalon, when I know what it all means, I will tell you everything."

"All right, but please, don't ever pull away from me like you did in the pass."

"I promise I will stay close to you for the rest of my life," replied Koyne, not realizing exactly what he had promised that beautiful woman.

Just then, a warm breeze blew through the hidden campsite, and with it came a great desire to sleep.

"Now lie down here by me tonight." Wrapping his arms around her a bit tighter, they settled in and were soon embraced in a deep slumber.

The men around the fire had also risen to get their beds in order and lay down for the night.

"Do we need to set watch?" asked Jace, yawning from his blankets.

McKray and the Bard looked at each other. "No, there will be no need for a watch tonight," replied the Bard.

Several miles away, on top of Watcher's Hill at the base of the White Mountains, an old man stood humming to himself and smiling.

*****

Morning brought clear skies and, compared to what they had eaten in the passage, a feast. Sterling and Damien had awakened early, built up the fire, and started cooking. Avalon and the others woke to the smells of bacon and eggs frying over the fire.

"I'm starving," she said, approaching the fire. They took their time that morning and ate a grand breakfast.

"Will we be leaving soon?" asked Graham.

"Not until tomorrow," replied the Bard. "Now that we are through the pass, we can pace ourselves a bit more. I know we are all worried about the creature that Oaran has sent after us, but rest assured, very few creatures will have been able to track us through the plains, swamp, and pass."

"Besides, the crystal spiders are agitated and won't settle again for several days. So if anything does try to follow us, it will find it hard to do so," said McKray.

"I need to scout the way ahead to be sure we are still going the right direction. I will be back before sunset," stated the Bard.

"Would you like some company?" Graham asked, jumping to his feet.

"Not this time, it will be best if everyone uses the day to rest." He inclined his head at Avalon. "Also, I wish to know what the terrain will be like tomorrow."

"We know the terrain and can get you safely through," said Damien of himself and Sterling.

"There are signs that I go to find that even your keen eyes would miss," said the Bard. Mounting his horse, he disappeared through the thick boughs of the immense pine tree.

"What is he talking about? First, he is checking terrain, then he is looking for signs. Who does he think he is?" asked Damien looking at McKray.

"He is the Bard of Souvac, he does what he wants, and what do you mean you will get us through? You're not even invited. However, if you two want to go exploring, look for snowberries and see if you can catch a few rabbits for dinner."

Knowing McKray as well as anyone, the brothers simply smiled. "Yes, Your Majesty, anything you ask will be granted, Your Majesty." They mocked before rushing from the cover of their campsite.

McKray grumbled and threw a pine cone at the retreating pair.

Stepping clear of the pine boughs revealed a bright green forest of mostly deciduous trees and scattered pines; the movement of animals filled the forest. Taking a deep breath of the forest air, the Bard turned his mount due west and rode through the clear morning at a trot. A couple hours after midday, he came to a stream. Filling his waterskins, he allowed his horse refreshment, then turned north. The cloud cover increased as he traveled another couple of hours; the forest began to thin as the mostly flat terrain began to give way to rolling grass covered hills. He wound his way through these until he came to the foot of the White Mountains; by this time the clouds had thickened and gave the look of rain. As he continued to ride up the ravines of the foothills, the trees again changed and patches of aspens became the dominant tree. The Bard stopped when he reached a rather large treeless, grassy hill. Tethering his horse to a sturdy bush, he started up an old animal trail toward the top. After thirty minutes of labored hiking, he reached the summit and began looking around. The ground was torn up in several places, and footsteps marred the grass in several others. Besides that, the Bard found no physical signs of anyone being there in the recent past. Yet he knew by the feel of the place that someone had been there the night before—someone very old and very powerful; both he and McKray had felt it.

Sighing, the Bard sat down on the only rock atop the hill and pulled out a pipe. He knew Odin had been here, but what other creature could have disturbed the ground like this? *Are these areas of overturned earth supposed to be signs for me to follow?* he wondered after smoking his pipe. Again he looked around the top of the hill. A few patches of grass trodden by the footsteps of a man, great areas of overturned earth, and the single small boulder on top of this hill where he had smoked his pipe were all he could see. *What am I to make of this? There seems to be no pattern, nothing I can follow or make out,* thought the Bard once again, sitting on the boulder that suddenly seemed very out of place.

Standing, he looked at the boulder. After several moments, he smiled. Placing his hand on top of the stone, he spoke a word of power he had found in an old scroll McKray had shown him once, "Akeru." He watched as the stone started to glow then change shape. It spread along the ground like molten lava. Hills and mountains quickly formed on its surface. Before long, a miniature of the White Hills and Mountains lay on the ground at his feet. Crouching down, he peered at it with his intense green eyes. Pulling maps from his pack, he began to compare them to the miniature that lay before him. He searched for a path that would take them to the Hall of Odin. He worked at it for hours until frustration began to set in. Finally, a ray of sunlight broke through the clouds, lighting up a path of small crystals embedded in the stone. Marking the path on his map that most resembled what he had before him, he smiled.

"We are coming, Odin. Be patient with us." Reaching out, he touched the stone again. "Shimeru," he spoke and watched as the model returned to its original shape.

The Bard made his way down the hill to where his horse was contentedly nibbling at the grass. Looking around, he realized just how late it had gotten. Mounting his horse, he made the return journey to where his companions were camping. He rode at a brisk pace through the evening, as the sun descended further behind the White Mountains the clouds broke and pink and purple hues painted the sky. A feeling of peace filled the Bard's heart and mind then, unlike anything he had known since his son had been born. The light faded to darkness, and a half-moon lit the path for the Bard. Like a rustle of wind in the leaves, he made his way through the pine boughs tethered his horse and lay down to sleep.

Before he drifted off, he heard McKray's gruff voice nearby. "Did you find it?"

"Find what?" he mumbled, already half asleep.

"Whatever you went off to find."

"Oh yes. I found it, and I'll show you when we get there."

McKray grunted and rolled over, allowing the Bard to drift into a comforting sleep.

*****

Once they were asleep, a shadow detached itself from the surrounding darkness, mounted a black horse, and slipped quietly into the darkened forest. It traveled back into the foothills from where it had followed the Bard. Traveling at speed, it arrived at the hill the Bard had climbed within five hours' time. Continuing north, it followed a broken stone path into a dense, bush-choked canyon, sometime later it finally turned east, following a small game trail. After thirty minutes of more travel, the shadow reined its steed to an abrupt halt in a small grass-covered clearing. Dismounting, it silently lit a torch and held it above its head. An answering torch flared to light several paces ahead of him in a tree; still he remained motionless. Two minutes later, large torches to his immediate right and left were lit, bathing the clearing in light. Revealed, the man held his left hand straight out in front of him with the palm up.

"You may proceed," said a powerful voice from the dark.

Without hesitation, the man continued forward across the clearing. Cliffs rose around the clearing to immense heights. At the opposite side of the clearing, the man dismounted, tethered his horse to a small tree, and entered a large cave hidden by brush. The cave was dimly lit by torches hanging at intervals along the walls. The floor, walls, and ceiling of the cave were smooth as glass. Smaller tunnels were occasionally glimpsed leading off to the right. The man quickly made his way to the last tunnel leading off this main passage. Different from the rest, it led to the left, was closed off by a door, and guarded by a somewhat hidden sentinel.

"You are slipping, Dale. If you cannot do a better job hiding, perhaps you will be relieved of your duties," growled the man coming up the passage.

"I'm sorry, Jotham," said Dale, gently pressing a dagger into the small of his back.

"Ah. Very good, Dale, subterfuge and trickery. But I am really in no mood tonight. I need to speak with Garen now," said Jotham. Grabbing Dale's wrist and spinning, he pressed a knife point to Dale's throat. "Now go in there and tell Garen I am here," he continued, nicking Dale's neck to prove his point.

Dale silently sheathed his dagger. Wiping the trickle of blood from his neck, he entered the closed door. A moment later, a gruff voice sounded from the dark chamber. "This had better be important, Jotham!" said Garen, leader of the Rogues.

Jotham entered the sleeping chamber, which was now lit by a small lantern on a table near Garen's bed. "It is the most important news you will have heard in quite some time, I assure you."

"Well then, get on with it," said Garen, lounging in his bed of pillows. A young dark-haired girl chained to a post to Garen's right watched the three men with loathing.

"I was watching the path near Watcher's Hill when I saw a large man riding toward me. He was alone and wore basic traveling clothes and a long sword at his side. He rode along as though looking for something. I waited for him to pass me and was about to attack him when he stopped. Dismounting his horse, he made his way up Watcher's Hill. Not wanting to spook his horse or draw his attention, I waited for him to return. Just before sunset he reappeared, looking very pleased with himself. He mounted his horse and returned the way he had come at a relatively quick pace. Curiosity won me over, and I followed him. Several miles to the east, amid the forest, I saw him ride into the boughs of a huge pine. I followed him in and saw that he has companions—five men, a woman, and a dwarf."

At mention of a dwarf, Garen's eyes opened wide, and he sat upright in his pillows. "Dwarves have been gone from these lands for hundreds of years. You must be mistaken!" said Garen.

"If all the legends we have heard about dwarves are true, then this is most definitely a dwarf. They will be coming back to Watcher's Hill tomorrow. The large man is going to show something to the dwarf."

"Then let us prepare a surprise for them. Take forty men and attack them at your discretion. Take the dwarf and girl alive, kill the rest." Thoughts of what the dwarf could tell him brought a smile to his face and drove the presence of the dark-haired woman from his mind.

The next morning, the Bard and his companions woke with the rising sun, packed their gear, and started their journey again. The Bard told the others to ride close together.

"Sterling, Damien, do you know the way to Watcher's Hill?" asked the Bard.

They looked at each other. "Of course, we do," they answered in unison.

Damien continued, "I find myself offended that you would even ask. McKray, have you told the good Bard nothing of us?"

"Of course not."

"Damien considers these wild lands our kingdom. We know the land from the Great North Road, west to the ancient land, and from the Kraggs to the base of the White Mountains as well as anyone."

"Very well, you can lead us," stated the Bard.

"Follow us then," replied Damien, as he and Sterling moved to the front of the column by the Bard.

As the group began riding, the Bard spoke, "Do you all remember what I told you about Odin's Hall?"

"Yes, you told us it was a myth according to McKray," responded Jace.

"You told them I said that? Are you trying to keep me from my people forever, Bard?"

"I didn't want to get everyone riled up, and until yesterday I didn't know for sure that it was our destination. Now, listen carefully as McKray tells you the tale of Odin. It is important that you know a little about him when we get there."

"Are you telling us that Odin is alive? Just how many immortal beings are we going to meet on this trip?" asked Koyne.

"At least six by my count," said Graham with a half smile.

"I'm beginning to think there might be more immortal beings living here than mortal ones, and it's a bit disconcerting," said Koyne.

"Oh, don't get your knickers in a twist. The fight yer in is just a small piece of a bigger picture. There are always the same number of immortal beings on each side," said McKray

"What do you mean?" asked Avalon.

"What he means," replied Damien, turning backward in his saddle, "is there are two sides, light and dark. They have been at war for millennia. If there are people granted immortality for one side, then the other side gets the same number to maintain balance."

"Well put, Damien, a simple yet complete answer," replied the Bard.

Damien turned again in his saddle, with a look and wink at Avalon.

"Yes, very good, Damien has always been the teacher's pet and a bit of a showoff," snarled McKray with a look of pride twinkling in his eye. "I suppose you want me to tell them all I know of Odin." The Bard just nodded. "Aye, very well, Odin is the oldest man to ever live," began McKray. "There are reports and stories of him going all the way back to when dwarves first came out of the mountains. There were many clans in those days, anywhere there were mountains, there were dwarves. But the greatest clan lived in the White Mountains. We thrived there building and creating beautiful halls and cities carved from the very stone. Odin was there too. He taught us from the beginning about the stone, minerals, and ores. He began teaching us about the God of the Living and what this life should mean to us. He told us about other people like him who had gone to teach the clans throughout the land. We could pass communications from clan to clan through Odin and his people. He told us with good came evil. And so it was, because the God of the Living had a brother that had dissented from the ideals that made life sweet and full of joy. His name was Kish the Evil One.

"Once we had learned all that Odin could teach us about the God of the Living, we were given greater knowledge concerning the forging and purifying of metals. We used this knowledge to make beautiful designs in the rock and jewels to wear. After many years, Odin told our king that a great good and evil was coming to these lands. He then said he and his people would do what they could to help us, but he had to go to a great council and would return as soon as possible.

"Shortly after that, we found that humans were building cities on the coasts. Through the years they spread from the coasts and moved toward the mountains and plains. We went among them to trade and learn about them. They taught us your language, and we paid them in gold, silver, gems, and other precious things for food, material for clothes, almost anything they had to sell, we wanted in order to understand them. They learned of our wealth and skills. As we became more and more open to them, the dragons came. We didn't know where they came from, but they came, stealing our treasure and hiding it in large chambers inside the mountains. We killed many of them in an attempt to reclaim what was ours. Odin returned and was angry with us. He told us to stop killing the dragons. He said he had sent them, they were trying to help us. He told our king that the humans were planning to attack and kill all the dwarves, taking what was ours. Pride had crept into the hearts of my people, especially our king. He and our people had grown to love man's praises, their precious things as well as gold, silver, and precious stones. The love of those things became greater than our love for Odin. The king at the time, King Flintfire, was angry with Odin and attacked him, that is when all dwarves were sent from Odin's presence. Since then, the location of Odin's Hall has been lost to the knowledge of all beings. It wasn't until later we learned that King Flintfire knew the dragons were good, sent by Odin to help, they were not stealing our treasure but hiding it from the humans. That is the sad tale of the dwarves."

The horses continued along the path, flicking their ears as the flies buzzed nearby.

"Do you know where Odin's Hall is?" asked Graham.

"No, nobody knows where it is."

"If no one knows where it is, how are we going to find it?" asked Graham.

"There is someone that knows where it is, Odin himself, and it appears he is helping us find the location," replied the Bard. "He left a map for us to follow on Watcher's Hill."

"So Odin just left a map on top of a hill that you knew would somehow be there. A map that leads to Odin's Hall. Can anyone else see or read this map?" asked Koyne incredulously.

"Yes, actually, McKray can. The map is an Odin stone," said the Bard.

"Oh well, that explains everything. Thank you for clearing that up," replied Koyne sarcastically.

"We will show you when we get there. After McKray and I have examined it, of course," stated the Bard.

"What happened after the dwarves left and the dragons came?" asked Avalon. Her curiosity about Odin was piqued. She urged her horse closer to McKray.

"Well, after the dwarves left Odin's Hall, dragons started attacking some of the humans, burning and killing them. The humans begged us to let them into any of our fortifications as the dragons did not attack those. So dwarves worked with the humans, allowing them into our cities and halls. The humans then begged for help to stop the dragons. Their pleas were so strong that all dwarf clans joined them." As McKray continued, a silence fell on the forest, and the light even seemed to dim. "Together we hunted and killed the dragons. When dragons became sparse, the humans turned on us, accusing us of employing the dragons to kill them. Battle and war raged throughout the land between dwarves and men. We in the White Mountains were the last clan to survive. As far as we knew, humans killed off all the other dwarf clans. We closed the passes and our cities, hiding from men. We learned as we watched them that the humans were the good and evil Odin had spoken of. My great-grandfather, King Greyhame, son of King Flintfire, felt guilty for the death of so many dwarves. Wanting to somehow make amends, he went in search of Odin. He pleaded with him to return and teach the dwarves, for they were angry and hateful and had started for the first time in history to fight amongst themselves. Odin returned with King Greyhame and began to teach us again. He explained that the dragons had only killed men who were wicked and had plotted against us dwarves. He told us if dragons should return, to protect them, for they were our allies, they had been hiding our treasure in a very special place and would one day return it to us. Many dwarves began to speak out against him, but my great-grandfather stood forth. He told our people we needed to listen to Odin. If we attempted to kill another living dragon, we would be put to death as punishment. Odin then blessed my great-grandfather with the ability to see images of the near future. In this way, he could ensure our lives and the lives of our allies.

"After that, Odin stayed with our people. He left occasionally, but only for a few months at the longest. He stayed teaching and helping us. Dragons never returned, and Odin never really seemed to have true joy, until my father returned from his rights of passage journey. I don't know what he told Odin, but ever after Odin had joy." As he said this, the heavy feeling that had come over the group dissipated, the light increased, and the birds resumed their singing, even the horses seemed to gain new vigor. "Odin stayed in the White Mountains. When we left, he returned to Odin's Hall. He said he would stay until it was time. I don't know what that means, but I suppose he is there waiting for us, but since I am the last dwarf, perhaps he waits for me. That is a brief history of Odin and his time among my people."

Jace's horse nickered. "Why did your people leave the mountains and go to the Kraggs?" asked Jace.

"It had to do with my father's rites-of-passage journey. I was so young then, only ten years old, I barely remember anything specific. Only that history and lore that all dwarves learn so we never forget the truth."

"I can't wait to meet Odin. I wonder if he can answer my questions," stated Avalon.

"Of course, he will answer your questions. I have heard he is fond of beautiful young maidens," said Damien with a wink; he moved his horse to ride beside Avalon. Both brothers were considered good-looking, but Damien had a witty charm to go with his dark-brown hair and olive skin. He flashed an easy smile, and his green eyes were the talk of the village maidens. He had been immediately attracted to Avalon, a fact that Koyne didn't miss. Sterling was more cautious and always kept two sharp eyes on his brother. He had had to pull him out of more than a few scrapes. Damien had a way of wooing a young lady, whether he was interested or not. He was mostly interested in being adored.

Koyne hadn't missed the wink or the looks Damien kept giving Avalon over his shoulder. So when he made this last comment and brought his horse alongside Avalon's, Koyne made a move, pushing forward to place himself between the young man and Avalon.

"So what's your story?" he asked. "What brings you and Sterling on this adventure?"

"Honestly, the adventure is what brings us. Right, brother?" said Damien casually.

"The adventure brings you, and you bring me. Damien is always out to prove something to someone. It seems you, Avalon, are his new audience," said Sterling, turning in his saddle.

"Well, I am very flattered, but I already have someone to impress me, who no longer has anything to prove," said Avalon with a smile toward Koyne, which caused him to sit a bit taller in his saddle.

"Very well, I can see that there is no use trying to steal your heart," replied Damien with a wan smile.

"See, fickle as the weather, I don't think I have ever seen you really fight for a woman's attention. If it isn't given immediately, you give up," stated Sterling, still looking at those behind him.

"Oh, you know so, little brother. It's the long game." Damien winked at Avalon again before returning to his place beside Sterling.

Somewhat irritated by the recent conversation, Graham chimed in, "What did bring you to be at the mouth of the pass when we arrived?" he asked.

Sterling looked at Damien. The brothers both turned completely in their saddles to face the others, letting their horses continue forward without guidance.

"We were coming to find McKray," said Damien.

"Were you expecting him at this end of the pass?" asked Koyne ever suspicious.

"No, we needed some new arrows and real armor, so we were going to him. We like to explore these regions, they have been relatively empty these last hundred years. Farmers and herdsmen have begun cultivating the land again recently. However, we have heard rumors of a band of rogues that have taken to the foothills in this area. They are robbing, looting, and murdering the settlers that are trying to build a life here," said Sterling.

"We have been trying to track them, so we can end the threat to the region and allow people to make a life here again. Plus, we have heard that they kidnapped a farmer's daughter who lives just a few miles east of here. I suppose you could say we have become the unofficial sheriffs of the west," said Damien.

"We think the rogues have a secret camp somewhere near Watcher's Hill. We were going to go to the farmers after seeing McKray, but since you are already going our way, we thought we would join you and ask for a bit of help dealing with these ruffians," added Sterling.

"What do you think, Bard, can we help them out?" asked McKray.

"We really don't have a lot of extra time, further delays could allow Oaran's boarhounds to find us," replied the Bard.

"Very well, after Watcher's Hill, you go about your business, I'll help the boys with the rogues and catch up to ya," stated the dwarf.

They continued speaking as they rode the constant hum of conversation drifting around them. The forest was alive with birds flying back and forth chasing each other in play. Squirrels, rabbits, and an occasional deer would cross their path. They were all very relaxed when they reached the stream where the Bard had turned north the day before. Here they allowed the horses a rest and refreshed their own waterskins.

"Watcher's Hill is just a two-hour ride up this trail. If there are bandits in the area, I recommend we silence unnecessary conversation and keep our eyes open," said Sterling.

"It would also be beneficial to wrap ourselves in our cloaks to hide our identities, as well as our rich armor and weapons," suggested Damien.

"True but have your weapons loose and ready for a fight just in case," replied Sterling. "If the rogues are already aware of us, they will attack, which means a fight to the death. Well, not for McKray or Avalon, or the Bard since he is immortal, but the rest of us surely will be killed."

"Why wouldn't they kill McKray or Avalon?" asked Graham

"Well, McKray is the last living dwarf in these lands that anyone knows of, which means he can make dwarven weapons and armor as well as show the rogues where Odin's Hall and all its wondrous treasures are. And Avalon is a perfect specimen of womanhood," said Damien with a wink and a sigh. "Use your imagination."

"If you keep talking like that, you won't have to worry about the rogues killing you, Damien," said Koyne, spurring his horse forward to once again block Damien's view of Avalon.

"Don't worry, hero, I know her heart belongs only to you."

"All right, let's all just settle down and stop this nonsense," said McKray. "Damien is correct, however, so let's at least follow his advice."

They did as instructed and rode on in silence, while loosening their weapons and trying to look as poor and pitiful as possible.

*****

"What do you mean you've lost them?" Jerec asked Oaran.

"The boarhound is unable to pick up their scent. It tracked all three scents and killed all the pack horses it found, but the Bard's scent is gone."

"Where is that useless creature now?"

"He is at the swamp where the scents split."

"Good, send him into the swamp."

"But, Jerec, he won't be able to make it through. He will die in there," stated Oaran, a hint of concern barely discernible in his tone.

"You should have thought about that before you decided to make a decision about how to use the other one in Souvac. I believe it's dead also, isn't it, killed by the whelp that followed the Bard to the forest?" stated Jerec, the words practically dripping with venom.

"How did you know about that?"

"I know everything that you do. Now send the beast into the swamp."

Oaran could see all that his boarhound saw; he could feel the panic in his pet as it stepped from spongy earth into the sucking, oozing mud of the marsh. The heavy bodied creature moved deeper into the marsh. Panic continued as it sought firm ground to step on. The mud and water rose higher and higher; hours of slow painstaking travel ended as the terrified beast was pulled under the marsh's surface. Oaran gasped for breath as the creature sucked in a mouthful of muddy water, then he shuddered as the animal died. "It is dead, I told you it would be a pointless attempt."

"Send the rest," said Jerec in quiet anger.

"I don't know if I can keep that many under control."

"I don't care, just find them!"

Unable to control himself any longer, he stomped away to his shelter.

"We may need to do something about him," said Kell quietly as he stepped beside Oaran.

"What are you talking about?" replied Oaran as he prepared to send the remaining fifteen boarhounds in search of the Bard's party.

"Jerec has completely lost his mind to his hate and anger, just like Souvac. If we do ever get out of here, he will destroy not only Bowen's posterity, whoever they may be, but us as well."

"I also want Bowen's posterity dead."

"Do you really? Think, Oaran, we have lived for a hundred years in this ridiculous state. My hatred is directed at me now. We were the ones that made the oath. We are the ones that killed Souvac. I don't want anything to do with this anymore. I'm tired," replied Kell.

"You better hope I don't tell Jerec what you just said, Kell. Remember, we are together, all or none."

“Says the man that attacked Jerec with a boarhound,” replied Kell as he walked away from Oaran.

Oaran’s gaze followed Kell all the way back to where he sat by Souvac’s corpse, before turning to the north. Oaran, still thinking about what Kell had said, bent his will on the remaining fifteen boarhounds and sent them from the forest.

Kell watched Oaran with a wicked light dancing in his eyes. The first seed of his plan was effectively planted.

Chapter 7

"Dale, you and I will climb to the top of Watcher's Hill with half of the men. The rest of you will stay hidden at the base of these hills. As soon as the man and dwarf get to the top of the hill, I will put an arrow through the man's heart. Then we will grab the dwarf, killing any others that come with them. As soon as you see the big man fall, you lot will attack whomever stays behind. Keep only the girl alive," said Jotham to the men gathered around him.

"Perhaps I should stay with the men down here," stated Dale.

"I have already given the orders, Dale, and you will follow them. We have suffered through enough of your mistakes. Why Garen keeps you alive is beyond me." This last comment was muttered.

Time passed slowly as the sun rose ever higher into the sky warming the surrounding hills. Having arrived just before sunrise, the rouges knew they would be waiting hours for their victims to arrive. As the sun crawled toward midday, some of the men began to wonder if anyone would be falling into their trap. Just as Dale was going to open his mouth to speak with Jotham, they heard a horse whinny in the distance.

"They should be to the top of this hill within the hour," whispered Jotham, smiling.

At the bottom of Watcher's Hill, the Bard called a halt. "This is Watcher's Hill, McKray and I will be investigating the map at its top. We will probably be gone for a couple of hours. Make yourselves comfortable amongst the shade of the trees," stated the Bard.

The group of travelers dismounted and tethered the horses. The Bard and McKray started up the hill using the same old game trail the Bard used the day before. All around the air filled tense and full of energy.

"Do you feel that?" McKray asked the Bard.

"I do. It feels as though this area is about to explode," replied the Bard. "Perhaps we should have reminded the others to keep a watchful eye." Stopping momentarily, the Bard peered down the hill to where the others were resting. Jace sat with his back against a tree, watching everything that passed around him. Sterling was also concentrating deeply on the hills and forest around them while eating a piece of bread.

"I think they will be just fine."

It was warm now, and by the time dwarf and Bard reached the summit of the hill, they were sweating freely. The Bard had just lifted his arm to point to the large stone at the center of the hill when an arrow buried itself deep in his chest. As he slumped to the ground, wild cries broke out from the base as well as the summit of the hill. McKray jumped in front of the Bard as if to protect him from the men now charging at them. An instant later, the men who so bravely started the charge faltered, slowed, and then stopped, gaping in McKray's direction.

"Scared of a single dwarf, are ye?" spat McKray.

A bloodied arrow fell at his feet. "I think they are surprised to see me alive," said the Bard fiercely. "Well, what are you waiting for? Come on!" he shouted at the stunned rogues.

Below, Jace had been watching the progress of Bard and dwarf. As soon as the Bard fell, he was on his feet.

"To arms!" he shouted, gaining the attention of those that remained with him. In the same instant, wild cries sounded around them.

"Protect Avalon!" yelled Koyne.

Avalon, Graham, and Damien immediately grabbed bows, firing arrows at the men charging toward them from all directions, the arrows effectively clearing the ranks of the rogues from twenty to eight. Soon, however, they were engaged in vicious hand-to-hand combat with the remaining attackers. Jace and Sterling stood together to repel the first assault that reached them through the arrows being fired. The second assault knocked them aside. Damien, seeing a large man coming straight at Avalon, jumped to her aid and fell, a dagger protruding from his chest. Before she could draw her slender, short sword, the large man grabbed her with one strong arm and turned to flee. Graham blocked the way with his father's broadsword.

"You will die, boy," threatened the man with a vicious grin.

"This sword repelled the knights of Souvac, vermin, it will see you dead." His eyes flashed as he prepared to fight the large man.

The large rogue placed his gloved hand over Avalon's mouth and nose; she immediately slumped to the ground unconscious. Graham's shock at Avalon suddenly lying prostrate on the ground gave the rogue an opening to attack. It was good fortune alone that saved Graham then. Koyne, engaged in battle with another rogue, spun his attacker around and pushed him to gain an advantage. The off-balanced man knocked Graham to the ground and died with his large comrade's short sword in his chest. In the next moment, Graham kicked out hard at the large rogue's leg, catching him in the knee, sending him to the ground howling in pain. Taking the advantage, Graham climbed to his feet and struck out with his sword; the large man was trying to scramble to his feet but fell an instant later, Graham's sword cutting through leather armor and flesh. Graham, looking around, saw the fight was over. All of the rogues lay dead. Sterling had suffered a few minor cuts to the face and hands. Koyne stumbled to Avalon's side and knelt beside her, gripping his shoulder to stop the flow of blood from a knife wound. Jace stood untouched, wiping blood from his sword on his enemy's tunic. Avalon was lying in the grass, her chest rising and falling with life. But where was Damien? Sterling spotted him first, lying facedown and motionless beneath the crumpled form of one of the rogues.

Sterling ran to his brother's side, dropping to his knees. He rolled the rogue's body away. "Damien! Damien! Talk to me, brother, please talk to me!" Rolling his brother to his back, he was met with sightless eyes staring back at him. Tears began flowing from his eyes as he pulled the knife from Damien's chest and tossed it away. "Please talk to me." Overcome with grief, Sterling lifted Damien into his arms and wept openly.

"I am sorry for your loss, Sterling," said Graham, laying a hand on his shuddering shoulders. They could hear the sounds of fighting on the top of the hill. "I think we need to go help the Bard and McKray."

"Stay here, Graham," commanded Jace. "The Bard and Dwarf will be fine. You are needed here, others may still try to attack."

Graham did not question the command; he merely nodded. "What shall I do?"

"Help me tend to Koyne and Sterling's wounds," responded Jace. Within moments, sounds of metal clanging together on top of the hill ceased. It was apparent the fight there had also come to its end.

Dead rogues lay strewn about in bloody gore on the hilltop. The Bard and the dwarf had charged into the group of men, cutting and slashing like wild beasts until none remained to stand against them. Only Jotham and Dale, who had stayed back temporarily during the battle, lived. Jotham lay on the ground, writhing in pain; a well-thrown hand axe had crushed his left knee. Dale had suffered a shallow gash along the left side of his ribs, compliments of the Bard's long sword.

"What are you?" Jotham hissed, his voice filled with fear and anger.

"I am the Bard of Souvac, and I cannot die," replied the Bard quietly.

Dale looked at Jotham with hate. "Fool! You have led us against this man. We never had a chance to succeed," he said, wincing in pain.

"You have started a war here that will end with the death of all rogues," said McKray. "It may not be immediate, but in the near future, I will return with others, and we will clear your miserable hides from these mountains."

"Please, my lord, I am Dale Barnes. I beg thee to grant me forgiveness. I will travel with you, indebted always to your mercy," Dale said, bowing painfully at McKray's feet, his right hand pressed tightly to the gash in an effort to stem the flow of blood.

"Barnes, huh, from the south?" The man nodded. "Do you swear to serve me, and to be more loyal than you have been to these filthy thieves?"

"Yes, my lord, I swear by the blood of my family to serve in loyalty."

"Very well then, but I swear to you if you so much as think about disloyalty, I will know it, and then I will kill you slowly. Now if you are still ready to swear loyalty, remove your tunic, and I will dress your wound."

"You," said the Bard, addressing Jotham, "I leave you alive to take this message to your worthless kind. Leave these mountains if you value your hides, or it will be as McKray has said. You will all be wiped from the face of the land."

Picking up a fallen staff, Jotham stood slowly, grimacing with pain. He stood a moment, looking at each of the men before him in the eyes; then turning, he started toward the far side of the hill. He did not reply to what the Bard had said; he simply left.

In the moments that he had looked them in the eyes, the Bard saw fear dancing in Jotham's eyes, but greater than fear was the hate. Hate that was directed mostly at Dale. By the time Jotham had disappeared over the edge of the hilltop, McKray had finished binding Dale's wounds.

"Now, Dale, go slowly down the game trail to our friends. Keep your hands high above your head, and when you get to the base of the hill, turn around and lie facedown in the grass. Then say, 'Jason Lye, I am in your care,'" instructed McKray.

With a nod of understanding, Dale made his way down the face of Watcher's Hill.

Once they were alone, the Bard turned to McKray, "Why did you so readily invite him to join us?"

"The Barnes family were noble people, they were true friends to my clan. When all other humans turned against us, they were loyal. I felt perhaps this man just needed a chance to redeem his family name." McKray could see the question remaining in the Bard's eyes.

"Barnes, from the south. Have you been so involved in this business with Souvac that you have forgotten the history of your own kingdom? Did you notice how poorly he fought? It was almost as if he was trying to interfere with his comrades' attacks."

Recognition dawned on the Bard. "Well, this is an interesting turn of events."

"Aye. I don't think we have to worry about his loyalty, but we may want to keep his true identity between us. I don't think he was ever truly loyal to these ruffians. Now we just need to prove that to the others."

"We will handle that later. On to other matters, but we should be quick about this, other rogues may be closer than we think." Walking over to the boulder, the Bard stretched his hand over it and spoke, "Akeru." The stone began to glow and melt as it had the night before. Seconds later, the three-dimensional map of the White Mountains was laid out before them.

McKray smiled. "This is Odin's doing." Stepping away from the model before him, McKray walked around the hilltop for a few moments and returned. "This was brought here recently, by a dragon."

"I believe Odin was here also," replied the Bard. "So many pieces of the puzzle coming into play that have been out of these lands for so long."

"Why didn't he just wait for us here? It would have saved us a lot of trouble."

"You know more about Odin and his unusual ways than I do, but I imagine it has something to do with making the journey that lies ahead of us. You know, because what doesn't kill us makes us stronger."

"Or leaves a gaping, bloody hole in your chest," said McKray, indicating the Bard's wound. "Do you want me to do something about that?"

The Bard simply shook his head. "I marked this path on a map I have, but the real question is, do you know where this is?" The Bard indicated the last jewel that appeared to be high up in the White Mountains.

"Aye, that must be Odin's Hall. It sits near Greyhammer's Dale where I grew up. I once knew the way blindfolded, but now I'm glad we have the map. I suppose we should get going."

The Bard held his hand out over the boulder and spoke, "Shimeru." By the time the model of the White Mountains had returned to its nondescript appearance, the two were starting down the trail that had brought them up. At the base of Watcher's Hill, Jace sat questioning Dale while Koyne was tending to Avalon. Graham was helping to dress wounds, and Sterling sat holding his dead brother's hands.

"What happened here?" asked the Bard.

Jace looked up at him "We were ambushed. Damien was killed, and we don't know what's wrong with Avalon. Graham says the large dead fellow over there put his hand over her mouth, and she just fell to the ground. She doesn't appear hurt or anything, just sleeping."

"Dale, what happened to her?" asked McKray.

"That large dead fellow over there was a friend of mine named Jord. He was a retriever. He has a powder on his gloves that if inhaled causes the victim to fall into a deep sleep. In my pack is a small vial of smelling salts, open it and wave it under her nose. She will wake up."

Jace did as instructed, and a bewildered Avalon woke up. "You should try to stop sleeping through all the excitement, my dear." Helping her to a sitting position, he patted her shoulder.

She looked up at him with a wry smile. "Maybe I should have just stayed home."

Sterling was looking at Dale with murder in his eyes. "Enough of this. So he helped with Avalon, but why is he still alive? I say we kill him, make him pay for what has happened to my brother."

"He has entered my service and is protected under our agreement. It is possible he knows the White Mountains better than anyone, he will be our guide. Besides, from the looks of things, the man responsible for your brother's death has already paid with his life."

"He is a rogue and will lead us into another trap to kill the rest of us!"

"I had nothing to do with setting this trap. It was done by Jotham and Garen. They wanted the girl and dwarf for their own purposes," Dale said defensively.

"Hold, all of you!" said the Bard, the sound of his voice rising like the wind to dispel the anger. "Dale, do not act like the innocent. You would readily have carried out your leader's orders and slaughtered us to the man. That said, you will spend the rest of your life making restitution for the crimes you have committed. You are now oath bound to McKray, but should he be killed while on this journey, your life is Sterling's to do with as he will."

"On that day, you will wake up with this sword in your pitiful guts," said Sterling, holding up Damien's sword.

"Don't be so quick to be rid of me, boy. After all, without me, you and your brother would have been dead long ago, remember?" said the dwarf, pity in his eyes.

"I'm sorry, McKray, I just…I just…" Sterling trailed off and turned back to look at his silent brother. "Graham will you help me bury Damien?"

"We will all help you bury your brother."

"Where do you want his final resting place to be?" asked the Bard.

"We will bury him on top of Watcher's Hill. The boulder on top can be his headstone," said McKray, looking up the hill.

They wrapped Damien's body in a blanket, and those that could carried him to the top of Watcher's Hill in solemn procession. They buried him there by the boulder that had been placed by a dragon. On the stone, McKray carved Damien's name and an epitaph that read, 'Brave soul, beloved brother, and loyal friend, he died to protect a fair maiden.' It took him hours to complete, but by the time Damien had been laid to rest and the earth restored to its place, the words could be easily read.

"May the God of the Living always watch over and keep this ground sacred," said McKray.

Before their eyes, the stone began to glow slightly. It took on a molten quality running over the burial site; it reformed into a rectangular block and covered Damien's grave. When it once again appeared solid, the words that had been carved remained, but appeared to be sparkling crystal.

"It appears the God of the Living heard your request, old friend," stated the Bard.

"Aye, that he has. This proves to all of us that he not only approves of Damien and his life but has accepted him into the heavens," McKray said, looking Sterling in the eyes.

"Thank you, everyone. May I have some time alone with my brother please?"

The others simply nodded and made their way back down the hill. The sun descending in the west caused the horizon to blaze like a wildfire. Sterling spent hours sitting beside his brother's grave, reflecting on the adventures he shared in with Damien, laughing and crying in turn. Finally, he stood and bid his brother farewell. He quickly descended Watcher's Hill; the others were sitting together, discussing what they should do. "I apologize for taking so long. My grief and anger have slowed our journey, and now we are probably in greater need of haste. I am ready to go if you are. Is there anyone that would take Damien's place and come with me to find the farmer's daughter that was taken by the rogues?"

Dale looked up momentarily, his eyes burning.

McKray spoke for the group. "We will travel a little farther into the hills tonight and make camp in Girder's Gorge. It is well hidden, and there is only one way in or out."

"I'm afraid that is not a good idea. Girder's Gorge is the location of the rogues' hidden encampment," replied Dale.

"What do you suggest then?" asked McKray.

"We can make camp above the gorge on Girder's Bluff. I imagine the rogues won't expect us to camp so close. Now that you have me as your ally."

"Do you have a horse?" the Bard asked Dale.

"There are several tied in the forest over there," said Dale, waving toward the heavily wooded area just east of them.

"Koyne, Graham, go and get three or four horses, cut the rest free," ordered the Bard. The two men followed the Bard's orders, returning thirty minutes later with four horses.

The Bard spoke as they arrived, "Let's mount up and make for Girder's Bluff. McKray, you and Dale lead."

It was a somewhat treacherous climb over uneven, rocky terrain. The horses slipped more than once, but by midnight the weary group was safely positioned high up on a flat grassy bluff. As they looked over the edge, they could see a thick forest illuminated by a nearly full moon. From their vantage point, they could easily see the barren top of Watcher's Hill. It might have been the sleep in their eyes, but each of them would have sworn (if they had been willing to mention it to each other), they could see something glitter white and then fade.

"Do not wander around up here in the dark. Just over that edge is a sheer, four-hundred-foot drop to the bottom of Girder's Gorge. I recommend staying well away," warned McKray.

It only took a few moments to tether the horses and lay out the bedding before falling asleep.

*****

It had taken Jotham hours to make his way down the hill and back to his horse. He tripped and tumbled numerous times, causing further injury to his mangled knee, as well as other parts of his body. He had given into pain and exhaustion once he got to the grassy area where his horse stood tied to a tree and passed out for several hours. When he came to, it was already hours past sunset. Despite his stiffness and throbbing pain, he managed with a great effort and force of will to pull himself into the saddle of his horse.

"Back to the Gorge," he said to his horse through gritted teeth. His horse, a rather intelligent animal, understood the command and began the trek back to the rogues' encampment. It was an hour past midnight when he rode through the trees into the clearing before the mouth of the caves. He reined in his mount and held up his left hand, thumb extended, with the next two fingers crossed, making the signal of the rogues.

"I cannot get off of this horse because of a grievous injury to my knee," he said into the darkness. "I am Jotham and must speak with Garen immediately."

Two men came out of the shadows of the trees at the edge of the clearing and walked right up to the horse. The man on the right investigated Jotham's face, holding up a shielded lantern, letting only a single ray of light fall on the mounted rogue's face.

"Garen has been waiting all day for you, friend. Where is everyone else and the prize?" asked the man, not masking his thoughts about the beautiful young woman that was to be coming with Jotham.

"That is what I need to see Garen about, obviously. Now get out of my way or help me to him," growled Jotham, pain and anger building.

The man with the lantern knew Jotham well and knew to fear his anger. "Sorry," he said quickly and took the reins, leading the horse to the caves, where he called two men to carry Jotham to Garen's chambers.

The ride on the makeshift stretcher through the dimly lit caves that were the home of the rouges was even more uncomfortable than the ride from Watcher's Hill. To Jotham it seemed almost as long. He tried, once again, to plan the words he would say to the unforgiving leader of the rogues. It wouldn't matter that the man calling himself the Bard of Souvac was immortal; only that Jotham had failed, and with that failure came the deaths of thirty-eight of Garen's men. Not to mention the betrayal of Dale Barnes, who had been Garen's personal bodyguard and attendant. Of all the men that were under Garen's power, Dale had been the only one he truly trusted, which was why Garen had insisted that Dale accompany the attacking party. It was he that was to ensure the safe and unspoiled return of both the girl and the dwarf. The men stopped in front of Garen's door, where two guards were stationed.

Upon seeing Jotham lying on the stretcher, the guard to the left of the door, opened it, and stepped through. A moment later he returned.

"Garen will see you now," he said, stepping aside. The other guard also stepped aside a pace.

The men carrying the stretcher began to step forward, but Jotham called them to a halt. "Stop. Set me down and help me stand. I will face Garen on my feet."

The men looked at each other and shrugged before following the order. Jotham staggered into Garen's chamber, using his staff as a makeshift crutch. The guards closed the door behind him, resuming their post.

Garen's chambers were well lit, and the imposing man sat on his stuffed cushions wearing full armor and sword. It looked uncomfortable, but rumor had it that the ruthless leader of the rogues only took his armor and weapons off to wash and take care of other personal matters.

"Where is my prize, Jotham?" he asked, speaking more of the dwarf and his knowledge than the girl that was supposed to be brought back to him. "Why is my faithful Dale not here announcing you?"

"My lord," Jotham began, dropping to his knees in submission before his leader, pain exploding through his body as he landed with more force than intended. The pain silenced him momentarily; he hoped the show of servitude would help his case. "I regret to inform you," he trembled with pain and fear as he spoke, "that the mission failed. All of the men that went with me are dead, except for the traitor Dale Barnes. To save his own skin, he betrayed his loyalty to us and swore himself to the dwarf." He hadn't intended for the truth to come rushing out as it had, but the pain in his knee was unbearable, and he could only think of getting this over with as soon as possible.

Garen jumped to his feet and crossed the open space to Jotham's kneeling form faster than Jotham would have thought possible given the rogue leader's size and position in the cushions. He thought once again about the reasons this man was leader of such a ruthless band of dissidents.

"So you come here to tell me that not only did you fail to procure the prize which you were sent to retrieve, but you also allowed thirty-eight of my men to be killed, and my most trusted bodyguard is now helping the enemy."

"My lord, there was a man, he could not be killed, and the people with him fought like devils. The dwarf crippled me with a single axe throw."

"Yet here you are alone, alive, a little worse for wear but not even mortally wounded. Perhaps your injury came while you were fleeing for your pathetic life."

"No, you must believe me. The man that cannot be killed sent me to give you a message. The rogues must disband and leave this area, or we will all be killed. I believe him. He is coming for us. I don't know when, but he will, unless we leave."

"You seem afraid of this man that can't be killed. Tell me, what was his name? If you spoke with him, he would have given his name." Garen was walking circles around the kneeling Jotham as he spoke.

"He said he was the Bard of Souvac. I don't know what that means, but Dale seemed to know."

Garen spun about as soon as the name left Jotham's lips. "You fool! The Bard of Souvac! Souvac, the most powerful and evil human king to ever rule these lands. You set a plan in motion to kill the one man that literally cannot be killed and abduct his companions."

"He doesn't know where we are yet," stated Jotham, interrupting Garen's tirade.

Garen looked down on Jotham, his eyes smoldering with anger. Jotham shrank back in fear.

"He doesn't know where we are? He has with him Dale Barnes, the only person besides me that knows everything about these caves. The man that you always thought beneath you. The man that would have killed you at any moment had I asked it of him. You don't think he will sell us out to save his own skin? I should have listened to him, he always said you were useless."

"But I…" It happened so fast. Garen's short sword flew from its sheath, plunging into Jotham's heart, cutting off the defense that was mounting.

"I guess it is time to go." Garen pulled the sword from Jotham's body.

The farm girl that had hidden in the shadows let out an involuntary scream as Jotham's body fell to the floor.

"Don't worry, dear, I will take you with us. I have yet to make you mine." He sat back on his pillows, thinking and planning his next move. Thinking about the traitor Dale Barnes, Barnes joining the dwarf, the lack of success of his raids when Dale was present. Slowly understanding crept into his mind. Dale Barnes had never been loyal to him. *I will kill Dale for his treachery*, thought the rogue leader.

The girl shackled to a chain connected to the wall shifted her position, trying to get farther away from her captor, the movement and noise regaining Garen's attention.

"Don't struggle, you will only hurt yourself. Plus, you need not fear me tonight, I will have a visitor soon. One that needs to join Jotham in eternal slumber," he said, indicating the lifeless form lying on the ground.

The girl tried desperately to avert her eyes from this scene of gore, causing Garen to laugh.

Chapter 8

Sterling sat under the shadows of the surrounding trees cast by the moon, keeping watch as the others slept. He kept going over the events of the day in his mind, the battles, the pain of losing his brother, the funeral. He couldn't believe that it had all happened just a few hours ago, and now here he sat keeping watch while a man that was responsible for this whole thing lay sleeping just a short distance away. His anger, once abated, began to rise once more. *What should I care about McKray's oath to this murderer. I don't owe allegiance to anyone but my brother. I will avenge his death*, thought Sterling.

Despite his anger, Sterling knew he had to be careful. The minutes passed by as a plan began to take shape. Several plans began to take shape, but the elaborate nature pushed each one to the back of his mind. Finally, he told himself keep it simple. He would awaken Dale and make him walk away as if he were trying to escape. Once they were a hundred yards down the trail they had come up, he could kill Dale. It would be easy to convince the others that the man was going to betray them. Sterling smiled to himself; it was perfect he would have his vengeance tonight.

Looking up, he noticed clouds were moving silently across the sky nearly covering the light of the moon. Now was the time to act. Standing, he crept to the sleeping forms of his companions until he found the bedding that was Dale's. Kneeling, he gently reached out and shook the sleeping form; to his surprise his hand pressed into nothing more than wadded-up blankets. He jumped to his feet and was about to shout, bringing everyone awake, when he realized this is exactly what he wanted. Sterling knew the man had not come past him on the narrow trail that they had ascended; that left only the cliff and the trail leading away from the camp. A feeling of dread rose inside of his chest; quietly but swiftly he moved to the tethered horses and found that much of the rope they had brought was gone. *So he has gone over the cliff*, thought sterling. He moved cautiously to the edge of the cliff and started walking along it, searching for the ropes that would allow descent. It only took a couple of minutes to find the rope. It was tied to a sturdy pine tree and disappeared over the edge of the cliff.

Sterling looked down the rope and saw a man partially visible in the limited moonlight descending the rope. Quickly deciding he would cut the rope, he drew his knife and set it against the coarse braids, looking down once more he saw the man disappear into the face of the cliff and felt the rope go slack. Sheathing his knife, he grabbed the rope in both hands and without stopping to think slipped over the cliff edge. He began descending rapidly hand over hand, not wanting his enemy to escape. He kept watch on the cliff face, trying to see where an opening might be. He failed to see anything and after just a few minutes found his feet dangling in open space with no rope between them. It had been a long day, and Sterling started to realize how tired he was. He felt his strength waning and his grip loosening. Looking up the cliff face, he knew he did not have the strength to pull himself all the way up. Searching the rock with his feet, he managed to find a small outcropping that he could rest some of his weight on and relieve the burning in his arms. After a few seconds' rest, he tried to pull himself up the rope a short distance. He began to tire after pulling himself up only two feet; he again searched the rock for something to rest his weight on but could find nothing this time. He began to resign himself to the fact that he would be dead soon when he heard a whispered voice from somewhere nearby. Looking up and to the right a few feet, he saw a face staring down at him.

"Hold on to the rope as tight as you can," it whispered just loud enough for him to hear.

Gripping the rope with the last of his remaining strength, he felt the rope jerk to the right, and then he felt himself rising. He used his feet to help with the ascent and seconds later felt a strong hand grab his shirt, pulling him into a nearly invisible opening in the cliff face. His rescuer turned him around, pushing him farther into the tunnel, away from the opening.

Relieved and exhausted, Sterling looked at his rescuer and started to say thanks. His blood froze as he realized the man who had saved his life was the man he had come to kill.

"Why? Why did you do that? You could have let me fall, you could have let me die. I came here to kill you, Dale. I followed you so that I could avenge the death of my brother." The words spewed out like poison. "You are going to betray us all, and I can do nothing to stop you."

Dale moved past Sterling and turned around to face him once again, his back to the tunnel. "Sterling, please listen to me. I will not be betraying any of you. I have some unfinished business here with the rogues. I am simply here to remedy the problems that I held a part in making. You can wait here. I will return when I am finished. Then I will lead you back to our party and continue the quest that awaits us," he said, lowering the volume of his voice even further.

Sterling looked at Dale; suddenly his mouth opened, wanting to scream. Dale reacted instantly, spinning around and pulling a knife from a hidden sheath. It sailed down the tunnel, embedding itself in the heart of a rogue scout.

"I am here to destroy the rogues and set my brother free," he whispered as he walked down the tunnel. He stopped by the man he had killed and pulled the knife from his body. He wiped the blood on the dead man's clothes before sheathing it again. He then searched the body, taking the man's sword, and a small pouch of gold.

"Wait, I'll help you," Sterling whispered.

Dale looked up from where he was kneeling and found Sterling's hand outstretched. Reaching out, he took the offered hand and by so doing established a bond of trust and friendship.

"Where do we begin?" asked Sterling as he pulled Dale to his feet.

"Follow me, stay in the shadows, and only attack when I call for you. We should be able to dispatch the rest of the rogues before morning."

They began walking quietly through a series of mazelike tunnels, turning one way then the other. After just a few turns, Sterling was completely lost. Every so often Dale signaled Sterling to stop and wait; in those moments he would disappear into some secret alcove and dispatch a guard. They continued on until they came to a large opening, where Sterling was asked to wait once again. Minutes later, Dale returned with a young man no older than seventeen. The boy carried a long bow, a quiver of arrows on his back, and a slender sword, which rested comfortably on his hip.

"Sterling, this is my brother, Mathias."

Sterling shook the boy's hand and nodded.

"Mathias, I need you to go to the vale and dispatch all four of the lookouts."

Mathias looked toward his brother. "The time has finally come, we are going on the quest that we have prepared for." Mathias smiled and without a word vanished into the tunnels.

"Well, Sterling, there are about fifty men in that room that are in serious need of punishment for crimes against humanity. Will you join me?"

"It's about time I got involved in this business, but I don't feel right about killing sleeping men, no matter how evil they might be."

"Oh, don't worry, they're awake. Intruder!" yelled Dale.

Smiling, he charged back into the cavern. Sterling could hear the ring of metal. Drawing his own sword, he charged into the fray. The battle lasted less than twenty minutes. The dim lighting and sleep kept the rogues from being very dangerous, especially since they didn't know who or where the "intruder" was. Sterling was amazed by the speed and grace of movement that Dale exhibited during the fight, dispatching well over half of the enemy's numbers.

When the rogues were dead, Dale and Sterling cleaned their weapons and exited the cavernous room. Mathias was there waiting for them.

"All four guards have been dispatched," he told his brother.

"Good work. Now lead Sterling to the gorge, ready three horses with supplies you feel are needed for a journey deep into the White Mountains. I need to have a talk with our fearless leader. I will meet you in thirty minutes or not at all."

Mathias nodded and turned away from his brother. "Follow me," he said to Sterling.

Sterling, mind reeling, followed the young man. Dale ran off into the darkness as soon as he had given Mathias instruction, leaving Sterling to follow the boy outside. Sterling didn't want to go; he wanted to fight to help end the threat of the rogues for good. He knew what damage had been done to innocent people in this area by these evil men, but here he was being led blindly through caves by a boy. Once they were outside, Mathias led Sterling to a picket area with horses. Each horse was tied to the picket line with a lead rope connected to a halter.

Mathias untied three horses and started leading them back to the cave. "Sterling, get four more horses, and wait at the cave entrance," he said as he hurried away.

"But Dale said get three horses, not seven."

"That is what he said, but it's not what he wants," stated Mathias, continuing away.

Shaking his head, Sterling looked at the line of horses still tied to the picket. On the ground in front of each was a saddle. *Well, I imagine we'll need them saddled,* he thought. Sterling saddled the horses he felt would be the best. Looking again at the remaining horses, he decided to set them free before leaving. The freed horses bolted away into the darkness. He led the saddled mounts back to the cave entrance where he would await Dale and Mathias. When he got back to the cave, Mathias was already leading his three horses from the cave, each loaded with bags and packages.

"Dale should be along shortly," stated Mathias.

The two stood quietly in the silent black of the early morning. Sterling had not had a chance to really look Mathias over but now took the opportunity. Mathias was on the smaller side for a seventeen-year-old young man; he stood a foot shorter than the six-and-a-half-foot Dale. He was lean, wearing leather breeches and a plain tunic. His shoulder-length hair was tied up behind his ears, which were more pointed than round at the tip. He had sharp facial features, which made him look a little younger than what he really was. He appeared for the most part unremarkable, until Sterling noticed his eyes. They were white with a slightly gray area where the dark pupil should have been. Sterling shivered involuntarily as he looked at those eyes.

Mathias laughed slightly. "What's wrong, you've never met a blind person before?"

"Not with eyes like yours." Moments of silence passed as Sterling thought about the last few hours of events. "Mathias, if you're blind, how is it that you dispatched four guards in the dark with a bow and arrow and led me out of the caves?"

"I may be blind, but I can still see. I just see differently."

*****

Dale ran through the dark caves as if he were running across a grassy field in the sunlight, pausing only briefly to dispatch the remaining guards outside of Garen's chambers. Kicking the custom fit door open, he entered the small cavern; bright torches assailed his eyes. Bringing his sword up defensively, and ducking to the left reflexively, saved his life. A heavy ringing blow struck his sword and sent vibrations through his arms. Garen was a large man whose heavy stature belied his true strength and agility. You didn't become leader of a cutthroat gang of dissidents by being weak of body or mind.

Dale stood and began circling his foe; he saw Jotham's mangled body still lying in a pool of blood near the center of the room.

"So you killed your proud general, I see."

"You should have been my general, Dale. You were the most skilled with weapons, the best at strategy, the deadliest in a fight, but you were the weakest regarding our questionable activities."

"I wasn't weak, I just never believed it was right."

"Then why did you stay around? There was something about what we did that you enjoyed."

"I stayed because I knew this day would come. Mathias and I have been biding our time watching, waiting, interfering with your plans when we could. Your men have killed fewer innocent people than you think because of my brother and me, and only when I wasn't on a raid did you manage to kidnap a single girl for your heinous desires. Now your precious lot of rogues are dead. You are the last, and you will die for your crimes." The cold edge to his voice was surprising to the rogue leader.

"You really think you can defeat me? I am Garen, leader of the rogues!" Charging at Dale, he struck hard and fast.

Dale deflected his attack and spun away to the right. Garen spun left and brought his sword down in an overhead attack. Dale blocked again, both hands holding the hilt of his sword, but another blow was already coming. Again and again the large man rained blows down on Dale. Dale's arms were beginning to ache with the effort of blocking each heavy attack; he was slowly being backed into the cave wall. Knowing he was getting into real danger, he released his left hand grip on his sword and drew a dagger, which he stabbed at Garen's midsection. Garen twisted his body slightly against the dagger attack, which altered the course of his sword slash. Dale with one hand deflected his opponent's sword and danced away to the left. Now with some room to work, he came on the offensive. Slashing and jabbing at Garen with blinding speed, he connected several times with Garen's body, but each attack glanced from plate mail.

Both men were starting to tire with the efforts they were exerting. The attacks were alternating between both men. Finally Garen, stepping forward, stepped in the blood on the floor; he slipped slightly and lost his footing. Dale took the opportunity and attacked hard. As Dale closed, his sword raised for deadly stroke; he saw a faint smile on Garen's face. He couldn't stop his swing and realized his mistake. Garen's misstep was false.

Dropping his left shoulder, Garen pushed hard with his legs driving his shoulder into Dale's exposed chest. Dale felt his ribs crack and his sword leave his fingers. His body flew back, landing on the large pillows that Garen usually sat in. Pain exploded through his body as he tried to catch his breath. His eyes cleared as he heard Garen's deep rolling laugh.

"You thought you could defeat me? You were good, Dale, but no man has ever bested me in a fight. This has been amusing though, I admit it will take some time to gather enough men to be a threat here again, but rest assured I will wreak havoc once more. In the meantime I have my little jewel to play with to pass the time," he said, indicating the girl. "You know, Dale, I think I will go back to the farms and villages that you admittedly helped, but this time I will personally kill every man and child. I will take every woman as my slave, and you will know that you, Dale, are responsible, because you were incapable of defeating me.'

Dale had finally recovered his breath and his senses. Reaching his arms out to the sides to push himself up, he felt his right hand close on the handle of a weapon. He hadn't really heard anything that Garen had said until his last statement. Looking up, he saw Garen's large sword rising to deliver the final blow. Dale moved, pushing up to the left, knowing Garen's swing would come with a slight angle to his right side. As he came up and Garen came down, Dale swung the weapon he had grasped with all his might. The large spiked mace connected with the left side of Garen's chest plate; this time Dale felt the metal give. He heard the air leave Garen's body, the sound of armor smashing against stone, and the gasping that came from his downed foe. Dale stood and watched as Garen struggled to his left side from his back. Swinging the mace again, he drove the weapon into the right front of Garen's chest, rolling him onto his back, sending the sword flying from his grasp. Dale viewed the damaged plate armor beneath the torn tunic; he saw the most vulnerable spot right in the center between the two dents from the previous attacks. Without another word, he raised the spiked mace high above his head and with both hands brought it crashing down. He felt the metal give way, the spikes biting through metal and flesh. He saw Garen's eyes open wide and then flutter shut as life ebbed from his body. The pain that exploded through his own body racked him, and his vision went black.

When Dale woke, he was lying in his blankets on Girder's Bluff. The sun was breaking over the White Mountains, and he could hear a camp stirring to life. Had his journey into the rogue caves been a dream, his fight, and ultimate defeat of Garen a nightmare? Pushing himself up onto his elbows, he felt a new rush of pain through his chest. Mathias, Sterling, and a pretty young woman were at his side as he lay back.

"Careful, brother, you were badly injured. Lucky for you, Sterling is an impatient man. We found you passed out with Amalia here holding your hand," he said, indicating the dark-haired young woman.

"That is where the mace came from," stated Dale as he lay back in pain.

"I slid it to you after you fell, thank you for saving me, I am ever in your debt." She took his hand in hers and held it tightly.

Moments later, the Bard and McKray walked over to Dale's bedside. Crouching down, they set to work on his injuries; soon his chest was rebandaged with herb poultices. The pain was subsiding into ache, and much-deserved sleep was taking Dale into a healing rest. Once Dale was sleeping peacefully, the Bard stood. He took note of the way Amalia had been holding Dale's hand when they had first walked over, as well as how she had taken his hand as soon as he and McKray finished with the bandages.

"Sterling, I believe we need to have a talk. Mathias, Amalia, I will ask you to keep watch over Dale for the time being."

Mathias nodded his understanding. Amalia smiled, slightly averting her eyes, and Sterling followed the Bard and McKray to the fire where the others sat eating breakfast, waiting for an explanation.

"Sterling, tell us what happened last night," coaxed the Bard.

Sterling looked around; his companions' eyes were on him, some filled with curiosity, some with anger, some with nothing at all. *Those eyes are the most disconcerting, what is wrong with Koyne?* thought Sterling.

"Well, get on with it," said McKray in his rough voice.

Sterling then recounted the events of the night. He told how he discovered Dale missing and, fearing betrayal, followed him. He explained how Dale saved him and they had freed Mathias. He told them about the battle wherein Dale and himself killed the rest of the rogues and concluded with finding Dale and Amalia in the rogue leader's quarters and the subsequent journey through the remaining dark morning hours to reach the camp.

"I know I should have woken one of you to continue the watch, but I was afraid I would be too late as it was, so I took rash actions. I potentially put you all in danger while you slept, and I understand if you want me to depart from your company."

"I do not believe you will do something so foolish again, plus we may need your skills as a fighter before the end of this journey," replied the Bard.

"I think we should have a say in what happens here. After all, he did put all our lives in jeopardy by running off like that," stated an angry Graham.

"Our lives were never in danger. I remained awake. I saw both men leave over the cliff and expected their return by this morning," replied the Bard.

Jace looked at the Bard questioningly. "You saw both men leave and did nothing to prevent them?"

"I am not a babysitter. If two grown men want to throw themselves over a cliff and risk their lives in a cause that they see fit to follow, then it is none of my affair to intercede."

McKray shook his head and smiled.

Avalon nudged Koyne and whispered in his ear, "What do you think of all this?"

"Huh um, well, I guess the Bard is right. It makes for a mildly entertaining tale," said Koyne.

Confusion was evident on all faces in the group as they tried to understand what Koyne's comment meant.

McKray spoke then, turning everyone's attention to another matter entirely, "So you said the boy Mathias is a skilled bowman when you arrived this morning. I'm curious how that is possible given the fact that he is blind."

"He can't be blind. I saw him taking care of Dale and walking around without anything to aid him," stated Avalon.

"Well, why is he wearing that cloth over his eyes now?" asked McKray.

Everyone's attention was now turned to the boy sitting by Dale. He wore a clean white band around his eyes.

"I saw his eyes when they came into camp, they are mostly white with just a bit of dull gray where the pupil of his eye should be. I have known blind men and blind dwarves, they each had a similar look to their eyes."

"He is blind," confirmed Sterling. "He told me so while we were waiting for Dale. He also told me that just because he is blind doesn't mean he can't see or something like that. Each man he killed had an arrow through the heart. I don't know how he does it, but somehow he can see."

They all watched Mathias for several seconds; as they watched it was apparent that the boy was getting uncomfortable by his body language.

"We will have to spend a couple of more days here in order for Dale's injuries to heal enough to travel," stated the Bard, drawing the group's attention away from the uncomfortable-looking Mathias. As their eyes turned from him to the Bard, Mathias relaxed noticeably.

"I thought we were in a hurry to get this whole thing over with. We should just keep going. We can leave supplies here with Mathias, and he can take care of his brother. They obviously know the area and will be fine, we can pick them up on the way back if they are still here," stated Graham with an edge to his voice.

"Calm down, boy, the end of this journey will come all too soon for us. We are currently in no danger, and a couple of days' rest could be good for all of us, given the events of yesterday," replied McKray.

Graham looked at McKray and nodded; some of the anger left his face, and he calmed. "I am going to introduce myself to Mathias. And Amalia."

"That is a fine idea," stated McKray with a smile and a wink.

Graham shook his head as he stood, then walked away.

McKray looked at the others. "He's a good kid, maybe he will make a good king someday."

"I think maybe you will too," said the Bard, then added with a smile. "It's good to see kids grow up."

"Now you hold your tongue, you little upstart. Just because you're immortal for now don't think you can call me a kid."

"Calm yourself, old friend, I was merely referring to your attitude, not your age," he said with a grin.

Those remaining around the fire got a much-needed laugh from the look that crossed the surly dwarf's face.

The sun had risen well above the peaks, and the bright sunlight was warming the mountain air as Graham strode across the green grass on top of the bluff. Mathias was sitting at his older brother's side, his back to the approaching Graham. When Graham was still several paces away, Mathias turned.

"Hello, I didn't mean to startle you," said Graham.

Mathias smiled. "No offense, but you couldn't startle me, not approaching so loudly. You are called Graham, I am Mathias, this is Amalia," he gestured to the girl who still held Dale's hand. "It is a pleasure to meet you."

Graham began to stammer a bit in response.

"I can tell by your inability to form speech that you were not expecting a young blind ruffian to know your name, or to have manners."

"I apologize, I am mostly awed that you knew my name specifically."

"Well, when you are blind, your other senses take over at an incredible level. I could hear everything that you were all talking about by the fire. So naturally, I heard you announce that you were coming to introduce yourself."

"Is that how you are able to be so accurate with a bow and arrow?" asked Graham.

"Something like that."

Graham sat down, and soon the two young men were deep in discussion about various subjects. As they spoke, Graham furtively looked at Amalia, taking in and committing to memory each detail of her face. From the delicate features to the color of her eyes and lips, her slender neck, and dark hair, as well as the way she held Dale's hand, her fingers gently interlocking his.

On the other side of camp, Avalon was leading Koyne away from the fire up a slight incline to a secluded spot in a small grove of pine trees. The rest of the group remained at the fire discussing how they would continue their journey.

Once they were alone, Avalon turned to Koyne, who still had a blank look in his eyes. "Koyne, are you okay?"

"I'm fine."

"Be honest with me please, you're not acting like yourself at all. Something has happened to you, please talk to me."

Koyne looked at her. "Avalon, I am afraid that I am a danger to everyone on this quest. I had a dream last night, a man came to me and told me I was his son. I know who this man was, he was tried and killed as a murderer. He told me I would become just like him and murder in cold blood. He said I would enjoy it just as he did, just as all the men in our family did. I was told there is no way for me to escape my future, my destiny."

"Koyne, it was just a dream," she said, looking deep into his eyes.

"No, no, it was more than a dream. Avalon, I believe he really was my father. He was a murderer, I will be a murderer as well."

"Look at me," said Avalon, taking Koyne's face in her hands. "You are not a murderer, you are a good man that has always done everything you can to help others."

"But I killed those rogues, and I have started to feel things in my heart, dark things."

"You are not the only one that killed rogues, and you only killed them in self-defense to preserve your life, my life, and the lives of our companions. You would not have killed those men if they had not attacked us."

He looked at her then, seeing the light that shone through her eyes. He saw her as if he was seeing her for the first time, and his heart opened completely. A sensation of warmth washed through his whole body, and he completely relaxed; a smile spread across his face.

"I love you, Avalon," he whispered.

"I love you too."

They embraced then and let themselves feel a full measure of peace.

*****

The Evil One, Lord Kish, was busy spreading his influence across the expanse of the world when a twinge of interest pulled his thoughts to the top of Girder's Bluff. Something was happening there that would have direct repercussions for him. His sight was drawn across time and space where it settled on a young man and woman. He listened to their conversation; he could feel the fear in the man's voice, sense the turmoil in his soul. Suddenly he saw it.

"Oh, this is just perfect," he said to no one in particular. "Whelp, come and see this." He came from the shadows, his skin almost shining in the light cast by both torch and fire; it was so pale.

"What is it, my lord?"

"Look in the Oracle, do you see the man and woman?"

"Yes, my lord."

"I want you to watch this man, he has a sickness growing in his heart. It is due to a curse put on his forebear who still resides in the King's Forest. You can see that he is in love with the woman, and she is in love with him. That will all change soon, for love is weak and leads to the greatest pain and suffering man can endure. He has doubt about himself, which will allow my influence to overcome him. He will give into the evil growing in his heart. It will consume him until he commits the cold-blooded murder that he so fears. Once he does, he will be mine. He will run from this desire to kill so hard that he will run right into his destiny. In so doing, he will break the heart of that poor, helpless woman."

Reaching both hands into the strange pool that hung on the natural stone wall of the underground cavern, he smiled. Then he put a finger on the man's image, touching his chest and forehead. "Embrace the anger that lives in your heart, let it fill your mind until you see the necessity to kill." The words flew across time and space like a poisonous dart embedding deep into Koyne's heart and mind.

Kish turned to the pale man at his side, "You will watch and eventually prove to me that you are more than the worthless son of your mother. You will learn, or I shall send you once and for all from my presence."

"It is my will and pleasure to serve thee, master. I wish to learn about all your powers, that I may assist you in your glorious work, my lord." Dropping to one knee, he bowed down to Kish.

From the shadows, his mother was watching, hoping that her son would finally find the Evil One's favor.

*****

A half hour had passed since Koyne and Avalon had walked away from the group, before Jace walked over.

"Koyne, Avalon, I am sorry to interfere, but we need to counsel and make some decisions, the Bard and McKray wish to discuss this with everyone."

"Thank you, we will be over momentarily," stated Avalon.

Jace walked away. Koyne stood and helped Avalon to her feet.

"Avalon, when this is over, I am going to ask Haven for your hand in marriage." As he said the words, he felt something prick his heart and mind.

Avalon smiled again, throwing her arms around Koyne's neck, turning his attention back to her. "If he says no, we will just run away together."

They kissed then, taking hands, walked away from the small grove of trees. They joined the group around the fire where Mathias was introducing himself to the full group.

"Dale, as you know, is my older brother, he has always looked out for me. When I was two and he was ten, a group of outlaws came to our village in the south. They looted and pillaged our homes before they raped the woman in front of the men, then they killed everyone and burned the village to the ground. Dale saved me and four other kids by hiding us in a cellar. We survived the fire that burned above us, but I lost my eyesight. We wandered for several months, Dale leading us providing for us until we reached the base of the White Hills at the westernmost point.

"Here an old man found us, he told us he was a friend and led us to a cabin where another man lived, then the old man left. The man in the cabin told us he had no name, so we simply called him master. He taught all of us how to use weapons, how to fight, and how to survive. We spent years traveling all over the White Mountains learning their secrets. Finally, three years ago, the master told us he had information regarding the men who had destroyed our village. These men had formed a large band called the rogues. On the day he told us about the rogues, he told Dale something else. Being the master's best student, Dale was told things the rest of us never were. So it was that Dale and I left; initially I believed we were going to destroy the group, but Dale had other plans.

"We joined the rogues and worked against them from inside their ranks, disturbing their plans as much as possible. Then last night Dale told me it was time to follow a new course. Apparently, that course lies with you.

The others listening were speechless at the tale Mathias had shared.

Amalia, who was sitting next to Mathias, reached out, putting her hand on his. "I am sorry you have endured such a hard life."

"We all endure a hard life."

"Well spoken, Mathias, now, Amalia, would you mind telling us about yourself, dear?" asked the Bard.

"I really don't have much to tell. I grew up on a small farm east of here, two nights ago I was gathering wild berries in the forest. Three men came out of the trees and grabbed me." She shuddered as the memory came flooding back. "I, uh, spent two frightening days and nights tied to that post in the rogue leader's lair." Tears began rolling from her eyes as she continued, "Garon told me all the horrible things he was going to do to me. He would laugh and reach to touch me." She shuddered again. "Dale came in several times. In fact, he seemed to always interrupt Garon just as he was getting ready to touch me. I am very grateful to him, for his bravery that saved me."

"Are ye sure that's all there is to tell us about your life?" asked McKray.

"How interesting can the life of a farm girl be compared to the lives you have all led? No, there is nothing more to say about me."

The Bard could tell there was more to Amalia's story, but thought it best to leave it for the moment. "Now that we all know a bit about our new friends, it is time to let them know where we are going and what we are doing. That way they can decide if they wish to come with us."

"Dale has already said we are going with you," stated Mathias.

"Yes, but he doesn't know what he is getting the two of you into," replied the Bard. "Plus, Amalia will need someone to help her get back to her home. Therefore, we will go speak with Dale." Standing up, he did not wait but strode purposefully across the green grass to where Dale was lying.

The group looked around at each other. Mathias stood, the white linen cloth still covering his eyes, and turned following the path of the Bard.

Chapter 9

The group had moved to where Dale was lying.

The Bard looked at the group, and a feeling of peace washed over him. A voice sounded in the depths of his mind, *Now you have everyone, bring them to me.* He knew they would all come, but he also knew it had to be their choice.

"Now that we are all gathered, those of you who have most recently joined us must know the dangers you face should you choose to join us. We are traveling to find Odin's Hall high up in the White Mountains. We are searching for a way to destroy the knights of Souvac once and for all. We are surely being tracked by creatures that will only obey their master and would kill any one of us without hesitation. We do have a map to follow, but no one honestly knows exactly where we are going."

"May we see the map?" asked Dale.

McKray pulled the map they had marked on Watcher's Hill from a pocket and laid it out for Dale to see. Dale studied it for several minutes.

"Mathias should lead you, we have been in many of the areas on your map in the last four years, he will know how to get you to your destination. I can take Amalia back to her home," said Dale, grimacing as he shifted his body.

"Actually, I want to come with all of you, if you will allow me," said Amalia quietly.

"How old are you, dear?" asked McKray. "I am twenty years old." Her statement was met with questioning looks. "I know I look younger," she said in response to those looks. "I know I look younger than Avalon, but I was going to leave my father's farm this summer anyway."

"Well, that's good enough for me," said McKray. "She is old enough to make her own decisions."

"Won't your parents be worried about you?" asked Sterling.

"No, they have each other, and lately my father has made comments to me," she looked around at everyone looking back at her. Steeling her tone, she continued, "No, they won't miss me, besides, I can always visit them when the journey is over. I think it best that I stay with all of you for now."

"I'm happy to have her along, it gets lonely being the only girl," said Avalon, reaching out and squeezing Amalia's hand, hoping to take the focus off the young woman. It was obvious to her that Amalia had something she did not want the others to know about her past.

"Well, if Amalia is going with the rest of you, I suppose that means we are all going," stated Dale.

"Very well. When do we leave?" asked Graham.

"Dale is still in too much pain to travel," replied Mathias.

"Actually, I think everything is mending quite well. We should be able to leave tomorrow morning," Dale said, wincing with pain.

"You're a terrible liar, brother, but you're right, we should leave tomorrow morning. If we are going to be tracked by vicious creatures, we need as much distance between us and them as we can get."

"Does anyone else have anything to add?" asked the Bard. Looking around at the group, all shook their heads. "We will leave at first light. For now I suggest we move a bit higher into those trees and build lean-tos big enough for two people and a small fire. It is going to rain tonight and get quite cold."

"How do you know that?" asked Amalia, looking up at the mostly clear sky.

"After living a hundred years, you begin to understand the subtlety of the weather among other things."

The group spent the day moving and building their shelters around fires to keep warm. Dale was healing well due to the Bard and McKray's skill with poultices and healing knowledge, but he continued to be sore where the ribs were broken; even the small amount of traveling they did that day was exhausting.

Avalon and Amalia paired up and built a shelter to share; they were getting along well and becoming fast friends. The others paired as well. Dale and Mathias, Sterling and Koyne, Jace and Graham, McKray and the Bard.

"You know, Bard, we have picked up four new companions that may not know the full story of yourself and the knights of Souvac, perhaps you should rehearse it to them," said McKray.

"I was thinking along the same lines. Tonight I will rehearse my tale and reveal all I can, however something recently told me that each of us on this journey is meant to be here. Do you not feel an almost-perceptible hand guiding each of us together?" asked the Bard

"Aye, that I do, but I don't want to see anyone else getting hurt," he said, looking over at Avalon and Amalia.

"You truly are more sentimental than you show."

"That's true, but we'll keep that between you and me."

That night they gathered around a large fire, and the Bard rehearsed once again his tale, the purpose behind the journey, and the inherent danger. He then asked the four new companions if they still wished to proceed. They all nodded their agreement to continue.

Shortly thereafter, the rain began. The group dispersed by twos to their shelters. Soon rain was pouring from the skies, and the temperature dropped drastically. It rained throughout most of the night, and despite the well-built shelters, almost everyone's bedding was at least a little damp by morning.

The morning sun chased away the wet night's chill. The group awoke anxious to be on their way from this place. The sooner they found Odin, the sooner this little adventure would be over. By midmorning the bedding was dried out, packed, and Dale informed everyone that he felt good enough to travel despite lingering pain. The group, energized by the news that they would be moving on, packed the rest of their supplies and belongings with speed. Within an hour, the group was mounted on their horses and waiting for McKray and Mathias to lead them.

"I can't believe we are being led by a blind kid," mumbled Koyne to Avalon, who seemed to have fallen into a sullen mood again.

"It fits with the expression 'the blind leading the blind,' does it not?" replied Mathias with a smile.

"You should be careful what you say, that young man has the hearing of an owl," said the Bard to Koyne as he rode by.

"Yeah, well, I have the vision of a hawk," replied Koyne.

"What are you trying to prove, Koyne?" asked Avalon.

Koyne merely huffed and spurred his horse to movement.

Looking back down toward the valley, the small group of people could see the distance they had already come. It didn't seem that far; they could see the forested mountain slopes turn into the rolling White Hills. They had really just started onto the base of the White Mountains when they met with delays. Looking forward, they could see the vast expanse and height of the White Mountains looming before them. Green grass, pine trees, and large, silver-trunked trees still covered this area of the mountains, but higher up they could see that growing things gave way to the gray and browns of earth, which then gave way to the white snow that existed continuously on the peaks of these mountains, giving them their name.

They traveled the rest of the day on horseback, the ground gently sloping ever upward. The large, silver-trunked trees created a large canopy of giant, dark-green leaves that spread out above them. A variety of animals began to be more apparent the higher into the mountains they traveled. At one point they rode upon a herd of elk, mostly cows and calves with a dozen or so bulls, one of which was enormous in body size as well as antlers that spread beyond the animal's rear flanks. Other animals of all sizes and types could be seen and heard running away from the approaching group of riders. Colorful mountain birds sang and flitted from tree to tree throughout the forest. Everyone's spirits were rising with the sunny warm weather and the beautiful scenery. As day waned into evening, Mathias, who had been leading them in a fairly straight line all day, veered his horse to the left, angling toward a towering cliff that seemed to have jumped out of the ground amidst the forest.

"A bit further on will be the best place for us to camp tonight, we will be there in an hour," he said.

"We still have at least two hours' worth of light to travel by. Perhaps we should continue a bit longer," suggested McKray.

"The place we will stop has a fresh spring of water and shelter from the strong winds that will be pouring down this canyon tonight," replied Mathias.

"What winds and what canyon? One cliff face doesn't make a canyon," stated Koyne, who continued to fall into himself as Avalon and Amalia rode together and talked.

"You cannot see it, but a hundred yards ahead of us, this cliff begins to turn to the right. That is where the right side of this canyon begins, it starts as a ridgeline several miles back, which grows in size until it rises from the trees. It is that cliff that you see in the distance. Winds come down this canyon every night, these winds are powerful enough to blow a large horse around like a leaf. I know because Dale and I were unfortunate enough to see its power last year," replied Mathias.

"How did you know we were here?" asked Avalon amazed.

"The echo," replied Dale from behind her. "He can hear the change in the way the horses' hoofbeats echoed as you approached this spot."

Each member of the group began to listen more intently as they rode toward the west side of the cliff face. "I hear it," said Amalia after a few minutes. "It's subtle, but I can hear it."

A couple of hours later, camp had been set, and the adventurers were sitting around a blazing fire eating dinner. As they ate they spoke, nothing more than idle chat, as the last bit of light faded from the sky, the camp fell into complete darkness. Seconds later a roaring sound reached their ears. It was a mixture of noise, sometimes sounding like thunder, sometimes the crash of large waves against stone; at other times it was like the bellows of some giant. Avalon had scooted into Koyne's waiting arms as the sounds continued to rise and fall in fluctuating tones.

"Don't worry, we are safe here, the sounds decrease in the night despite the winds maintaining force and power," stated Dale in an attempt to calm Avalon.

Amalia was also looking scared but had no one to comfort her.

They sat silently listening to the noises from the canyon. As the minutes ticked by, the noises lessened, and the group calmed down further.

Graham broke the silence that enveloped the camp. "What do you think is out there?" he asked, pointing vaguely at the heavens. The others followed his gaze to the stars shining brightly above them.

McKray snorted, looking into the sky. "Who knows, I guess there could be just about anything out there."

Amalia looked up as well and began singing. Her song began softly, building in strength, filling the mind with images of peace and beauty.

The stars look down and see us all
Recognizing how we fall
The sun rises each morning sweet
Lifting us back to our weary feet

Marching through the green forests we see
Life working in harmony
The animals and birds to
Without gold or even food

Find a way to live their lives
Without the need for war and strife
These creatures great and small
Make families and love them all

We are blessed to find true love
If we choose to rise above
The weakness of our mortal frame
We are granted a new name

When you look into the heart
Of the one you can be a part
You see their eyes looking back at you
Shining with love, truly seeing you

So look around, you see true friends
With them you will find great ends
Those who love you lift you up
Like the sunshine in the morn

Adventure and life are a test
Allowing us to find our best
From housewives and farmers to
Great warriors, kings, and especially you

Each must make choices while on earth
To chart successfully a course
Leading to freedom, life, and love
Once obtained look again above

The stars look down and see us all
Recognizing how we fall
The sun rises each morning sweet
Lifting us back to our feet

Follow the sun, it leads us all
That we may no longer at evening fall
But stay upon our strengthened feet
Moving forward always toward the sun

When she finished, she looked around at her audience and noticed Jace had tears welling up in his eyes.

"That was beautiful, my dear. Who taught you that song?" asked McKray.

"My mother used to sing it to me when I was young. She told me to never forget and always cherish what the words mean. Whenever I am scared, I sing it to myself, and I always feel peace in my heart and mind." She would have continued, but Dale interrupted her.

"What is it, brother?" he asked Mathias.

"Something approaches, it moves very quietly, unlike anything I have heard before," replied Mathias.

The rest of the group was now completely silent. The Bard had closed his eyes and appeared to be trying to sense rather than hear whatever was approaching them.

"I think it came from the Canyon of Wind."

Mathias continued to sit very still, looking into the blackness surrounding them; those that could see in the dark were peering into the engulfing blackness. Suddenly Mathias picked up his bow and with fluid grace fitted an arrow to the string; with lightning speed he sent it flying between Jace and Graham's heads. A startled growl came back to the group from the shadows just yards away. A few moments of silence passed.

"Whatever it was, it has fled back toward the Canyon of Wind," said Mathias sitting back down.

"Hey, I don't appreciate blind people shooting arrows past my head," stated Jace. "I don't care how well you hear or shoot."

Graham sat quietly with a pale color to his face. "I think I am going to bed now," he said standing up. He shakily walked to his bedroll and lay down. The fletching of the arrow had tickled his ear as it shot past and unsettled him.

Dale smiled. "Don't worry, from the first time Mathias picked up a bow, he has never missed a shot."

"That is very impressive," stated the Bard.

"Do you think it was Oaran's?" asked McKray, changing the subject.

"No, it was not. It did not have malice in it, just interest," declared the Bard.

"Koyne, Jace, did either of you see it?" asked McKray.

"It is completely black out there, how are we supposed to have seen it?" asked Koyne.

"It is a simple question, lad," replied McKray

"I didn't see anything," stated Jace.

"Neither did I," agreed Koyne.

The Bard looked around at the others. "I told you all about the boarhounds earlier. I had hoped we lost them in Bishop's Swamp, but I suppose others if sent might be catching up to us, given the delays we have encountered."

"You told us about the boarhounds, but what are these creatures?" asked Mathias.

"Truth be told, they are vicious, dangerous creatures, and they will do whatever their master tells them to do. They will try to stop us if we are deemed a threat by the knights. I expected them to try and track our progress, but Oaran, who created these creatures, could snap at any moment and set them on a new course of action, specifically killing any one or more of this group. Therefore, if anyone sees anything, I need you to be forthright and tell me."

"How did he create these boarhounds?" asked Amalia.

"Through torture and breeding different animals, over several decades. I don't know how many animals have been used in the creation of these unholy creatures, but I have seen what they can do. Oaran can link his mind with their minds to control them, but that is not all, he sees what they see and hears what they hear. I have been close enough to feel the malice, hatred, and desire for destruction that they possess. To put you all at ease, whatever the creature was that you heard, Mathias, it was not one of Oaran's."

"We need to get a very early start tomorrow, it takes an entire day of riding to get to the top of the Canyon of Wind, and we don't want to get stuck in there when the sun goes down," stated Mathias. "If these creatures are gaining on us, I don't want them to catch up."

"You say the winds blow all night long?" asked McKray.

"Yes."

"That will give us an advantage, you told us these monsters can only travel at night," said Jace, turning toward the Bard.

The bard looked at Jace. "That is true, but I do not know if they can adapt to the sunlight. I do not believe Oaran has ever sent them on this long of a journey."

"Good point, I will take the first watch, the rest of you get some sleep," replied Jace.

Once the others were settled in, Jace put the fire out and turned his back to the dying embers. Two hours later, McKray came to relieve him.

"I may have an idea about that creature Mathias shot," McKray said later that night as the Bard sat down beside him. "When I still lived in these mountains, my father told me of an animal that only a few of our ancestors had ever seen. It was able to travel anywhere in the White Mountains even the highest peaks, that means it is able to fly. When it wants to be invisible, it can be especially at night. It was described as being very dangerous, highly intelligent, and even capable of communication with people of all races. My ancestors held them in high regard and believed them to be protected by the God of the Living. That is why they never made physical descriptions of them. I am concerned that injuring one could be very bad for us."

"I understand your concern, I will do some scouting if you will keep watch over the others."

Amalia slept poorly that night, her dreams turning to nightmares filled with black, hairy ferocious animals that were trying to rip into her flesh. She also dreamed that a being in a heavy, dark-colored cloak grabbed her from behind, pinning her arms to her side. This being was about to whisper something in her ear, but she woke with a start, moving to a sitting position. Looking around, she could see McKray sitting with his back to her. Koyne and Avalon had moved their bedding closer together, one of his strong hands rested on her side. Amalia secretly wished she had someone to comfort her; lying back down, she fell back into a restless sleep.

The rest of the group slept fitfully despite the tumultuous sounds of the wind that continued throughout the night.

Just before dawn, the Bard returned and sat by McKray.

"Well, what did you find?"

"I found a few droplets of blood right at the base of that tree," he said, pointing vaguely toward the canyon. "Along with this," he said, holding up a sixteen-inch-long golden feather. "There were no footprints of any type on the ground, there were no further signs of blood, and nothing else to indicate that anything was nearby in any direction. We should keep our eyes open as we travel today, not only on the ground before us but the skies above as well."

Avalon was awake listening intently to the muffled conversation between the Bard and McKray. She was starting to wish she had not come on this journey. She was finally starting to realize just how dangerous things were going to get before they even got to the King's Forest. Needing to do something, she began rustling in her bedding to give the impression that she was just waking up. She sat up slowly and stretched, looking around with a blank look.

"What time is it?" she asked.

"Time to get up," replied the Bard.

"I will get the fire going and start some breakfast," stated McKray.

"You get the fire going, and I will make breakfast. I'm not sure I trust your cooking," said Avalon with a smile and a wink at McKray.

"If you are going to cook breakfast, I will pack your things," he said, smiling back. Leaning over, Avalon gave Koyne a gentle kiss. "Rise and shine time to get moving, boy." Avalon had been calling Koyne boy since childhood but had stopped doing so in the last year or so. He wasn't sure why she had slipped back into it this morning, but as much as he had hated it growing up, he relished in it now.

A few minutes later, the entire group was awake, and the smell of bacon was emanating from the fire. "We should probably save some of this good fare for when we are sick of traveling, it will boost our spirits," stated Jace.

"Save it for too long and it will go rancid," replied Dale. "Besides, I don't think we had much bacon to begin with."

Jace made a face and shrugged his shoulders. "I guess things could be worse."

During the different exchanges, Mathias made his way over to where the Bard was standing by his horse. "There was something there last night, I know I hit it but not seriously, that has never happened to me. I have never failed to hit a target I have shot at."

The Bard turned to face Mathias. "What that creature was, we do not know for sure. It is something that may or may not be a threat. If you feel that one is that close again, I suggest that you do not shoot. We will be patient and see if it truly means us harm."

"In my experience, anything that creeps in the dark means you harm," replied Mathias "However, your wisdom and life are greater than mine, so I will heed your words." Turning, he walked back to his own horse and finished preparing it for the day's travel.

With breakfast cooked and the horses and group ready to travel, Dale spoke out, "Mathias feels we should leave now if we are going to make it to the top of the canyon. We should eat as we ride."

Taking some bread eggs and bacon, Dale made a quick sandwich and mounted his horse. Mathias, despite his blindness, followed Dale's lead and was soon sitting in the saddle upon his horse, gazing around at the others with his glazed eyes, before he urged his horse forward.

Realizing that they would be left behind, the rest of the group quickly followed suit, and moments later they were entering the Canyon of Wind. The canyon started just as Dale and Mathias said it would it was narrow with towering cliffs on both sides; the ground remained covered with a thick carpet of green grass. No trees grew in the canyon. Dale said it was due to the high winds. McKray felt that there was another reason. Despite the narrowness of the canyon, it was quite comforting, and by midafternoon Koyne was voicing his feelings about stopping for a rest in the cool grass. Mathias, however, did not allow them to stop, and so they ate lunch while on horseback. They rode at a quick pace throughout the morning and afternoon; as the sun began to set, they were spurred into an even quicker pace.

As soon as the suns remaining rays turned to red and pink, Mathias yelled, "Ride, ride as fast as you can!"

Without waiting for encouragement, the horses jumped forward, their gait opening into a full out run. The sensation of air building in front of them became a palpable presence. The feeling of something about to be unleashed could be felt like a wave rising to break against a rocky shoreline, and then the canyon walls fell away, the sky opening above them. Mathias rode like a madman, reeling to the right as soon as he cleared the canyon walls; the remainder of the group followed him. Jace, bringing up the rear, guiding the terrified pack horses, had just cleared the canyon walls when the wind's fury unleashed. The force of it was like an explosion. Jace was thrown from his horse by a backflow of the air. The sound of the wind ripping through the canyon was like a massive giant bellowing its hatred and frustration at the top of its lungs. Four of the pack animals made it beyond the powerful winds; the rest were lost, taken by the winds as easily as a man blows salt from his hand.

The group, getting their horses under control, dismounted and hurried to Jace's aid. He was already getting up from the ground, shaking his head as if trying to clear it of dizziness. Graham got to his side before the others and helped to steady him.

"I think we lost the rest of the bacon," said Jace with a smile.

Koyne turned to look at Mathias still sitting on his horse. "You should have led us through faster."

"If we had tried to go any faster, we all would have perished. These horses barely had enough to make the final sprint out of the canyon," replied Mathias.

"Maybe if we had stopped for a rest, the horses could have gone at a faster pace between breaks!" yelled Koyne, saliva at the corners of his mouth.

"Koyne! Mathias has done what needed to be done to get us through. Please calm down," said Avalon.

Koyne looked around at the others. Jace, still a little groggy-looking, stepped over with Graham's help and put his hand on Koyne's shoulder. "Don't worry, I'll find us some more bacon," he said still smiling.

Koyne relaxed slightly, but the look he gave Mathias's back was murderous.

"I think it is time for you to lead us, McKray," said Mathias. "It is obvious my leadership is not trusted."

"I will lead with you and Dale by my side. You men know the area better than I for the time being, after all I haven't been in these mountains for many years."

They traveled in the darkness for another hour before making camp; the entire group wanted to be away from the canyon of wind and its constant howling. They ate a cheerless dinner and went to bed quickly, keeping watch in turn, McKray taking the last watch. In the growing morning light, he pulled out the map the Bard had made on Watcher's Hill from his pack, looking at it closely. He noticed the path that he had copied was slightly different from the one they had just taken to reach this spot. At the moment, the sun peeked over the distant horizon; a faint rustle in the treetops above made McKray look up. He saw sunlight glisten on the golden feathers and fur of a large animal. Standing there mouth agape, he watched the messenger of Odin soar away. He was still staring at the sky when the ear-piercing shriek of an eagle split the morning silence.

The others awakened by the eagle's cry were slowly getting up, Jace moving a bit slower than everyone else, except maybe Dale. McKray was still staring at the sky when the Bard stepped over to his side.

"Are you okay, old friend?"

McKray looked at the Bard with an almost-dreamy look. Seeing the stern face, he shook his head and came back to himself. "Uh, yeah, I'm fine, I just saw something fly away." Lowering his voice he continued on, "It was a messenger of Odin, I saw it briefly, it had golden wings and fur. It had four legs and a long tail, and that eagle's cry you all heard came from the animal."

The Bard smiled. "Then it appears our progress is being closely monitored."

"That's not all. I should have been looking at this map more closely. We didn't have to come through the Canyon of Wind. It appears that there is another route to this spot. I didn't know about either of these paths given that the main dwarf road is still several miles to the east and possibly gone from existence after all these years."

The Bard nodded. "I think we should keep this between us for the time being. If some of the others knew our journey yesterday was riskier than it had to be, we might see some serious contention."

"Agreed."

*****

“I don’t need your excuses, Oaran,” stated Jerec, captain of the knights of Souvac. “I want to know what that loathsome Bard and his little band are up to.”

“I am sorry, my lord, I have sent out all my trackers. One has perished in Bishop’s Swamp, and two in that canyon, they had almost caught up to the Bard.”

“What information do you have for me then?”

“I know that the Bard and four others left from the inn. Now he travels with an additional five. It would have been six, but one was killed and buried on top of Watcher’s Hill in the foothills of the White Mountains. They are making progress in their journey.”

“I wonder what the Bard is up to, it would appear he is trying to amass a small army. I believe he thinks he has found a way to destroy us. I am no longer complacent to have you track them. I want your beasts to attack and kill the members of the original chosen. The Bard picked those four for a reason, I want them all dead.”

“As you wish, Captain,” replied Oaran, turning away to communicate mentally with his trackers. He gave a dark look at Jerec’s back. *I will kill you when the time comes*, he thought.

“I have not seen you this scared in a very long time, Captain,” stated Kell.

“I am not scared.”

“We have been brothers a long time, Jerec, I know when you are scared. I wonder if we are going about this the wrong way. I mean, we know they must come back. They are avoiding the easily traveled paths to stay hidden and out of site. Once they get to wherever it is they are going, they will turn around and come back. I imagine they will then come by the fastest road possible, perhaps we should just set a trap and ambush them,” stated Kell.

“Should my plan fail, I will take that under advisement.” Jerec’s teeth gritted together; he hated the smug look on his brother’s face. He knew it was the most logical plan, but he would not admit that. *I will kill both of these traitors when I am free*, he thought, smiling to himself.

"I am just saying, Oaran only has so many of his little beasties. If they all get killed in the pursuit through the mountains, we will have no way to stop the Bard," said Kell in matter-of-fact tone.

Captain Jerec, glaring at Kell, turned and walked away.

Kell walked to Oaran's side. "I believe he wants to kill us as soon as we are free of the curse."

"Of course he does, but I will have a surprise ready."

"Do you intend to kill me as well?" said Kell, a bit louder than Oaran liked.

"Of course not, you have never betrayed or attacked me, and I don't believe you will, if you know what's good for you."

"I prefer the unveiled threats, honest and straightforward, they leave no margin for error. You leave me alone, and I will leave you alone."

"Agreed," said Oaran, again turning his focus on the twelve remaining creatures he had sent to follow the Bard. The final beast lay crouched in the dark branches of the trees above Jerec's shelter, quietly listening.

*****

They began traveling again, following the route marked on McKray's map. It took them in a winding path through the seemingly never-ending mountains, keeping them in areas that were covered with lush green grass and large trees. As the days passed, they continued to climb higher, the green leafy trees eventually giving way to hardier pine trees. McKray listened for an eagle like cry that he had noticed coming from high above and out of sight. He heard it only when there was more than one path to follow. He smiled to himself, knowing that, indeed, this journey was being guided by Odin.

As the sun set on the weary travelers once again, the ear-piercing eagle like cry sounded.

Jace spoke up, "It may be my imagination, but I swear that is the same bird that wakes us up every morning. I think it's following us."

"You are right, it is the same creature. It isn't, however, a bird, and it isn't following us," replied the Bard.

"I think we should make camp here," stated McKray. "We all need the rest, and we should have a little talk."

"Dale, Mathias, do you know this area?" asked the Bard.

"It is familiar, but I am afraid we are not that knowledgeable about the mountains beyond this point. I have hunted some of these paths but have not ventured much further as the mountains begin to climb steeply and the vegetation becomes sparse, as does the water," replied Dale.

"Very well." The Bard turned and walked into the gathering darkness. "I will return shortly, do not follow me."

"You know sometimes I get the feeling that he is just a crazy old wanderer that is leading us to our deaths," stated Koyne, whose mood had been souring further over the past several days, especially toward Mathias.

"You might have something there," replied Graham. "I mean, when he showed up, he was leading right. Now he lets everyone else do the leading while he follows along. Oh, and every once in a while, he decides he needs to disappear into the darkness."

"I thought you believed in the Bard, after all you, like me, sought him out," said Jace.

"I know he seems odd at times, but have you ever thought that there might be something for you all to learn on this journey?" said McKray in his gruff voice.

Dale, who had been very quiet the last few days, spoke, "I think McKray is right. I have been thinking a lot about how this journey has gone for me, and honestly, it's starting to feel pointless. But now with what McKray has said, it's starting to make sense again. We all have things to learn and experience here."

Koyne shook his head. "I'm with Graham. I'm wondering if abandoning this fool idea isn't the best choice for us. I mean, the people we thought knew these mountains have gotten us as far as they can." He looked pointedly in Mathias's direction.

"Look, I know I'm younger than you and blind, but I'm getting sick of your constant attacks at Dale and me," said Mathias, stepping toward Koyne.

"Just step back, since you are blind, I'll let this go and save you some dignity," replied Koyne.

Mathias balled up his fists and stepped closer. Dale put a calming hand on Mathias's chest. "This is not what we need, little brother. We both know you are meant for bigger things, don't let him stop you."

Mathias turned his head, as if trying to look at Dale's face, then walked away.

Koyne was about to say something at the retreating figure when Avalon put her hand over his mouth. "I think you need to learn to keep your thoughts to yourself sometimes." The fire of defense started to shine in Koyne's eyes; Avalon moved her hand and kissed him softly on the mouth. The fire vanished instantly, replaced by a look of love. "See, there is more to you than an angry boy," she said.

The two walked away hand in hand.

"We'll be back, we are just going to gather some firewood," stated Koyne.

They went the opposite way of the Bard.

"Come on, Graham, you can help me get the fire started. I think they might be a little while before they get back with any wood," stated McKray. Laying a hand on Graham's shoulder, he turned away, giving Dale, Sterling, and Jace a knowing look.

Sterling looked at Dale. "I believe you are right, my friend. We all have a lot to learn on this journey. I think before too long, our paths are going to diverge and take us to who knows where."

Dale nodded. "I just wish I knew what is in store for us."

Sterling continued, "I never thought I would live life without my brother, and the farther I get from when he died, the more his death weighs on my mind."

"Perhaps your brother isn't as far away as you think," said the Bard, reappearing from the shadows. "Did I miss anything while I was gone?"

"Just a bit of a philosophical debate," replied Jace. "Where did you go, if I may ask?"

"We have been a long time in the saddle, and I like privacy when answering nature's call."

"I think the long journey is starting to get to everyone, putting us a bit on edge," said Dale smiling.

"Ah, am I up to no good?" asked the Bard.

"There is a good chance of that," replied Jace.

"Has anyone seen Amalia?" asked Dale, looking around. The men looked at each other, blank looks on their faces.

A sudden heart-piercing scream caught everyone's attention. The sounds of commotion, twigs snapping, and yelling could be heard from the direction Koyne and Avalon had gone. Drawing swords and bows, the group ran toward sounds.

Moments later, the feral growls of some wild creature and the cry of a bird of prey could be heard. Koyne and Avalon burst from the trees into the path of their companions.

"There was something out there something that wanted to kill us," said Avalon shaking.

"I don't know what it is, but—" Koyne's comment was cut off by the sounds of two animals fighting loudly nearby.

"Sterling, I want you and Jace to come with me. McKray, take the others back to the fire, keep your weapons drawn, there may be more of these creatures."

The Bard, his sword drawn, and Sterling and Jace with bows ready proceeded toward the sounds moving as quietly as the night. The sounds of battle raged on, broken only by the ferocious growls of a beast and the eagle-like cry of the animal it was fighting. After just a few moments of creeping through the darkened forest, the Bard and his companions came to an area that was more open, the small trees in the area were bent over, some were broken, the ground was torn up as though a farmer's plow had just been through. In the middle of the chaos was a large creature with thick, black, matted fur and piercing orange eyes. It crouched low to the ground, its head pointed into the air as if searching the treetops for its enemy. It could be heard sniffing the air, and when it caught a scent, it would let out a menacing growl and slowly circle toward its attacker.

Sterling turned his head slightly to face the Bard. "That is a creature of evil, not just an animal of this forest."

"You are right, that, I am sorry to say, is one of Oaran's boarhounds," replied the Bard.

Jace and Sterling simultaneously fitted arrows to their bowstrings and drew back taking aim. The slight creek in the bow limbs as they were bent caught the beast's attention; it immediately turned on the three men. It took a mighty leap forward Jace, and Sterling loosed their arrows, both of which found their mark in the creature's chest. At almost the same instant, the eagle's cry broke with ear-shattering volume right above the men, and the boarhound's body, which never hit the ground after it leaped, climbed higher in the air carried by some great winged bird.

Several seconds later, the black thing slammed into the softened earth, the sound of bones breaking gave evidence that it must have been dropped from a great height. A cry of victory sounded far above, and then the night became silent again. The Bard led Sterling and Jace to the shattered, lifeless body of the creature. Quickly lighting a makeshift torch, they were able to inspect the beast. It was the size of a small black bear with similar fur, but its body was slender and lean. It had claws on each foot, four inches long, and the many three-inch teeth in its elongated maw were in a double row at opposite angles. It appeared that this animal had been made with an enhanced sense of smell and vision, but not hearing, as it had smallish ears for a creature this size. This was an animal of dark creation with two reasons for existence: seek and destroy.

*****

"Captain Jerec, my lord, another of my boarhounds was killed. It was about to kill two of the Bard's original chosen when it was attacked by some winged creature of the White Mountains. I have put the rest of the animals on hold for now. What would you have me do?" asked Oaran.

Jerec looked over at Kell, who was smiling smugly to himself. "Draw all your creatures back but one. I want them to set an ambush on the Great North Road where it splits the Kraggs. The remaining beast will continue to track the Bard's movements in case we need time to alter our ambush location."

Kell smiled to himself even more. He had grown tired of being second to Jerec. He wanted to rid himself of his captain and rule his own destiny, and now he saw his opportunity growing. In the end you can only be loyal for so long, and that time was running out.

The Evil One sat in his dark abyss with his witch and her son watching the petty lives of these mortals that he had enslaved. His work kept him busy across the breadth of all the inhabited lands, but this little game that he had started was unfolding again, keeping his interest for the first time in over a hundred years. He loved to see betrayal, murder, and chaos; it appeared Kell could be a way for this investment of time and power to continue playing out.

*****

"Where have you two been?" asked McKray of Mathias and Amalia as they came running back to the group after hearing the screams.

"I followed Mathias, I didn't want him to be alone after what Koyne said," stated Amalia, glancing darkly in Koyne's direction.

"What is going on out there?" asked Mathias.

"We don't know, the Bard told us to wait here," said Graham.

"Maybe I should join the Bard," said Mathias.

"Let's just all stay put until the Bard returns," stated McKray, putting his sturdy hand on Mathias's shoulder.

Chapter 10

McKray and the others sat tensely by the fire, waiting for the Bard to return. They were quietly discussing the situation when the three men walked into the fire light.

"So what was it?" asked McKray.

"It was a boarhound, it seems the knights wish to bring death to our group. I fear I may have underestimated them. It appears these creatures have adapted to traveling in the sunlight. They are gaining on us. We should get some rest, but we will begin traveling again in a few hours," stated the Bard.

"Is it dead? asked Avalon with fear in her voice.

"Yes, it is dead, but it seems we are in greater peril than I had imagined."

"Is it wise to travel so soon? There is a lot of cloud cover, which means little light from the moon, we will be traveling in nearly complete darkness," stated Koyne.

"I can lead you," replied Mathias. "This darkness does not affect my ability to see," he said smugly as Amalia took his hand in hers.

"I can also see in the dark and will assist in guiding," stated McKray before Koyne could respond. "We will rest for a time we need it and the horses need it. I will watch and then wake all of you when the time is right," replied the Bard bringing the discussion to a close.

The next few hours passed slowly as the band of travelers found themselves unable to sleep. They knew it was a miracle that no one had been killed by the creature. It was very likely that more of these beasts were on their trail, and death was now a very real part of their journey. They arose from their beds at the Bard's signal, each member of the group feeling a new urgency. Little was said as they packed their meager camp and prepared to depart. Despite the heavy darkness the group continued into the White Mountains, gradually climbing toward the snow-covered peaks. Just after midday, darker clouds began to amass in the sky above them.

McKray eyed the clouds wearily. "I know I haven't been in these mountains for many years, but that is a large storm that is going to unleash some wrath on us, we had better find someplace to get under cover," he said.

"It looks like sheer cliffs rise ahead of us, is it possible that we might find a cave there to shelter in?" asked Graham.

"It's a definite possibility, plus it appears that is where we are headed anyway according to the map," replied McKray.

They continued, even after the clouds descended on them like an advancing army. Before long the travelers could feel the moisture in the clouds working into their clothes. It started raining on them at first, soaking them to the skin. After an hour the rain slackened, turning into large white snowflakes. The temperature of the air around them dropped drastically, and misery set in. If it had not been for the map that McKray carried and the ever-constant eagle cry that led them in the right direction, panic would easily have crept in. The clouds around them got so thick that they decided they needed to tether the horses together to prevent anyone from getting separated.

The bad weather had slowed their progress and with the now-freezing conditions and monotonous passage of time, patience began to slip.

"Are you sure you know where you are going?" hollered Koyne from near the back of the line.

"Actually, I have no idea, but if you think you can do better, I welcome you up here to give it a try," McKray growled back.

"We have to be getting close," stated Dale. "The cliff face was maybe nine to ten miles distant when the storm first settled in. Our progress has slowed a bit, but that was at least three to four hours ago, so we should be there soon."

"I hope so," replied Avalon through chattering teeth. "I don't think I can take this cold much longer I feel like my fingers and toes are going to fall off."

Another thirty minutes passed, and even McKray began to doubt that they would ever find the cliff face when a great craggy shadow rose in front of his horse. Startled by the sudden appearance of the rock face, McKray let out a yell.

"What is it?" called the Bard.

"It appears to be a cliff," replied McKray. "I'm getting a bit jumpy in my old age."

The others brought their horses up into a tight group.

"Now which way do we go?" asked Jace.

As if in answer, the shrill eagle cry that had guided them through the impenetrable mist cried out ahead of them.

"Any more questions?" asked Sterling.

"No, that was the only one I had," replied Jace.

They took a moment to untether the horses, knowing that all they had to do was stay close to the cliff face, keeping it on their right hand, and they would not get lost. At first the sight of the cliff gave them hope that they would find shelter quickly. An agonizing twenty minutes later, they were again losing hope. Avalon began to fear that they would all die from exposure to the cold. They had not heard the eagle cry since finding the cliff, so when it rang out again louder than they had yet heard it and with an echo, they all jumped in their saddles.

McKray's strong voice carried back to the others through the noise-stifling clouds. "There is a large opening in the cliff right here, we can get in out of the weather."

Soon they were all inside an enormous cavern. A large stash of firewood lay piled against the wall near the opening. McKray, moving as fast as his frozen body would allow, began building a fire near the cavern opening.

"I'm sorry, everyone, usually I can build a fire in seconds, my frozen hands just don't want to move," he said as he fumbled with the task. However, minutes later, a large blaze was chasing the cold from everyone's bones and drying their soaked clothes.

As the warmth settled through their bodies, sleep began to tug at their minds. Avalon had already fallen into a fitful sleep, leaning against Koyne; the others, even the Bard, began to doze—until Mathias sat up sharply.

"There is something out there. I thought I could sense it while we were riding, but the cold was affecting my hearing."

The Bard stood and moved to the opening. He looked into the swirling snow and white bank of clouds as if trying to peer through it. He could feel something tugging at his mind just beyond his sight, but whatever it was, it was trying to stay hidden. The tension in the air woke those who had fallen asleep; they were looking at the Bard with bleary eyes. He turned from the opening, and several things happened at once. Jace yelled, Avalon and Amalia screamed, the Bard rolled forward onto the ground as if forcefully pushed, and the cavern opening was swallowed by stone. The muffled sound of claws tearing at the rock could be heard.

The Bard was back to his feet instantly with his back once again to his companions. He stared blankly at the rock wall before him, not noticing the blood that was soaking his travel-worn cloths.

"Are you okay? Your back is bleeding," said Amalia, rushing to stand at his side.

The Bard turned to look at her and smiled. "Yes, I am fine, in a few minutes that scrape will just be another bad memory." He patted her shoulder and returned to the fire. "I have no doubt that the creature was one of Oaran's. I can normally tell when dangerous animals are close, but this was trying to stay hidden. Mathias, you thought you could sense something near us as we traveled?"

"Yes, I never heard it, but there was a feeling of suppressed malice. I think you are right about it trying to stay hidden though, it felt like it was trying to mask its intentions."

"I don't think it was the creature masking its intentions but Oaran controlling it. I don't know what to make of these actions, earlier it seemed the boarhound was trying to kill Koyne and Avalon. Now he is trying to hide and only attacked me. It doesn't make sense. Perhaps the knights are fighting about what to do. In the end that could prove beneficial to us." These last statements were said to no one in particular, as if the Bard was speaking to himself.

The others sat quietly, taking in the information they had just received. None of them knew what to think about this revelation, let alone what to say.

Koyne, as usual, was the first one to break the silence, "So here we are safe from the monster that wants us dead but stuck in a hole unable to get where we need to go."

"Not exactly. I believe we have found Odin's Stair. Legend says that only those permitted by Odin can attain it. As a man who supposedly speaks for the God of the Living, he has been granted great power, power enough to control the earth if he desires, and so he built this, a way to lead those that he wants to his door or to trap and destroy those that he finds unworthy," said McKray.

"Well, if we're safe for now I think I'm going to get some sleep, even with the latest excitement, I can barely keep my eyes open," stated Jace. Rolling into his blanket, he was asleep within seconds. The others following suit were soon breathing deeply and soundly as they slept, all except the Bard and McKray.

The Bard stood shakily to his feet and motioned for the dwarf to follow him. He walked to his horse, pulled a small bottle from the saddlebag, and walked deeper into the cavern. McKray walked with him, occasionally reaching out a steadying hand. Thirty minutes later, the Bard was leaning on McKray for support. McKray had never seen his friend like this and was beginning to worry.

The Bard, seeing the worry in the dwarf's eyes, smiled. "Don't worry, friend, I cannot die, but I imagine the poison that infiltrated my blood from the creature's claws takes a long time to dissipate without a cure," he said, holding up the vial he had taken from the saddlebag. "This should be far enough away that the others won't hear me scream." He slumped against the cave wall and rolled slightly to his left side, removing his cloak and tunic. "I need you to pour some of this into each of the wounds and then leave, please."

McKray, kneeling at the Bard's side, took the vial, removed the stopper, and slowly poured the liquid into the open wounds. The Bard shook, the muscles of his body contracting with the pain that coursed through his body. McKray, finishing his work, could see clearly the many white scars that crisscrossed the Bard's back. Without a word, he stood, corked the vial, set it near the Bard, and left walking at a quick pace. He did not want to hear the screams that he knew were going to erupt from his injured friend's mouth. He heard the first scream minutes later, echoing behind him, then came a great, sobbing cry. Unable to bear any more, McKray began to run until the sounds were no longer discernible. He lay awake for some time, wondering how long the Bard would suffer. Sleep took his awareness, and unpleasant dreams gave way to the comforting sensation of being watched over and protected.

The man stepped from the covering blackness of the alcove he had been sitting in since the arrival of these travelers. He added wood to the fire, spoke some words of command, and watched as each member of the party relaxed even deeper into sleep. He knew it would take two days for the Bard's pain to ease, and the others would grow worried. It was for that reason that he blessed them with sleep. He walked to where the Bard lay sobbing, giving way to the screams, which then gave way once again to sobbing. It was a terrible vision to behold, and it pained the man to see it, but he knew the Bard would refuse his blessing. The Bard viewed the pain and suffering of mind and body as a penance for things he considered his fault, like the death of his wife and son. Therefore, the man simply laid a skin of cold, refreshing water by his side and departed up Odin's Stair.

*****

Oaran struggled for several minutes to bring his beast under control. The creature which typically followed his master's immediate commands had resisted until it had torn the flesh of its feet and even left part of its claws embedded in the rock face. Oaran had even begun to feel the undeniable rage of the beast creeping into his own body and mind. He had allowed it to lash out at the Bard as Jerec had instructed and, in so doing, nearly lost his mind to the creature. Exhausted by the efforts it had taken to restore control of the beast and himself, he moved to his own little section of the cursed glade.

Kell had watched as Jerec gave the order to have the beast attack the Bard. He watched Oaran struggle mentally and physically during the apparent confrontation. He saw that Oaran was weakened and would be vulnerable to suggestion. Kell approached his brother knight with false worry on his face.

"Are you all right? It appeared something was going terribly wrong."

Oaran looked into Kell's dark eyes. Too tired to try and penetrate the thoughts of the knight, he simply nodded his head.

"What happened?" asked Kell again, false worry filling his words.

Oaran was suspicious of Kell; truthfully, they were all suspicious of each other ever since the night that King Souvac fell to their oath-breaking blades, and so it was that Oaran hesitantly answered, "I'm not sure, I started to lose control of the beast after it attacked the Bard."

"Why did you have it attack the Bard I thought the plan was to just watch and wait until they reached the ambush point?" stated Kell, turning his gaze to Jerec, who paced the glade some distance away.

"Captain Jerec wanted the Bard to suffer a bit, so he demanded the attack."

"I've never seen you lose control of a tracker like that before. Do you think Jerec had something to do with your struggle?" he asked again, letting his eyes wander to the pacing captain.

Oaran let his own eyes follow Kell's gaze. "What are you trying to say?" he asked suspiciously.

"Captain Jerec has been different since the Bard showed up for his last meeting with us. He was unwilling to accept my strategy initially and only accepted it as his own plan, after the first boarhound failed. I worry that he is becoming distrustful of us and plans to continue life outside of this cursed glade alone."

Oaran allowed his gaze to stay on Jerec. "You have said as much numerous times over the last couple of weeks. Is there something you know that I don't about your brother?" Thoughts of betrayal were swirling through his mind.

Kell placed his hand on Oaran's shoulder. "I just fear that these past hundred years have caused a tear between all of us. I don't know how freedom will affect us. Be careful, let yourself get your strength back before you do anything like that again."

Oaran nodded as Kell stood and walked away. Oaran once alone began to think deeply about all that Kell had said. Kell knew Jerec better than anyone; being brothers they had always been inseparable, and Oaran had felt honored to be a part of their brotherhood. Now he could see that it was all starting to unravel, and he wondered what would happen to himself as it did.

*****

When McKray awoke, he knew he should go and check on the Bard but did not relish the idea of seeing his friend still writhing in pain. Then there would be the lies he would have to tell his companions. McKray hated to lie to people he considered family. After several minutes of contemplation, however, he decided to get up and go before the others woke up.

"Good morning," stated the Bard, sitting at a small fire.

Startled, McKray nearly jumped out of his bedroll. "Ahh, you scared the daylights out of me," he said with a smile. "I'm glad to see you are feeling better, but giving someone a start like that could easily take ten years off their life."

"My apologies."

"Speaking of feeling better, how did you get feeling better so fast? I thought it would take a couple of days at least."

"It has been two full nights and a day," replied the Bard. "When my pain began to subside and I could think of other things, I began wondering if you would come and check on me. I then slept the entire night through and awoke with a skin of cold water by my side, so I figured that you had come by to check on me."

"Regretfully, it wasn't me, apparently I and the others have been asleep for a very long time."

"I believe you all have been asleep for the same amount of time, and since everyone will be starving when they wake, we should make a decent breakfast."

Before long, the other members of the party awoke to the smell of breakfast. They were all ravenous from the lack of food, and so they ate cheese and dried fruits as well. Dale even opened a skin of golden ale that he passed around. For the first time since Dale and Mathias joined the group, they were all feeling well fed and optimistic. They would have remained where they were for a while longer had the Bard not encouraged them to make haste for the first leg of journey was coming to its end.

They spent two more full days traveling through the enormous caverns that were Odin's stair. Shortly after they passed the spot where the Bard had recovered from his injury, the cavern began to change. It had been solid gray rock with the walls, ceiling, and floor appearing smooth as if some great craftsman had spent centuries carving. That, however, gave way to more exotic formations that appeared to have been made by nature itself. Mighty stalactites and stalagmites in different stages of creation glittered in the light of torches that were carried by the companions. In some places, the formations had become giant stone pillars that seemingly held up the cavernous roof.

They saw formations of stone that appeared to be piles of gold coins the size of McKray's hands. Other formations of varying shape size and color dazzled the eye as well. At the end of the first day of travel, they began to see large streaks of gold and silver running through the very walls of the cavern; some veins were hundreds of feet long and as wide as a man is tall. All the companions wondered about the wealth of treasure that was still in its natural form in these caverns.

The second day of travel allowed even more glimpses of fascinating rock formations and even more natural treasure of gold and silver found not only in the walls but in the ceiling and the floor as well. Even gems of various sizes and colors began to be visible everywhere they looked. In fact, as one began to look more closely, they would have noticed that the natural veins of gold and silver, the setting of the gems in their places. And even the natural formations were taking on very unique patterns, patterns that did not naturally occur. McKray, who had been studying everything he saw as they rode, suddenly let out a gasp. The sudden sound broke through the silence, causing everybody's heart to jump in their chests.

"What is it?" asked Jace, drawing his sword. Sudden fear washed over the entire group as thoughts of underground creatures attacking careened through their minds in seconds.

"Nothing, nothing, I am sorry to startle everyone. I just realized that I recognize this workmanship."

"Yeah, it's called nature," replied Koyne cynically.

"Boy, I am a dwarf, and if there is one thing a dwarf knows better than anything else in this world, it is stonework. This stonework is subtle, only a trained eye would see it, and only a trained eye would see that it was done by my father and my people."

The others, of course, did not see the subtle stonework, but as they continued to travel, the workmanship became more noticeable and magnificent. The light of their torches danced from the myriad of facets cut into the precious stones that were now placed in intricate designs along the walls and ceiling of the cavern.

"This looks less like a cave and more like a grand palace," stated Graham.

"My guess is that we are approaching the gate of Odin's Hall," remarked McKray.

The road that they had been following had been steadily climbing but remained fairly straight throughout their travel; now it began to climb more sharply in a great spiral. The gems and gold in the wall changed again from beautiful intricate designs to strong runes, delicate lettering, and words in the common language surrounded by pictograms. Each member of the party could read the common language welcoming travelers to the kingdom of Odin and peaceful rest.

The runes that were being read by McKray, however, gave warnings and messages of caution. So it was that they made their way safely up the great spiral that so beautifully hid traps of death. After two more hours of constant climbing up the spiral, they found their way blocked by an enormous door standing easily thirty feet tall and half that wide.

"How are we going to get through that?" Avalon wondered aloud.

"Perhaps we should knock," suggested Mathias. Riding forward, he turned as he neared the door and knocked heavily on the dark wood with his shield. To everyone's surprise, the great door swung back noiselessly.

The group shielded their eyes as bright rays of sunlight assaulted their vision. As their eyes adjusted to the sunlight, fragrant air filled their nostrils. Lush green grass spread away like a great carpet; the singing of numerous songbirds filled the air. The warmth of the air that washed over them was like a warm blanket fresh off the line in the summer sun. McKray rode his horse forward, and through the giant doorway, the others followed, some more tentative than others. Once through the doorway, they could see that the sun was filtering down through an expansive dome of clear crystal that let one see the snowy peaks, the light-blue sky, and the blazing sun overhead. Under the crystal dome amongst the grass, all manners of flowers bloomed; trees and bushes held fruits of common and exotic nature. Colorful birds flew through the air, filling it with their songs and chatter. There were even several forest animals hiding amongst the foliage.

McKray sat for a moment, looking around, when he turned to look at the members of the group. They could see that he was both impressed and upset by what he saw.

"What's wrong, McKray?" asked Avalon.

"It's as I feared—elves. That was the other writing on the walls, you know, the fancy, swirly stuff. Apparently, they are welcome here also."

"And that's a bad thing?" asked Dale.

"Look, I have no personal argument with elves, but overall, they're a stuffy bunch. I like what they've done here. I just hope we don't run into any of them."

"What is this place?" asked Jace.

"Someplace I only thought existed when you died. This is Odin's Garden," said McKray, his head drooping slightly.

"Well now, don't be so disappointed," said a deep voice.

Everyone looked around but could not locate the person who had spoken.

"I am glad you all arrived safely. I will say there was great effort on my part, but you all did well to follow my directions."

Again the members of the group looked around, trying to find the source of the words.

"Please dismount and allow your horses to wander freely here in Odin's Garden."

Suddenly the great doors closed with a bang. Looking up, the group saw three large golden animals. Two, it appeared, had closed the heavy doors while the third descended on golden wings to stand before the startled group. To their surprise, the horses remained calm.

"My name is Gold Wing, I am captain of Odin's royal guard, welcome," said the animal with its eagle-like beak.

"Not to be disrespectful, but what are you?" asked Sterling in awe.

"I and my brothers are griffins, the guards of Odin and his kingdom," replied the magnificent animal. "Now as I said, please dismount and give your loyal beasts their much-needed rest. I will guide you to Odin's house, from there another servant will lead you to your quarters where you will wash and put on fresh garments which have been laid out for you. After that you will dine, and Odin will speak with you."

The group of adventurers dismounted from their horses and were beginning the process of unpacking.

"Please leave things as they are, someone will be along shortly to see to your animals and bring your things to your rooms," stated one of the other griffins.

Gold Wing was already moving through the garden. It was difficult to tell for certain where he was headed because the garden was so vast. The travelers rushed to catch up and then had to keep a quick pace to stay close to the mighty griffin.

"Gold Wing, your brother mentioned that someone would be tending to our things. Who is it that serves Odin besides you and your kind?" asked McKray.

"Ah, my good dwarf, that is not for me to tell, but I imagine you will know before long."

"The workmanship in Odin's Stair, may I ask who is responsible for such beautiful craftsmanship, and how long ago was it done?" asked McKray prying for information.

Gold Wing appeared to smile, his large black eyes shining a bit brighter. "I believe you well know who is responsible for the stunning craft done on Odin's Stair, for it was your own clan. As to when was it done, let's just say work has commenced for centuries."

As they talked, the other members of the group looked in wonder around and above them as flocks of colorful birds flew from well-tended trees. Animals of all manners and sizes roamed the well-kept gardens. Avalon and Amalia walked together, their eyes often straying far above them to look at the crystal dome that allowed sunlight in but kept the frigid cold of the White Mountains out. Pools of crystal clear water were spread throughout the groves and glades that made Odin's Garden.

Avalon turned, taking Koyne's hand in her own, and whispered in his ear, "This is the most beautiful place I have ever seen. I feel like I could stay here forever."

Koyne looked back at her, a look of calm on his face and a tear glistening at the corner of his eye. "I feel peace, I feel peace in the very depths of my heart. I have never felt this way before," he whispered back.

Avalon squeezed his hand tighter, and they continued in silence.

Mathias and Dale walked side by side, Dale describing in as much detail the many things he was seeing to his younger brother. Mathias was smiling broadly. "Brother, I see colors in my mind, it's not the same black-and-white haze that I usually sense but colors and tastes and smells that are bringing the images that you speak to my mind in clear pictures. It is as if I truly can see," he said.

Dale put his hand on Mathias's shoulder. "I keep telling you, this is just the beginning of great things for you. Ever since I had that dream, I knew something big would happen in your life."

Jace and Sterling were walking side by side in silence, each man keeping his thoughts and feelings to himself.

The Bard brought up the rear with Graham. "May I ask you a question?" Graham asked.

"You may ask me anything you wish."

"McKray and I have spoken a fair amount on this trip, and anytime I talk of reclaiming the throne in Souvac, he discourages me. I will not try to subjugate the people, my father taught me well the proper way to rule a kingdom. I just want to try and make life better for the people."

The Bard looked at Graham with interest. "You are young, yet wisdom is in you, this is a most desirable virtue. It is important to understand a bit about McKray. He told you of his family and the reason he is alone, I believe. He saw himself becoming the worst thing a king can become, which is selfish and greedy. His family had ruled his clan for many centuries, and all the kings ruled with wisdom and goodness. Then despite all the teaching he had from his father, he became the very thing that could completely destroy his clan, a selfish person. He had to be left behind alone for centuries to learn the lessons that his father had tried to teach him. This is perhaps what he fears for you, not that you will be selfish, but through the years one of your sons or grandsons could fall to the same blindness that caught him."

"What do you think I should do?" Graham asked.

"I think you should follow the course of wisdom. I have my own life to lead, and so I can be of no use to you on this matter. You have your life to live, which will determine the choices you make. I suggest looking at all sides of the equation and making a decision when the time is right. I also imagine we will receive valuable counsel from Odin."

They finally reached the end of the garden; a solid cliff face without blemish rose to meet the crystal dome. An opening half the size of the door on the far side of the garden admitted them onto a broad stone staircase. Fine tapestries of various material ranging from silk to sturdy cotton and wool hung along the walls to either side. Each tapestry displayed images of great battles, glorious heroes, fascinating beasts, pastoral landscapes, ominous castles, fair maidens, and many other wonderful scenes.

"First, I see elven writing and decoration in Odin's Stair, now I see elven tapestries adorning the walls of Odin's Keep. I don't know if I can stomach this insult," stated McKray

Gold Wing smiled as they reached the landing at the top of the staircase. Below them a great hall opened. A staircase smaller than the one they had just ascended stretched down to the main floor on the right and rose to higher heights to their left.

"This is where I must leave you, for I have other business to attend to. However, my close friend Teran will show you to your rooms. I ask you to be nice, McKray." With that, Gold Wing turned and, spreading his wings, leaped into the air, gliding back down the way they had just come up, the tips of his outstretched wings just missing the stone walls.

The group watched the griffin disappear from sight; they did not see the small door at the base of the stairs open and a tall, lordly man of exquisite grace approach them until he called their attention with a small cough.

"Welcome to Odin's Keep," he said in a melodic voice. "My name is Teran, and I will be showing you to your rooms."

"An elf as a servant, I could get used to this," said McKray beaming.

"Master dwarf, I serve Odin, not you or anyone else. Now follow me."

He led them up a flight of stairs to another large landing. This also looked down onto the great hall, but there was a long corridor leading deeper into the keep and stairs at the far side of the landing that continued higher in more flights of stairs. Teran led them down the corridor a short distance.

"As you will see, your names are written on the door that will be your chambers while you are here with us. You are free to explore anything on this the second floor and the main floor, which is the great hall and the gardens. I must ask that you go nowhere else in the keep, for it is off-limits by order from Odin. If you are found outside of these areas, the instructions are clear, you are to be put in the dungeon. Should you need anything while you are here, please ring the bell in your room and speak into the griffin head by your door." Teran turned on his heel and strode back down the stairwell.

Avalon and Amalia's names were written on the door closest to the landing. They pushed it open, and everyone looked inside. There was a thick carpet covering the entire floor, the main room was handsomely furnished. To the left another door opened to a large four-poster bed. Straight ahead was a crystal door that opened onto a balcony.

They stepped inside turned around and closed the door, saying, "Goodbye, gentlemen," with a smile.

In the bedroom were two tubs of warm water. Each woman quickly undressed and climbed into the water, letting the warmth wash away their travel soreness. After the bath, they dressed in the simple white cotton dresses that were laid out for them and walked back into the main room. Crossing the room to the crystal door, they found it opened onto a balcony. Large, dark-brown birds flew through the air, landing on the cliff face and then jumping away again to soar through the open expanse. White snow glistened on the tops of the cliffs that extended high above where they stood. After several minutes of watching the great birds in their graceful dance, they noticed one great bird flying directly toward their balcony. There was something about this bird that was different from the others the women had been watching, but it was difficult to tell at such a distance. As it drew nearer, a stocky, well-built man could be seen riding the great bird. Seconds later, it was close enough to see a thick, black beard and long hair that almost completely obscured the man's facial features. The small bit of skin that was visible looked rough and red, but before they could get a better look at the man, the bird wheeled away, dropping into a dive, landing on a balcony thirty feet below.

"Did you see that?" asked Amalia looking at Avalon.

Avalon was smiling broadly "Of course I did. We must tell the others.

The women's companions met with similar experiences in their own rooms. Each man took a much-needed warm bath and, when finished bathing, dressed in the simple white woolen tunic and pants that had been laid out. After exploring their own rooms, Jace, Dale, and Sterling—being intrigued by the crystal doors—went to the balcony attached to each of their rooms. Each man saw the same thing that the women had seen, the great birds flying about and the black-haired dwarf that was riding one of the birds. The Bard slept heavily on his soft bed for the first time since they left the Travelers' Inn. McKray and Mathias both spent much more time soaking in their individual tubs. Graham spent extra time looking at all the beautiful items that decorated his rooms, thinking how nice these things would look in his own palace once he took his place as rightful king of Souvac.

Koyne was the only one who wasn't content; he had tried to lie down after his bath, but his restless mind which had been so full of peace in the gardens had begun to fill with the anger that had plagued him throughout the journey. He strode around his room for a time looking at nothing; however, a feeling of foreboding continued creeping into his mind. He had made it through this journey, he thought, with his anger mostly in check, thanks to Avalon's calming presence. He had even had a moment of complete peace in Odin's Garden, but now this feeling of rage again assaulted his mind and heart. This horrible desire to lash out and kill someone, anyone, not in self-defense, but just for the sake of killing. He had wanted to kill Mathias on more than one occasion. The young man gave him no real reason, yet the desire was still there. Finally, after several minutes, he left his room with no idea of where he was going or what he was going to do. He paused in front of Mathias's door as he walked back toward the stairs. Reaching out his left hand, he grasped the handle and tried to turn it; fortunately the door was locked as Mathias was still soaking in the bath. Koyne let his hand drop away from the handle and continued back toward the stairs. Once he was on the landing, he looked at the stairs leading down and then the stairs leading up. He had been instructed by the elf to not ascend any more stairs, but looking around, he saw that he was alone. That was enough. He turned and climbed the stairs flight after flight; the elf Teran stood hidden in a secret alcove and watched him go.

Koyne climbed stairs until his legs burned with the effort. Finally, when he felt he could climb no more, he reached a landing. There was a small hallway leading away to the left. This place was unadorned unlike the rest of the castle. He followed the hall back to its end where a plain wooden door faced him. Reaching out his left hand, he rested his hand on the latch for several seconds before opening the door.

Teran waited until Koyne was well out of sight before coming out of his hiding place and going to knock on the doors of his lord's guests. It took some extra time waiting for McKray and Mathias to finish soaking and get dressed, but soon they had all joined him, except for Koyne. He began leading them down the stairs to the great hall.

"Wait, Koyne isn't here. Shouldn't we wait for him?" stated Avalon.

"The young man had some business to attend to, he will join us as soon as he is ready," replied Teran.

"How will he find his way? Maybe I should wait here for him," countered Avalon.

"Worry not, my dear, he is with someone who will guide him to his place," replied the elf with a smile.

"Well then, let's go, this dwarf's not getting any fuller standing here yackin'," said McKray.

Teran smiled at the dwarf, a genuine smile of warmth and friendship, which took McKray by surprise. Teran finished leading the group down the two flights of stairs to the great hall they had seen earlier. Leading off from this room were several doors of varying material—stone, crystal, and wood of all kinds. They walked through a large crystal door into an enclosed garden with a large table. The floor covering was lush green grass with small lavender flowers that gave off the intoxicating aroma of spring. Golden dinnerware was laid out on the table. Each person took a place at the table, and beautiful elf maidens in the same simple white cotton dresses as Avalon and Amalia began to file in, carrying with them trays of food. Each elf maiden had the delicate features, slightly pointed ears and almond-shaped eyes that set their race apart. However, each was completely unique in appearance.

The Bard looked across the table at McKray. "Didn't you once tell me that if you have seen one elf, you have seen them all?" he asked with a smile, noting the looks of admiration being given to the women by the other men at the table.

"That's exactly what I said," replied McKray. "It appears that I was mistaken about these beautiful young women, but if you take a good look at Teran, you will admit he's an ugly creature."

"McKray! You stop it right now. Teran is a very handsome man, and you are just being rude and ignorant!" yelled Avalon.

"It is quite all right, my dear, McKray is a sincere and noble dwarf. To be honest, I miss the negative banter that this affords me," replied Teran, a smile on his lips. He sat down at the table and began dishing food onto his plate. Once they had filled their plates, Teran spoke again before anyone could eat, "Please hold hands as we say grace." The group obliged, and Teran offered grace.

Chapter 11

As the door opened, Koyne looked around the room uneasily. The room was sparsely furnished with plain but comfortable-looking furniture. The grandest thing in the room was the four-post bed, but it was again plain unlike the ornate bed Koyne had in his room. Koyne continued to look around thin white gossamer hung in sheets from the ceiling on one side of the room blocking an open doorway. Koyne was about to leave when he heard a cough; it came from the other side of the gossamer curtains. He went to investigate; he didn't know why he needed to do this. After all this was a stranger's room. He had never done anything like this, and yet he felt driven; he knew he was going to do something he would regret. One part of his mind was screaming, "Turn around and run" while another told him to find a weapon.

Koyne silently parted the gossamer with his left hand, letting his right hand reach around the wall. He felt a table. Opening the curtain a bit more, he could see a man sitting in a chair looking out of an open window straight across the room from where he was entering. He slid the rest of his body through the hangings, looking down at the table he had felt with his hand. He saw a tray of apples, one had been cut, and the knife was lying on the tray. Koyne picked up the knife and started forward, again the two sides of his brain screaming at him to do opposing actions. He could feel, however, that the one that wanted him to kill would win, and so he gave into it, embracing it. He walked silently across the room to stand just behind the man. Koyne's victim was older-looking with long, white hair and a well-groomed white beard; he wore a simple white robe.

Wrinkle lines lightly creased the side of the face that Koyne could see; the man's eyes were closed as if he slept. Koyne guessed his age to be in his late eighties. He raised the knife to strike. He began the downward thrust, and the man spoke.

Unable to stop the momentum of the blade, he felt it bite deep into the old man's neck and shoulder. Koyne stepped away as the red blood of life stained the man's white robe.

"What did you say?" he asked the bleeding man.

"I forgive you, Koyne."

*****

In the King's Forest, Oaran sat bolt upright, as if waking from a terrible nightmare, but it had not been a nightmare. Oaran had dreamed a dream of a beautiful woman, a woman he had loved with all his heart. She stood facing him, her delicate hands resting on his cheeks. She was looking deep into his eyes, into his soul. He felt all the evil that he had been a part of laid bare. He tried to turn from her, his regret deepening to a feeling of torment. Yet no matter how hard he tried to turn from her, to tear his face from her tender hands, she held him. As she looked at him he wept, the tears of a man who was drowning in anguish. That was when she spoke, three simple words: "I forgive you."

That was the moment he sat up from his slumber. The weight of the truth crashed down on him; his lost love had forgiven him. That night Oaran wept for the first time in more than a hundred years.

*****

Koyne turned and ran, straight into the curtains that blocked the doorway. In his hurry to get away from what he had done, he found himself entangled in the white gossamer. He frantically pulled on the curtains, tearing them from their mounts. The force of his struggling caused him to lose his balance and fall to the ground. He began to weep and stopped struggling with the curtains that held him trapped. He had killed an innocent man for no reason at all, and now he would have to face his companions. He would have to face Avalon, but most difficult, he had to face himself. He lay on the floor great sobs racking his body; soon he was lost to grief and misery. Avalon had been wrong about him, her faith misplaced; he had fallen, just as his father told him he would in his dream several days ago. As he lay there in shock, images of red staining white continued to run through his mind, reminding him of the blood he had shed. He could not tell how much time had passed, or how long he had cried, but slowly the images in his mind changed until there was no more blood. There was peace there was joy and laughter. He saw a man that he did not know; the man was holding a dark-haired woman in his arms professing his love. She was pleading with him to go with her. Another image flashed in his mind: the woman alone holding a baby boy. Then the images ended, and Koyne opened his eyes.

An older man with long white hair and neat white beard stood over him, wearing a simple white robe. The man reached his hand down toward Koyne, who had been freed of the white gossamer curtains. Koyne reached up to take the offered hand and then recoiled; it was the old man he had killed.

"Take my hand, Koyne," said the man.

"But you…you're dead, I killed you."

"You thought you killed me, but no, I am quite healthy and free of any mortal wounds. It would be quite impossible for you to really kill me. However, since you needed to kill someone, it is best that the attempt was made on my life rather than on anyone else's."

"Who are you, how do you know my name, what is going on here?"

"I am called many things, but here I am called Odin, and I know all about you, your family, and the curse that has plagued the men of your family since Oaran made his oath," replied Odin, helping Koyne to his feet.

"What are you talking about?"

"You are the direct descendent of Oaran, one of the knights of Souvac. In his youth he fell madly in love with a young maiden, they were secretly wed while Oaran was in King Souvac's service. His actions and betrayal, however, cost him the love of his life. He cursed himself and in so doing cursed the unborn child that was growing in his love's womb. Ever since that day, when a male child of Oaran's bloodline fell in love, he was driven by an unknown need to kill in cold blood. These men have never received the forgiveness that they needed to end the curse just as Oaran has never received forgiveness for his actions from the woman he so desperately loved," said Odin.

Koyne stared at the man. "Are you trying to tell me that the reason I have wanted to kill is because I am the descendant of a maniac that cursed himself?"

"Do you feel the need to kill any longer?"

"Well, I…" Koyne paused, searching inside himself for the feeling that had driven him here to this spot, this time, and this action. "No, I don't feel it anymore. What does this mean?" His thoughts that this old man was crazy were leaving him.

"What it means is that Oaran's curse on himself is broken, no longer will the insatiable drive to murder plague you or any sons that you might have. I forgave you of your actions and in so doing broke the curse, now I ask that you continue with this quest and end the curse that continues to bind your forebear."

"What curse still binds him?"

"He is bound to King Souvac."

"How do I do that?"

"That will be explained after dinner. I don't know about you, but I am famished. Walk with me to the dining room."

Koyne, quite beside himself with all that had happened in a relatively short span of time, stood speechless trying to sort through the thoughts and feelings that were now racing through his mind and body.

"I see you are a bit perplexed. Come follow me, I will guide you to the dinner table."

They left Odin's chambers and descended steps until they came to the great hall. Crossing this, they entered the room in which Koyne's companions were contentedly eating. Avalon stood and ran to his side.

"Koyne, where have you been, I was worried about you."

"The young man was assisting me down to dine with all of you. I wish to welcome you to my home," stated Odin.

The group sat in silence, looking at Odin and then at each other, a bit of confusion registering on their faces. Odin watched with amusement, then nudged Koyne with his elbow, which told Teran that Koyne would be introducing him. Koyne looked at the old man that seemed to have aged since descending the stairs. He looked slightly bent and withered, older than the man that had spoken with him earlier.

"Um, this is Odin, master of this house and our honored…"

"Say *revered*."

"Okay, our revered host."

Teran was smiling and rolling his eyes at his master.

McKray leaped to his feet and then fell to his knees. "I apologize for not recognizing your greatness."

"You're forgiven, stand up, there really is no need to grovel," replied Odin. He shuffled over and stood behind Dale. "You're in my seat."

Dale looked confused, for the seat at the head of the table remained open.

"I always sit here. Would you kindly take your dinner and move?" asked Odin

"Of course, I am terribly sorry," Dale quickly stood gathering the plates of food and moving them to the head of the table. He then returned, carrying the empty plates and set them before Odin, who had already sat down.

"So you are Mathias, I am so pleased to meet you," said Odin, extending his hand as he sat next to Mathias.

"The pleasure is all mine," replied Mathias, reaching out to take Odin's offered had.

Odin moved his hand slightly away as Mathias reached, causing him to miss the handshake. "It's all right, my boy, blindness has that effect on people," said Odin, his hand still extended. Mathias reached again, and again Odin moved his hand away. "Maybe you should just give up, I mean, you're starting to embarrass yourself."

This time Mathias's hand flashed forward, grabbing the old man's in a strong handshake. "As I said, the pleasure is all mine."

Sterling and Jace watched the exchange with confusion. They looked at each other, and the same thought raced through their minds. *This is who we came here to find. What was the Bard thinking? This old man is crazy.*

By now Teran was smiling broadly, unable to contain his mirth. "If you will all excuse me, I have some duties to attend to," he said as he stood.

Graham looked at the Bard, questions visible in his eyes. McKray was looking at Odin with a mix of adoration and disappointment.

The Bard sat watching the exchange; he had noted the reaction of Teran, as well as all those that had followed him. He knew that it was time to show them that Odin was more than he seemed. Taking a dagger from his belt, he readied himself to throw it at the old man.

Before he could complete his move, Odin raised his hand palm out. "Rest easy, young Bard, there is no such need for all that. Allow an old man his fun. You have all traveled through difficult terrain, weather, grief, and sorrow to reach me. You have questions that only I can answer, you need instruction and advice that only I can give. You must understand that everything you have gone through has been a test, everything you will continue to go through will be a test. You each have a destiny to fulfill, some of you will do so in the near future, others will take a bit longer."

Odin's appearance changed while he spoke. His wizened bent frame straightened and grew stronger in appearance. The lines of age on his face smoothed, and his hair became fuller and whiter until he seemed to shine with some inner light. His voice deepened and became strong.

"You have done very well, Bard, to find such a group of people to share in this important journey. You probably did not expect to find three future kings, a reunion of lost family, and allow love to flow through bloodlines once more. These things you have done."

"My lord Odin, I do not know of what you speak," replied the Bard. "I only answered the call I felt in my mind and heart."

"Often in our attempt to find one thing of importance, we find several things of remarkable value. It is the ability to see what we have found that truly separates the great from the mediocre," replied Odin. "Let us reveal secrets that each of you have, some of them known, some of them unknown, in this way you will discover a way to destroy the knights of Souvac once and for all. Those of you who have responsibility to destroy the knights know the story as the Bard has shared it to you in its truth. But now we have the question of how we destroy these men, for men they are—cursed men, but men nonetheless.

"In order to answer that question, we must answer others first. I will begin with Avalon. You did not know that you were an integral part of this story, but you are one of the most important parts. Without you, none of this could be done. One of the knights, Sir Kell, had a weakness, it was women. He never hurt a single woman because of the love he had for his mother that raised him, his brother, and his younger sister. You see, his mother died when he was fourteen. His older brother, Jerec, had already become a knight in King Tean's service. He alone raised his younger sister. Even as one of the knights of Souvac, he cared for this younger sister until he was trapped within the King's Forest. She married and moved far away to the south. You, Avalon, are the great-great-granddaughter of that woman—in fact, you are the first woman to be born of that bloodline since your great-great-grandmother, whose name was also Avalon.

"Next we come to Koyne. As he has learned tonight, he is the great-great-grandson of Oaran, one of the other knights. Oaran was ready to leave the lands of Souvac with his true love when he was ensnared in King Souvac's evil. He cursed himself for letting himself be blinded and losing his love forever. Since that time, when the men born of his bloodline fall in love, they are driven by an insatiable need and desire to murder in cold blood. Tonight, that curse was lifted, and Koyne is free of the destruction that follows those actions, as are any sons born of his bloodline now and forever.

"Now we come to Graham, whose father was, in fact, the son of the great King Tean—yes, King Bowen, who gave up his throne and left this land shortly after the disappearance of Souvac and his knights."

Those gathered at the table looked around at each other, somewhat in disbelief.

"Ah yes, you are all wondering about Graham's age. How could he be the son of King Bowen? I will explain. After the Bard spoke with King Bowen and was told the tale of Souvac and his knights, King Bowen's fear of the power that a ruler had over people was solidified. He found he disliked the notion of telling others what to do, and so he left. Bowen had no living family anymore, Souvac had seen to that. So it was that Bowen changed the way the kingdom of Souvac was ruled at which time he departed. He traveled the lands for many years, finding peace in adventuring until he found himself in the land called Tarshish. There he met a woman and fell deeply in love. For years they traveled the lands together, they fought side by side against wicked men and fell beasts of the southeast. They found numerous treasure vaults from ancient days and collected the riches for themselves. As they grew older, they finally settled down in Tarshish, they had given up on the idea of ever having a child. They remained vibrant and youthful even in their old age. When Bowen was ninety-eight, his wife Tsinsuri gave birth to their only child, Graham. The thing no one knows is that Jerec, captain of the knights of Souvac, is Bowen's first cousin and, therefore, Graham's second cousin."

"That means Graham and Avalon are also family, for Kell and Jerec are brothers," stated the Bard.

"Yes, you see, each of you that set out with the Bard have a direct relation to the knights of Souvac, and it is only a blood relative that can kill the knights and break the curse forever," said Odin.

"Forgive me for interrupting, but if we are all meant to be on this journey, then what is my purpose?" asked Jace.

"Jason Lye, you will have the most difficult task of all. This next part of the tale is one that will cause pain, I am sorry," said Odin, looking into the Bard's eyes. "For almost a hundred years, the Bard has been racked with the pain of loss. After speaking with Bowen, he traveled, telling the tale of the knights of Souvac. After a couple of years of being laughed at and scorned, he decided maybe the people were right. Maybe the knights were gone and could not hurt him. Even as he felt their summons, he ignored them, finding peace in the love of a woman from King Bareth's kingdom. They were wed and had a child together, a little boy. That boy had a little girl who was married and also had a daughter named Isabeau. Isabeau married a young warrior." As Odin spoke, both the Bard and Jace's eyes grew in size. "Isabeau had a son, she named him—"

"Jason Lye, after his father who died defending their small village from a band of raiders," said Jace.

"Yes, you are the great-great-grandson of the Bard of Souvac," said Odin.

The Bard's eyes widened further as he fought against the implications of this truth. His wife and son had not been killed, but if that were true, where had they gone?

"I am sorry, Bard, your wife and child both lived full lives. Your wife never remarried, her love for you and the hope that you would return someday remained. You were tricked by the knights of Souvac," stated Odin.

"But I went back to the house, no one was there, it was destroyed," replied the Bard in shock.

"Oaran sent one of his beasts to your home early the morning you found your wife and son missing. The beast caught hold of your wife's cloak and sent them running in fear. The beast then returned to the King's Forest, where Oaran set up the scene that you found, blood and the cloak of your wife. After your wife and son returned to your home, she feared the beast had killed you. In her frantic search to find you, a lamp was knocked over, and the home was burned down. They left then traveling to the west of Bareth's kingdom, where they settled and lived out their days. They left messages for you to find, but they were destroyed before you came back. A jealous man who had loved and courted your wife before you met her was the culprit. He followed her, trying to entice her into marriage, but her love for you was unwavering."

The Bard stood abruptly and left the chamber. He found a door that opened onto a balcony overlooking the canyon above which

Odin's Hall was perched. There he fell to the ground, weakened by the painful truths that he had heard. Tears rolled slowly down his cheeks as he thought about the life he had missed out on, the memories that were denied him, the love that he could never reclaim. Why had this been his lot in life, to have pure happiness and joy for a moment, and then have it ripped from him? As he thought about it, he began to imagine his son growing into a strong man, having a daughter whom he raised. His wife had the joy of raising his son and seeing his granddaughter. Now he had the opportunity to get to know his great-great-grandson. Once again he knew he would be able to find joy. Above him, in the darkness, a figure stood on a similar balcony, watching the pain that the Bard suffered and wept.

After a time, the Bard returned to the dining hall where the others were sitting in a state of silence. They were still reeling from the shock of truth that had been so plainly thrust before them. The Bard walked toward Jace. Jace stood as the Bard approached, a fire burning in his eyes. He looked as if he was about to kill someone, and then he opened his arms and pulled Jace into a strong embrace. Surprised at first, Jace let his arms hang limply at his side a moment before he returned the embrace. A moment later, the hug ended, and Jace spoke, "That is why my mother urged me to find you, she wanted me to reconnect our family."

"What can you tell me of our family?" asked the Bard.

"I have in my packs journals that each person kept, two are sealed, the others belonged to my mother and grandmother. I was told to give the sealed journals to you," replied Jace.

"You may peruse them later, for now we must finish the discussion that we began about how do you destroy the knights of Souvac," stated Odin.

The Bard and Jace took their seats, and Odin continued on.

"As I said, only a blood relative can kill those protected by the curse. In order for the knights to be destroyed, all those under the curse must die. Before you can kill the knights, three of you must swear to take on the responsibility of staying in the forest with King Souvac. In so doing, you will release the knights and the Bard from their immortal state."

"But then we will be trapped," said Koyne.

"One of the three that will pledge themselves must be Avalon."

Avalon looked up, fear dancing momentarily in her eyes before being extinguished by her will. Koyne was about to speak again when Odin raised his hand as if to push the thoughts and words back into Koyne's head and mouth.

"The knights ask that three men come to them to swear fealty to the corpse of King Souvac, in so doing they are freed to leave the forest. If a woman should pledge herself to the cause, the curse is put in a state of limbo. The knight's immortality will be gone, but they will be stuck in the forest. That is when you must strike. Each person must kill their blood relative. This is why it will be hardest for you, Jace."

All eyes were trained on the Bard and Jace as they looked at each other.

"Then this mission is failed. I cannot kill the Bard, I will not kill my grandfather," stated Jace.

"This mission will not fail, we have come too far to stop now. I have lived a long life and am ready for the rest that awaits me in death. You will strike me down when the time to do so is at hand," replied the Bard.

"If you do not complete this quest, no one will ever complete it. Eventually, greed and stupidity will lead three men to take the oath from the knights in an attempt to gain the treasure. At that point, the knights will be free to rain terror throughout the lands, for they may be mortal but they will maintain some of the powers granted them by Lord Kish the Evil One," said Odin. "It is, however, your choice to make. Those of you who are not pertinent to the endeavor will return to whatever place you desire, but you must not accompany the Bard and his companions further than the White Hills, if you do so the quest will be for naught. You will rest this day and the next, after that you must continue on your way. I desire to speak with Koyne and Dale before you depart. McKray, I will ask you to accompany me at this time."

With that, Odin stood and began walking toward the door. McKray quickly leaped to his feet and followed Odin out of the dining hall.

The companions looked around the table at each other in silence.

After a few moments, the Bard spoke, "We now know how to end this curse, we will all follow through just as we have been instructed."

"I don't think I can do this thing that is being asked of me. I don't know if I can kill you," said Jace, looking into the Bard's eyes.

"You can, and you will. I must be freed of this existence, and I would rather it come at your hand than any other. Let's speak no more of it, for now I desire to see those journals."

The two men stood and left the dining room.

Koyne and Avalon looked at each other, stood, and followed behind the Bard and Jace. Graham followed immediately after and then Sterling. Dale, Mathias, and Amalia sat together at the table.

"I'm glad that our part in this journey is nearly over," stated Dale.

"I have a feeling that our part isn't completely over," responded Mathias.

Dale shifted uncomfortably in his seat; he was feeling the same way. "What do you think Odin meant when he said there were three future kings here?"

"I don't know, I thought that Odin was speaking in some sort of riddle at first, and we would have to meet to decipher everything he said. Now that everything is out in the open plain as day, I don't quite know what to do or even think. Maybe what he said about the kings is the same. Graham is the son of kings, so he will probably become one. McKray is the son of a king from what Graham told me on the journey, so I expect he is one of the three."

"That makes two, who do you suppose the third is? I don't think it's Sterling, or anyone else that is going with the Bard," said Dale.

"Well then, that leaves one of us, you are the oldest, and Odin does want to speak with you personally, so that makes you the third king," said Mathias.

"I am not fit to be a king," stated Dale, bowing his head. "I have too much blood on my hands."

"We all have blood on our hands, brother."

"At any rate, we aren't descended from kings."

"Brother, we are orphans, we don't know where we come from, therein lies the possibility."

Dale sat quietly for several minutes, playing with his remaining food. "I think I am going to go to bed, are you coming up?"

"Not yet, I will stay here for a bit. You know, I like to be alone in the dark and haven't had the chance since joining this party."

Shortly after Dale had gone, Mathias arose and began to explore the house of Odin. He would spend all night learning about this mysterious place. He wanted to know everything. So it was that Mathias slipped quietly from the dining hall and moved through the castle like a shadow. Amalia, feeling forgotten, quietly followed him. Mathias decided to follow the staircase down first; he did not notice, nor could he sense, the shadow that would follow him and Amalia throughout their entire journey.

*****

Odin led McKray out of the dining room and across the great hall to a door that opened onto a large balcony. Scenic views of the White Mountains spread away before them. The large eagle-like birds could be seen soaring around the cliffs, landing on ledges high up and entering caves. McKray watched in awe of the majesty of the mighty creatures effortless and graceful movements.

"They are some of my favorite to watch also. Few creatures in this world move as beautifully as the mighty rock eagle. They are swift, powerful, deadly, and intelligent. Even my griffins have a hard time keeping pace with these," said Odin, gesturing toward the large birds with his hand, "although the rock eagle isn't as stubborn and picky as the griffins are. You know, McKray, your people were the first to ever take flight."

McKray turned to look at Odin. "What do you mean take flight?"

"I mean, to tame this eagle, climb on its back, and go flying around for fun. At first it was for fun, but then the dwarves found many uses for flight. Of course, not all dwarves love flight, many still prefer the solid foundation of the earth, shaping the living stone into works of beauty and finding marvelous treasure to store. One dwarf in particular, probably the most skilled dwarf I have ever seen in working stone and metal, and a few of his friends, never work stone or metal anymore. In fact, this particular dwarf hasn't gone underground in over a hundred years. He is almost becoming elfish, if you can believe that. He spends a lot of time walking the gardens with Teran, when not flying, that is."

McKray looked at Odin, completely perplexed. "Dwarves flying on giant birds rather than work the stones of the earth, I am not sure that I believe that. Who is it that is so skilled but refuses to use his craft? The thought of that would make my father turn in his grave."

"Funny that you should mention your father. He won't be turning in his grave about the thought of such a thing."

"What do you mean? He and my mother left with my people such a long time ago, and they were already getting old then, they must be dead," stated McKray.

"Oh no, he is very much alive. He is responsible for much of the work you saw on Odin's Stair, as well as in this castle, but he took to the air and never works the stone anymore. I saw the change happen gradually. His feelings about his son could not be resolved. Finally, one day a little over a hundred years ago, he tamed a rock eagle, and the rest is, as they say, 'history.'"

"Are you telling me my mother and father, my people, are here now?" asked McKray, his eyes shining.

"They come and go, freedom is theirs, they are, of course, welcome here as are the elves and some humans that have grown in wisdom."

"Do you know where they are now?"

"Yes, but I made a promise not to give out that information." Seeing the light in McKray's eyes fade slightly, Odin continued, "Your father's promise still holds true, when you are ready, the door will open, and you will be reunited with your people, you need but have the key."

"I don't have a key, my father didn't leave a key." McKray's head was starting to spin with the magnitude of information he had just received. In an effort to recover from his confusion, he asked a question, "What is this place exactly?"

"This is the home of the God of the Living. He comes and goes as he pleases, leaving caretakers to keep everything running properly. In truth, all who seek goodness are welcome here, but that is not your real question. McKray, you are becoming the king that your people need. That is why you came on this journey, your father has been completely distraught these many years. You are his pride and joy, and it nearly killed him to leave you the way he did. He has been slipping further and further away, it is time for you to come home and lead your people."

"I don't understand. Am I to remain here, am I to find my people in the mountains?"

"My dear boy, you are to do as your father directed. Go back to Kragg's Golden Valley to your home, open the sealed door, and lead your people."

"I told you there is no key. I have searched everywhere, there is no way for me to open the door."

"I say you are right, your father must still hold the only key to the door." Odin called out then, "Teran, I need your assistance."

"I thought he left."

"Oh, he did, but he is also always where I need him, the blasted elf won't give me any time to myself."

"The blasted elf is here," said Teran, appearing as if by magic at Odin's side.

"Excellent, I need two things. First go to McKray's father and retrieve the key to the sealed dwarven door."

"He no longer has the key, my lord, he lost it many years ago."

"Very well. Take McKray to the forges and help him make a key. Once you get there, he will know what he needs to complete the task. When that is finished, I need the amulet. It is time."

Teran's eyes opened a bit wider, but he said nothing. He simply turned and began walking away. McKray, unsure of what was happening, followed Teran in silence. Several levels below the dining hall, they entered the forges, which were silent this time of night, but McKray was feeling inspired.

"All right, you blasted elf, let's get this forge heated up."

"As you wish, filthy dwarf," replied Teran, causing McKray to smile broadly.

They worked for several hours together, trading insults through the night, as together they created a key that would open the door and bring McKray back to his people. When the work was done, McKray held up the key, a beautiful work of exquisite detail that combined the greatest craftsmanship of both dwarf and elf. The key was both sturdy and delicate made of a combination of metals, including gold, silver, and mythril. Small perfectly shaped jewels adorned the end, which was shaped like a tree.

"I am beginning to understand why Odin keeps you around, Teran," said McKray as he slowly turned the key over in his hands.

"I don't think I have ever been so warmly complimented by a dwarf," replied Teran.

McKray, smiling, said, "I will see it never happens again, but once I have returned to my kingdom, please come visit, bring some of your people and help me make Kragg's Golden Valley even more beautiful. I believe we could use gardens the likes of which I have seen here."

"If you continue speaking to me like this, I might begin to think we are becoming friends." After a brief pause, he continued, "It would be an honor to visit your kingdom and work with your people. I must tell you, I have never seen anyone create such a combination of metals that work together so perfectly. How did you learn to do this?"

"It has taken much work, but once I truly started learning all the lore of my father, I couldn't stop, I had to learn about every alloy, mineral, stone, and jewel. I have spent days working on a single knife blade to get it perfect. I probably sound crazy to you."

"No, you sound like a dwarf I know. Now if you will excuse me, I must attend to another matter, I trust you can find your way back to your room."

"Yes, I will be fine."

Teran departed, and McKray made his way to his room. Before going to bed he stepped onto the balcony, peering into the darkness. He could just make out a rock eagle, flying away. On his bed he found a note; it simply read, "I am proud of you."

A short time later, seven dwarves entered the forges.

"Light them up, we've got a lot of work to do, and only a few days to finish," said a gruff-looking dwarf. He picked up a hammer, closed his eyes, and let the memories of forging wash over him. Moments later, he opened his eyes, smiling. "Get me gold."

The dwarves with him were also smiling broadly, each with a forging hammer in hand. "Aye, my lord," they shouted in unison.

Moments later the sound of deep dwarven voices could be heard rolling through the forges in song that matched the beat of their hammers and tools.

*****

Oaran was still awake; he had been ever since his dream the night before. He thought of his wife his love for her and the pain of her leaving. She had been dead now for so many years. Could she really have forgiven him, he wondered. He began to think of all the things he had taken pleasure in, the things he thought had brought him joy. He realized for the first time how empty his life truly had become. He had had everything when he was with his darling wife. As soon as she had gone, he had nothing. This sudden realization made him angry, angrier than he had ever been. He needed a way to release his anger; he stood and started toward Jerec's shelter. He was going to tear into him like a savage animal; he knew he wouldn't be able to kill him, but at least he would be free for a moment of this horrible self-loathing.

Kell had been awakened the previous night by Oaran's scream; he had watched him and still watched him. He could feel the tension surrounding his unfortunate companion and had waited for this moment.

Kish was also watching, finding pleasure in the inner torment that was ripping Oaran apart inside. There were, however, those other feelings that were so evident on Oaran's face, love and regret—they could turn the worst person into a follower of the God of the Living. Kish the Evil One had done all in his power to gently fan the sparks of hatred in Oaran with memories. Now that hatred was about to fill the glade in a wonderful fight.

Oaran was just a few feet from Jerec; he readied himself to yell Jerec's cursed name. Suddenly panic swept through him. He could feel fear; it was coming at him from several locations at once. Screams rang out in his head; his creatures, his beautiful pets, were being killed. He tried to more fully link his mind with the beasts to see what was happening. By the time he succeeded, all but one of his boarhounds were dead or dying. The fading light of one beast's eyes showed him a large feathered creature ridden by a stocky man. Complete blackness fell across Oaran's mind and vision.

His anger increased further. "Jerec!" he yelled, bringing the captain to his feet.

Jerec ran to Oaran's side and pulled him to a sitting position, for Oaran had fallen as the blackness took his mind. "What is it, what is happening?"

"They are dead, they are dead!"

"Who is dead?"

"My boarhounds, something has killed them all." Jerec looked at Oaran, who was obviously upset about the deaths of his pets, but there was something more as well. "What is wrong with you? Weeping over your little animals. You act as if you lost something you loved, but we know none of us feel love."

At this Oaran jumped to his feet, drawing his sword, and sent out a single thought, *Attack.* His last remaining boarhound jumped from the tree it had secreted itself in, slamming into Jerec's back. Jerec fell forward, and Oaran's drawn sword plunged through his body. The beast continued to tear at Jerec, its claws making several deep cuts before Oaran called it off.

"We are done, Jerec. When we are free, I never want to see you again. If I do, I will kill you." With a thought, he sent his last boarhound from the clearing.

Jerec had fallen to the ground and languished in the pain of the poison that had entered his bloodstream. Oaran walked away and with a thought sent his boarhound away. Kell rushed to Jerec's side, a look of concern on his face. Without a word, he assisted his brother to his shelter.

"We must stop him when we are free. I fear he has grown too bold."

"I will kill him, as soon as the curse is lifted, I will kill him," muttered Jerec through gritted teeth. "Keep an eye on him for me."

"Yes, my lord," responded Kell, bowing in mock reverence. *Things are going very well*, he thought to himself as he made his way back to his shelter.

Chapter 12

Dale woke and went downstairs to the dining hall. The rest of the companions minus his brother and Amalia were all there eating breakfast.

"Have you seen Mathias yet this morning?" asked Dale.

Teran, entering the room behind Dale, answered the question. "Your brother had a rather late night. He will be taking his breakfast in his room after he has had some sleep. Amalia will also join us later."

Dale understood that his brother was more comfortable in the darkness of the night, and so he let the matter drop, joining the others for breakfast. After breakfast, they went out to Odin's garden to explore the beauty of the place. Now that they had time to relax and look around, the gardens appeared even more beautiful. Flowers of all shapes sizes and colors populated the grass and trees. Exotic-looking birds of all colors flew from tree to tree, some singing, others sounded as though they were talking. Some had crests of feathers on their heads; others had long tail feathers.

Animals of all varieties were spread throughout the gardens, quietly going about their lives, taking no notice of the bipedal observers. The group was wondering about some of the unique trees and plants that were foreign to the area when Gold Wing descended from the air to land before them.

"Ah, good day, I see that you are curious about the gardens," said the griffin.

"Yes, we are. What can you tell us of these strange plants and trees that grow here?" asked Graham.

"What can you tell us, oh, mighty Bard?" he asked, turning the question from himself. "For I know that you have traveled to lands that host not only these plants and trees but the birds and animals as well," replied Gold Wing.

The others looked at the Bard with interest. "When you live nearly a hundred years alone and in good health, you travel a lot. I have more tales and stories, but alas, I am unable to recite them while the curse of the knights is upon me."

"Surely, speaking of plants, trees, and animals is not telling tales you are unable to share."

"That is a fine point you make, Master Gold Wing, but surely, a lore master like yourself would be better suited to teach these students."

"Very well, many of these trees, plants, and animals come from the south where it is always warm. Odin loves all creatures and plant life, so he made this place for those that would otherwise die in the conditions of the White Mountains. Perhaps you have at times seen dark-skinned men and women in your villages selling strange-looking jewelry and fruits."

"I have, they sail great ships on the seas bringing goods to Tarshish where I lived," stated Graham.

"Yes, they are very seaworthy people. Have you, young Graham, ever been beyond the great sea?" asked Gold Wing.

"No, it can be very dangerous to even attempt sailing across the great sea."

Gold Wing looked at the Bard. "I have been across the great sea and to lands beyond that, as have your parents, Graham. Perhaps I can tell you of these things one day," stated the Bard.

"Do you have record of these experiences?" asked Jace. "Yes, my son, they are all written, waiting to be told," replied the Bard. "I will tell you of their location when I am ready."

Gold Wing then went on to describe a land that housed many large animals of thick, gray hides—some with horns, others with ivory tusks and long noses that could be used to lift trees and eat. He continued speaking of large cat animals with different markings that hunted on the great grass plains and many other types of animals.

He spoke of people of different-colored skins. Some with skin so dark it is almost black, others that have skin of red, and others yet with skin that looks yellowish; of course there are those with brown skin of various hues. The companions sat with rapt attention to the descriptions, fabulous pictures being created in their minds. Gold Wing spoke for a very long time, enjoying his audience's attention. Nobody else liked to listen to his tales anymore, or so he told the group of adventurers.

Teran was the one that eventually saved them from Gold Wing's musings. "It is well past midday, and I am sure that our guests are famished, Gold Wing."

"Forgive me, Master Teran, I do lose track of time when I am reliving the past, especially when I have such a captivated audience," replied Gold Wing.

"At least they are not a captive audience like I once was," stated Teran.

"Oh, will you never let me live that one down? It is not my fault that you were not taught properly about griffins and our affinity for storytelling," replied Gold Wing. "It is actually quite an amusing story," he began.

"Yes, it is, and I will tell it as I walk these poor innocents to their meal," stated Teran.

"Oh, pushaa."

"Please come with me," Teran said to the travelers.

They began walking away in silence. "Well, are you going to tell us the tale about you and Gold Wing?" asked Avalon.

Teran smiled. "It happened many years ago. As you may know, griffins and elves live terribly long lives. I was just a young man back then and lived a bit on the wild side of life, leaving home for weeks at a time to explore and learn about new things. I felt that experience would be a better teacher than the elven lore masters, especially lore master Fillian, he taught about nature and animals. Given the number of times I had skipped his lessons, he decided to teach me outside of class, that was when I met Gold Wing. Gold Wing and Fillian were good friends, and they got quite the laugh at my expense.

"It was a regular morning, and I was exploring nature for myself when this giant griffin flies out of the treetops and grabs me in his talons. He took me on a hair-raising ride, nearly dropping me on a couple of occasions. I finally stopped screaming after he plopped me down on a fairly narrow ledge high up in the White Mountains. I knew I was about to die, and so I pleaded with this creature to let me live. I knew griffins were intelligent but vicious creatures, other than that, I hadn't paid attention. Suddenly he spoke to me, which caused me to nearly fall off the ledge. He promised he would let me live if I listened to some stories. Three days later, he set me down outside of my village nearly starved to death, where we were greeted by lore master Fillian. I never missed another lesson."

Avalon was still giggling when they entered the dining room to eat.

"I suggest you begin getting ready for your journey back, we will help you, but you should be ready to depart late tomorrow evening. Odin has indicated that time is of the essence. He would if possible have you stay longer to regain your strength physically, emotionally, and spiritually. However, you must continue with what you now have," said Teran.

The Bard nodded. "I guess Odin has a plan for us if we are to depart in the darkness of night."

"Yes, he does, which he will explain tomorrow. Koyne and Dale, you will join Odin in his chambers as soon as you have eaten. I will gather your personal effects as you will be occupied until your departure," stated Teran.

Koyne and Dale looked at one another, questions burning in their minds.

"McKray, Odin would have you begin instructing Graham and Mathias in the ways of leadership, diplomacy, manners…" Teran stopped speaking while watching the dwarf ravenously eat. "Perhaps you should just start with leadership."

McKray stopped eating, picked up his napkin, and dabbed the sides of his mouth mockingly. "I can teach them manners that would make an elf proud as well, Teran," he said, extending his little fingers while holding his napkin to his bearded face.

Teran smiled, a small laugh nearly escaping his mouth. "I doubt that, my friend, I really doubt that," he replied. "Just do your best."

"Aye, Captain," replied McKray with a false salute.

After the laughing died down, Teran began walking away. "Remember, once you have eaten, go to your rooms and begin packing your things. I will be waiting for Koyne and Dale."

"If we are leaving tomorrow evening, why should we get packed now?" asked Sterling.

Everyone looked at the Bard. "I imagine it is best to follow the directions of Odin, don't you think?" The group nodded in agreement.

The meal passed with little conversation as the group contemplated their return journey and subsequent quest. Mathias never showed up for the meal, which caused Dale to be even more concerned. As the group finished eating, Dale and Koyne left the dining hall. Teran stood there waiting and led them to Odin's chambers. The others went to their rooms and began packing. The Bard went to Jace's room after packing his meager belongings.

"Jace, I am ready to reveal to you the location of all the tales I have collected over my lifetime. Each story has been written and bound in leather to protect them, and they are stored in chests that are impervious to water." The Bard reached in his tunic and removed a key on a chain. "This key opens each of the chests. You will find more than books inside. This map will lead you to their resting place. I will not say out loud where they are hidden, so you will have to follow the map. Use the journals of my wife and son, they will help you to understand the landmarks on the map."

"Maybe you could show me after this is all over," stated Jace.

"When this is all over, my body will finally be at rest," declared the Bard. Jace's face fell. "But if I can find a way to haunt you on occasion, I will."

Jace smiled at this, and the Bard turned away. "You better get some rest, old man, I know you didn't sleep at all last night."

With that the Bard went to his room.

Avalon finished getting her things together and woke Amalia, who had been sleeping all morning. "What were you doing all night?" she asked.

"I was following Mathias. After Odin told us everything, Mathias went exploring. I think we might have explored the entire place."

"Why didn't you come with me?"

"You seemed busy yourself. Besides, having been left out of the conversation and feeling alone, I just followed Mathias around."

"Are you sure that's all that happened?" pressed Avalon.

Amalia blushed slightly. "Of course I'm sure. He didn't even know I was there."

"What did you find out, as you explored?"

"It is very beautiful, everything is amazing. I honestly don't think there are words to even describe what this place is. I wish I could tell you more, but I can't describe it with words," she replied.

Avalon smiled. "I wish I had been with you, it sounds incredible. I should tell you, we are going to be leaving late tomorrow night. Teran said that time is of the essence, so we must go soon. I recommend you get some food and walk in the gardens, enjoy this place a little more before we must leave. While you are out there, you might bump into Mathias, he hasn't eaten yet either."

"Why are you so interested in me and Mathias?"

"It is obvious you like him, which is interesting, because you would be older than him by a couple of years according to what you told us."

Amalia bowed her head. "I am only eighteen. I lied so I could come with you guys. I don't want to go back home. You won't tell the others, will you?"

"Of course not. I will say this though. I am sure you have a purpose here. Odin said we were all meant to be here together."

"He may have said that, but it is obvious that I am not included. What can I be amongst kings and heroes? No, I am just a frightened girl. I ran away from my mother's husband and got caught in an even bigger mess. If not for Dale and Mathias, I don't know what my life might be like right now."

"Is that why you like Mathias so much?"

Amalia again blushed slightly. "Mathias has talked to me in the night. He has comforted me, protected me, he sees me for who I am, not what I look like."

"What do you mean not what you look like?"

"Well, being blind, he sees me, you know, who I am inside, not the ugly girl that my stepfather told me I was."

"Amalia, you are beautiful, your stepfather was an idiot. Is that why you ran away, because he was mean to you?"

"I would rather not discuss why I ran away."

"Amalia, did he hurt you, or did he try to hurt you? If he did, I will take care of him for you, and if not me, then any one of us will."

Amalia, smiling, replied, "He wasn't able to hurt me. I ran away, I met all of you, and that is enough. Do you think Mathias could really like me? I mean, according to Dale, Mathias could become a king."

"I am sure Mathias likes you, which means you better start thinking about being a queen," said Avalon smiling. "Go find him tell him how you feel. We are leaving tomorrow night, you should at least use this time when we are in a safe and peaceful place to talk with him."

"You're right, you think he may be in the gardens?"

"It is definitely a possibility. He wasn't at breakfast or lunch either."

Amalia was wandering in the gardens looking for Mathias when Goldwing approached. "Dear Amalia, what are you doing out here alone?"

"I was looking for Mathias," she said blushing.

"And yet it is I that have found you. How can I be of assistance?" asked Gold Wing.

A strange feeling of peace stole through Amalia's heart, and before she could stop herself, she was pouring out her thoughts to Gold Wing. "I'm scared, I have developed feelings for Mathias. I told Avalon, and she told me to tell Mathias, but I lied to everyone in the group. I fear that when my lie is discovered, Mathias and the others will be upset with me."

"Ah, matters of the heart most profound. May I ask you a question, dear child?"

"Yes."

"Does anyone know the truth?"

"Avalon does."

"What was her response?"

"She wasn't upset, she just encouraged me. She told me that I was supposed to be here as well. I guess she was trying to help me see that the others would feel the same way, but I don't tell lies. This is the first one ever that I can remember," replied Amalia.

"Do you remember what Odin said at dinner?"

"He said a lot of things, but none of them were about me."

"Actually, he did say something about you, just as your friend Avalon has said. Odin did say that everyone was here for a reason. That most definitely includes you, in fact it is not coincidence that brings us both here at this time. Odin sent me to speak with you. You have a role to play that is even more important than the Bard's quest or that of the three kings," stated Gold Wing, taking on a more serious tone. "What do you know of Odin?"

"I have heard McKray speak reverently about him. The Bard says he may be the speaker of the God of the Living, but I don't really know what that means. Other than that, I really don't know anything else," replied Amalia.

"And therein lies the problem. There are very few people that know Odin anymore. There was a time when all the world rejoiced at his name, but alas, that time is past. Let me explain. Being the speaker means to speak to the God of the Living directly and tell others what plans are in store for them or what the God of the Living would have them do," replied Gold Wing. "For many thousands of years, an ongoing battle has raged between the speaker and Kish the Evil One. Kish wants the world to forget the God of the Living so his influence can fill the hearts of mortal men." He stopped speaking and looked at Amalia.

She looked back at him for a moment with a blank look on her face. "But what does this have to do with me?"

"Yes, of course. Forgive me, I do get caught up in the story and expect others to understand what they cannot. Odin is not the speaker, he is the God of the Living."

Amalia's jaw dropped slightly as the idea that she had been in the presence of a God sank in.

Gold Wing, noting her change of countenance, continued, "That is not all. He has chosen you to be his new speaker."

Amalia stepped back, suddenly breathing fast. "Why would he choose me? I am but a simple girl."

"You are most definitely not just a simple girl. Your forebear was the last speaker."

"I don't know what to believe right now. I almost feel that I should just pick a direction and run as fast as I can from here."

"I can sense this news has caused some turmoil in your heart, let me tell you what I can. What I tell you must be kept a secret, you must never divulge this to anyone else until instructed to do so. I am putting at jeopardy much by telling you this, but I feel you must know. Odin is very powerful. He can take the shape of a man, a dwarf, an elf, even a dragon. He has been fighting the Evil One since the beginning of time. He will make sure that this quest succeeds. He cannot interfere directly, but he can encourage noble men and women to act according to his will and by his authority keep in balance this and other worlds he has created," stated Gold Wing.

Amalia sat in wonder as she tried to take in the full meaning of Gold Wing's words. She had sat in the presence of a God, spoken with him, explored his home. As she continued to sit in silence, Gold Wing spoke. Comprehension unfolded before her, and she felt that all would be well, possibly even perfect. Unfortunately, the frailty of being human kept her from complete peace.

"I am still feeling a bit on edge. Somehow I feel in my heart that all will be well, but my mind continues to scream at me. Can you help me, somehow, be more at ease?" she asked.

"It would be my honor," replied Gold Wing. He started into a long tale of romance and intrigue that he said came from islands from the southwest called the dream islands. Amalia listened for the first hour before the calming resonant tones of Gold Wing's voice sent her into a deep and revitalizing sleep. She would wake hours later in the soft confines of her bed carried there by Teran.

*****

McKray took to heart the charge given him by Odin, and as soon as he was finished eating, he went to find Mathias, Graham at his heels. They found Mathias coming out of his room. McKray took him by the arm and led him right back in.

"Mathias, you have probably figured out that Graham, myself, and you are the three kings that Odin spoke of. Now it's up to me to teach you some of the things that it takes to be a good king—diplomacy, leadership, manners for instance. Graham here was schooled by his father and mother who have both seen enough to know what it takes to be the kind of king that we all are going to need to be, so I brought him in to help." Mathias was smiling calmly while McKray droned on and on. Graham was looking at times nervous whenever McKray used terms like "see here." or "someday you'll see."

After nearly an hour of solid advice from McKray, Mathias thoughtfully raised his hand and asked permission to interject, at which point McKray grudgingly allowed.

"McKray, you have already taught me much about how a man, or dwarf," he added quickly, "should lead. You taught me these things by your example as we have traveled. I know that you are loyal, as a king should be, by how you treated my brother. You have given me many great lessons and have added upon those with the kind words of advice that you have given me over the last hour. I ask now, however, that you allow me to go eat something before I pass out."

"Well, why didn't you say something earlier? You see, I admire a man who is honest and not afraid to say what's in his heart or on his mind. I rather enjoy talking while I eat…"

"We know," stated Graham, which drew a smile from Mathias and a scowl from McKray.

"Now look here," said McKray, taking Mathias by the arm and leading him out the door. "If I am going to rule peacefully around, you two young kids, I gotta know that you are going to respect me as your elder."

Mathias gently removed his arm from McKray's iron grasp. "I have great respect for you, Your Majesty, but since we are such good friends, I believe Graham and I will make some jokes at your expense, all in good fun, of course, and we in turn expect you to treat us like terrible little beast children," said Mathias.

McKray looked at Graham, who was nodding his agreement. "Maybe I should double-check with Odin about you two becoming kings."

Graham and Mathias laughed.

"Come on, let's get Mathias some food," said Graham.

*****

Sterling felt very alone. He sat at the table poking at his food for a few moments before rising from the table and leaving the dining room. The others had already gone out of site, leaving Sterling to stand alone in the large hall. He thought of his brother and the fun that they could have had here together exploring the great Hall of Odin. As his thoughts wandered more to his deceased brother, he began to almost hear laughter and feel the punch in the shoulder that was so often received from his brother. Then looking up the stairwell as it curved in mighty ascension, he thought he saw his brother standing high above, on a landing, looking down at him. He was about to go running up the stairs when his attention was stolen by Teran's approach. Looking at the elf, he then returned his gaze to the landing where he thought he had seen his brother.

"Loneliness plays terrible tricks on the mind," stated Teran, "especially in this place where it seems so many lives are intertwined."

"What are you talking about?" asked Sterling.

"You thought you saw your deceased brother. He is not here. Very few men are permitted here after death, because of the choices they make in life," stated Teran mysteriously.

"I don't understand," replied Sterling. "I have a message for you from Odin." He handed an envelope to Sterling, who tried to open it. "It will only open when it is necessary for you to view the message," stated Teran, who bowed and walked away.

Sterling looked with confusion at the letter and the departing Teran before folding the envelope and tucking it into an inner pocket of his tunic.

Despite being in different places throughout Odin's Hall, the group of travelers were weighed down with the thought of leaving the next day. They had appreciated the amount of rest they were able to get here but felt the heaviness of travel approaching. As counseled, each member of the group went to bed early and slept late the next day. They were awakened by an elf that said she was Teran's assistant. They were asked to meet in the dining hall for a meal as soon as they could. The Bard, Jace, McKray, Graham, Mathias, and Sterling were there within twenty minutes. Koyne, Dale, Avalon, and Amalia arrived before an hour had passed. Koyne and Dale talked very little and looked furtively at each other throughout the meal.

Once they had eaten their fill and sat back to relax, Teran entered the dining hall.

"Good afternoon to you all. It is my pleasure to speak to you on behalf of Odin. He apologizes for not being able to be here, he had important business to attend to. However, he has spent the better part of the last two days putting together a plan to help you on your way. Bard, you told the knights of Souvac that you would return in a month with those that began their journey with you. That time is nearly spent, and the knights are getting nervous and agitated. According to Odin, there is a change being wrought in the knights because of the actions that have already occurred and the choices that some among this party have taken.

"In order to speed your departure from the mountains, it is critical that you leave this night. Oaran's tracking creatures that have wandered these mountains have all been destroyed, however time is of the essence, therefore you will be flying away from here. Most of you will be riding on the backs of griffins, your horses being carried by dragons."

At the mention of dragons, the soft hiss of breath leaving the lungs of nearly each person was heard.

"Fear not, dragons are not the terrible man-eating beasts they are made out to be by legend. Despite their fierceness, they are highly intelligent beings, and they are loved by the God of the Living. The leader of these great creatures has asked that Amalia ride upon him while he carries her horse. You will be taken to the spot where all your paths joined from there you will go separate ways. McKray, Sterling, Dale, Amalia, and Mathias will join you, and you will return to the Kraggs. There you will each be tested, and a new journey will begin. Bard, you, Jace, Graham, Avalon, and Koyne will follow the path on this map to the Great North Road. You will follow it as fast as you can until you come to your journey's end.

"Remember, you must not falter in your quest. When the time comes to follow a new path you must. When the time comes to strike with your blades, do not falter, do not hesitate, no matter how difficult it may seem. You have all slept the morning and a portion of the afternoon away, the sun will be setting in three hours' time. Your horses and belongings have been secured and are ready to depart with the sunlight. I recommend that you say farewell here so that upon landing, you can immediately begin your journeys. Also get with your companions and make plans for the return journey, it is important that you all go with as much speed as you can. It is a five-day journey from the point where you will part company to Kragg's Golden Valley. When McKray's group reaches Kragg's Golden Valley, the Bard's group must be at the south side of Kragg's Pass on the Great North Road. You should each reach these destinations at the same approximate time."

"Why do you mention the timing so specifically, is that important?" asked Avalon.

"You will all understand when the time comes. I must go now to double-check and finalize all the preparations for your departure. If you require anything, call my assistant, Eliana, she will do all she can to serve you." Teran then turned and left the dining room.

As he left, an unsettling feeling fell on the group.

"I have a bad feeling about this whole thing," said Koyne, looking around at the others.

"As do I," replied McKray.

"I believe that everything will be okay," stated Amalia. "I had a long talk with Gold Wing yesterday, and I believe we are all going to succeed."

Her comments were quickly swallowed up in the hollow silence that seemed to now be permeating the room.

"Let's go someplace brighter that we can say our farewells as Teran counseled," said the Bard.

They all stood and followed the Bard to the gardens. There, in the bright sunlight, they reminisced of their meeting and subsequent journey, and their hearts were eased. They spoke of the good times that they had shared as well as the close encounters with death. As the shadows lengthened and the sunlight lessened, a feeling of despair worked its way into their hearts and minds.

"I'm sure Teran will be here soon to get us on our way," said Koyne standing. Looking around at everyone, he apologized for his actions and poor attitude throughout the journey. "Mathias, I am especially sorry for the anger that I felt toward you and the disrespect that I showed you. Please forgive me."

"My friend, we all have reason to ask forgiveness, and I ask yours in return," replied Mathias. The two grasped arms and turned to the others.

The group was finishing their farewells as the sun set in the west, and Teran joined them. "Please follow me. I will take you to a place that none of you have been."

Teran led the way while Dale and Koyne brought up the rear, whispering quietly to each other.

They walked through the great hall toward a wall covered in skillfully crafted carvings of men, elves, dwarves, griffins, dragons, and other magnificent creatures. Many of them were painted, or covered, in gold leaf and adorned with sparkling jewels. As they approached, Teran stretched out his hand and spoke a few words in elven. The wall began to split and open outward, revealing a huge stone-paved square. In the square stood their riding horses and baggage horses, griffins, and dragons of various sizes. Silver-, copper-, blue-, white-, and gold-scaled bodies glistened in the fading sunlight. The largest dragon was gold, and as he saw the group, he dropped his left knee and bowed. The other dragons and griffins followed his lead. Teran bowed in return, as did those with him.

"Lord Teran, you are followed by the hope of these lands," said the great dragon.

"That I am. Yet I don't believe that these men, women, and dwarf fully appreciate their calling, oh, mighty Galeon," responded Teran.

"Perhaps they will see when their journey is completed," replied the golden dragon.

"I thought dragons had been hunted to extinction," said McKray in awe.

"We had to let all humankind believe that in order to survive," said Galeon. "I understand there is no time to waste, however so we will go into detail at some future time. Shall we, dwarf king?"

"It would be my honor," replied McKray, bowing low.

Teran urged and pushed the group into action, and in a few minutes' time they were sitting astride griffins, while Amalia alone sat in the dragon saddle attached to Galeon's lower neck. Without further ado, they took to the air in a swirl of dust, borne by the powerful wings of the griffins and dragons. Their horses hung suspended in leather harnesses carried in the mighty talons of the great dragons.

Once they were airborne and the initial churning in the stomach passed, the travelers allowed themselves to revel in the experience of flying. The cold night air bit at their faces, causing them to wrap themselves more tightly in the cloaks they had been given as departing gifts. They flew in silence, covering distances that took days in hours.

Amalia began to be restless after the first moments of takeoff. "You have a question for me," stated Galeon. The sudden statement startled Amalia.

"I do."

"Then ask it, child, for now is the best time for conversation. No one else can hear us."

"Why do I have the honor of riding on your neck, oh, mighty one?" she added awkwardly.

"You have another journey to fulfill once you have succeeded in this one," stated Galeon.

Silence followed for several minutes. "Are you going to tell me what it is?" she asked.

"First, I will ask a question of you. Do you know my true identity?" asked the dragon.

Suddenly Amalia's conversation with Gold Wing came flooding back. "You are Odin. You are the God of the Living. I…uh…." she trailed off into silence.

"Gold Wing has told you things that only a few mortals have known since the beginning of time."

"I don't understand," she replied.

"No, I don't suppose you do. There has always been me, and there have always been speakers or mouthpieces for me, until the time that Souvac swore allegiance to Kish and became a king. You see, Kish and I have been at war for as long as there has been time. I create, he destroys. I heal, he makes sick. I teach and organize, he fights for chaos and ignorance. Souvac, and other evil men, under Kish's guidance, tracked down and killed all my speakers. It has taken this long to find a suitable replacement to take the role as head speaker. You are the only living human—that includes elves and dwarves—that know my true identity."

"But what about Teran?" she asked, interrupting Galeon.

"He believes, as do all in my household, that I am Odin the Long Lived, a wise protector under the grace of the God of the Living. However, it is time that Odin passes from this earth, and a speaker is chosen to do what I cannot. When you have finished this quest and the lands are truly free of its curse, you will return to me at Odin's Hall. There I will bestow upon you all the rights and powers to which you are entitled. Then you must establish a school and choose others to become speakers as well."

"How will I do this without you?" asked Amalia, interrupting Galeon again.

"Once you are ordained as speaker, I will always be with you to guide you and instruct you. You will be able to call on me whenever you have need. There is something else you should know. Following the conclusion of this quest, you will find a protector and more. From you two will come a line of great and noble leaders. This earth is ready for a rebirth, and that will come as a result of this journey and the people who have joined to make it possible. In your midst are three kings who will join the lands of the north, west, south, and east kingdoms in peace. Once that is done, an age of peace and prosperity will reign over these lands. It will not be easy, and there will be plenty of bad with the good, but you and your friends are the beginning of it all," said Galeon.

"Will this age ever end?" asked Amalia.

"Yes, all things come to an end, but at that end is a new beginning, which will also end and begin anew. Do not fear, for you have the strength to be a part of this great change, as do all with whom you have traveled. Inside the storage pouch at the front of the saddle is a medallion. It is yours now, it marks you as a speaker and binds you to me." Amalia found the medallion and put it around her neck. "I suggest you keep that hidden until the time is right to reveal it."

"When will that be?" she asked as she studied the intricate carving on the round medallion. It appeared to have a light of its own, for she could make out the details as she ran her fingers over the emblazoned sun with a tree at its base, lifting its branches over miniature people, while a great dragon spread its wings over the tree.

"You will know the proper time. Now sleep, we have a few more hours of flying before we land."

"I'm not tired," she said through a yawn. Moments later she slept, kept in place by the ornate leather saddle on which she sat.

The sun was breaking over the horizon when the dragons and griffins set down in front of the cave that had been the Rogues' hideout. The dragons looked as if they could have flown for another ten hours straight. The griffins, proud and strong as they were, were showing signs of fatigue.

"Now that we are here, you all must go with haste. Do not tarry, ride through the day, sleep through the night. Fear no enemies from behind, for at this moment, all of Oaran's abominable boarhounds have been destroyed," said Galeon.

"We are…" began the Bard.

"I know of your gratitude, it swells in each of your hearts, now go," replied Galeon, urgency in his words.

With no further hesitation, the travelers mounted their horses and headed for the open end of the box canyon. As they exited the canyon, Amalia alone looked back. She saw sixteen people in colorful robes standing by nine griffins, Odin at their head in blazing white robes. She raised her hand in farewell, riding around a great pine tree. The view was lost from her sight. She touched her hand to the medallion she wore beneath her tunic.

"Be well, child, I am with you. Take strength, hold your courage and faith." The words came as clear to her mind as if Sterling had shouted them from his position in front of her.

Within the hour, they came to a point where the trail split, one fork going to the right and one to the left. McKray started down the right-hand trail with Dale, Mathias, Amalia, and Sterling.

"Farewell, Bard, I will see you later," he said.

"Not in this lifetime," was the Bard's sobering reply.

As the now two separate groups parted company, Avalon looked at those riding away.

"Avalon, be careful," said Dale, giving her a strange, almost-longing look.

"I will be there to watch over her. See to your brother," stated Koyne, a little defensively with a hint of agitation.

Dale turned and rode away without looking back.

"Koyne, what has gotten into you? He was just showing concern," said Avalon, now riding beside Koyne.

"He hasn't been overly protective of you until now," replied Koyne, agitation still present in his voice.

"Perhaps you haven't seen the furtive glances he has sent my way throughout the trip," stated Avalon.

"He has not," said Koyne, suddenly defensive. "I mean, I have watched everyone very closely, and he has not been looking at you."

"You weren't watching very closely then because even Mathias has made eyes at me," said Avalon.

"But he's blind," replied Koyne confused.

"You are the most jealous man I have ever met. I am only one of two women on a journey with eight men. You ought to know that they all find me beautiful." Koyne started to blush slightly. "Of course, being that they are all noble and perfect gentlemen, they avert their eyes and keep their distance. So you don't have to worry, they all know that we love each other," said Avalon with a smile.

Koyne was blushing even more now. "We better hurry, we're starting to fall behind," was all he said before riding forward, leaving Avalon in the back of the line. During all the days leading up to now, she had never been allowed to ride at the back of the group; now it appeared this might become her permanent spot.

The day grew warmer as the sun rose, and by midday they were all sweating profusely. The Bard called a stop when they came across a clear running stream in the shade of some Aspen trees. They had been riding east all day, and so they were still in the White Hills.

"We will be turning a bit more to the south soon, which will put us in the Summoner's Forest by nightfall. There we will find the main road and follow it due east until we come to the Great North Road. Once we reach that, it will be a long march to Souvac and then the King's Forest and the end of our quest together," said the Bard.

Hours later they made camp on the road in the Summoner's Forest. After eating they discussed who would take the first watch. Koyne volunteered, expressing his need to clear his head. Each man was to take a two-hour watch, leaving Avalon to sleep through the night. She had argued that she needed a chance to keep watch, but the others insisted she sleep. She fell into a deep sleep within minutes of lying down. When she awoke, the men were already packing and getting ready to move out. She hurriedly packed her own things and mounted her horse, before the others.

After all I had been through, I am still trying to prove myself to the others, she thought to herself.

Again, as they got underway, Avalon found herself at the back of the line. She had tried to speak with Koyne at first, but he had brushed aside the conversation, expressing his need to think for a while. The next three days followed the same pattern as the first: a brief midday stop for food and to rest the horses, followed by a long ride until sundown, with a quick, cheerless meal and Koyne always taking the first watch, followed by Graham, Jace, and the Bard. Avalon was always the first to sleep and the last to wake up. They spoke little, as it was clear each person was concerned with the undeniable destiny that awaited them.

On the fifth morning of travel, Avalon woke first. She wanted to feel the warmth of Koyne's body near hers. She rolled to her left (Koyne had been sleeping on her left throughout their journey) to see his sleeping face. He wasn't there; he was several feet away, rolled tightly in his blankets. At first, she was mad, but as she started thinking about it, she realized Koyne had been acting differently since they left the Rogues' lair.

*****

McKray and Mathias had been riding side by side throughout the morning talking about royal duties and protocols, how to tax appropriately to strengthen a kingdom, the role of a king and the king's army, for every kingdom should have an army especially during times of peace; it was McKray's thought on the matter. Mathias spoke his own opinions and thoughts, and the two got into a couple of very strong debates. During all this, Dale, Sterling, and Amalia rode in silence, listening to the banter.

"Shouldn't you be involved in some of this discussion?" Sterling asked Dale.

"I don't think I have anything to add that Mathias hasn't already said," replied Dale.

"But you are brother to the king, which means if something were to happen to him, you would be the king," said Sterling.

"Then I guess nothing can happen to the king," replied Dale coolly. "I'm sorry," he said after looking at Sterling's face. "I know this whole situation can't have been easy for you. I'm sorry you lost your brother."

"We've been through this. I forgave you, but I still envy you. You have your brother, and you get to see him become something great. I know my brother could have been something great. I just will never see what. I have been pretty lonely since reaching Odin's stair. While in Odin's Hall, everyone had someone but me. I felt like I was always alone, and it has been wearing on me," said Sterling, sharing his feelings for the first time.

Amalia, riding behind these two, felt a twinge of sadness enter her heart.

"I'm sorry, I swore to be your brother, but I failed in that, didn't I?"

"No, I'm the one that failed," replied Sterling.

"I need to ask you to do something for me. If anything should happen to me, I need you to be there for Mathias. I need you to step into my role and be the big brother that I can't be—should anything happen to me, that is," Dale added almost as an afterthought.

"It would be my honor and privilege, but let's just see that nothing happens to you," replied Sterling with a smile.

"Hey, now that's a good idea," said Dale, forcing a smile.

They rode on through the day at a leisurely pace, eating lunch while they rode. McKray and Mathias continued to drone on about politics, while Sterling began telling Dale about the area they were passing through and how it related to his childhood. Dale asked questions, keeping the focus on Sterling. This gave Sterling a chance to relive the adventures he experienced with his deceased brother. They stopped that night at the large pine tree where the group had camped the night before their encounter with the Rogues. Each man took a two-hour watch. Dale took the last watch, waking the others promptly when the sun began to lighten the eastern horizon.

"Rise and shine, we have to get going," Dale said as he urged the others to the long day's ride ahead. Since they had reached the valley floor, they were now able to ride four abreast. They quickly reached the hidden entrance to the underground pass that would take them to Kragg's Golden Valley.

Entering the pass, Dale spoke up, "Should we bind the horses' feet in cloth?"

"Why?" asked Mathias.

"Because of the crystal spiders," replied Dale.

"Good point, lad. Let's bind the horses' hooves," stated McKray.

They lit the lanterns, prepared the horses, and resumed their journey through the pass. The first day was spent listening to the deep, droning voice of McKray as he recounted tales from his youth.

As they rode, Dale wondered why they had been told it would be a five-day journey to Kragg's Golden Valley when he knew it would only take four.

They stopped to sleep when McKray let them know that the sun had set. Dale seemed reluctant but agreed before lying in his blanket and going to sleep, having again chosen to take the last watch. McKray woke when it was morning, coming to Dale's side. Dale, understanding that it was time to go, moved quickly around camp, waking everyone and urging them to be on their way.

"We need to be on the other side by the time the sun sets on the fifth day. If we push on, we can be through the pass in two more days," said Dale to the looks he received from his companions.

"How did you know it takes three days to get through the pass?" asked Mathias.

"Uh…the Bard told me that's how long it took to get through," replied Dale.

The others looked at each other, and McKray shrugged his shoulders. "All right, light the torches, and let's be on our way."

Once they began the morning ride, Dale fell to the back of the line and pulled his cloak close about him with the hood pulled low over his face. After what seemed to be a few hours of riding, Mathias dropped back to ride beside his brother.

"You seem to be a bit on edge. Is something wrong?" he asked.

"I just want this to be over. I miss…" Dale trailed off.

"You miss what?" asked Mathias.

"I miss having time to relax," replied Dale awkwardly.

"Oh," replied Mathias, looking in the direction of his brother.

They rode the rest of that day in silence, not wanting to alert the deadly crystal spiders to their presence. To Dale, the time seemed terribly long, and it was obvious to the others that he was getting increasingly tense.

The next morning, they rode for an hour when they found the passage blocked. McKray marveled, as this passage had never had a cave-in. It took the entire rest of the day to clear the debris that blocked the tunnel. Dale, in a near craze because of the delay, was pushing them to ride a bit more, but McKray wouldn't hear of it.

"We are all exhausted, as are the animals, we all need rest now," stated McKray.

The morning of the fifth day, Dale was urging McKray to lead them at a much faster pace. "McKray, it is the fifth day, we have to be out of here as quickly as possible."

"We have until sunset," replied McKray.

Dale, pacing back and forth during their conversation, was nervously drumming his fingers on the pommel of his sword, his face hidden by his hood. "I can't take it any longer, McKray. I have to be out of this infernal darkness," he said as the others approached him cautiously. "Are you all ready to go?" he asked from beneath his hood.

"We are," replied Mathias.

"All right, we can ride a bit faster, but we still have to be careful. There is a chance we could run upon another cave-in or into a group of crystal spiders," replied McKray, trying to peer under Dale's hood.

Dale turned abruptly, strode to his horse, and jumped into the saddle. "I will be leading today, try to keep up."

The others quickly mounted their horses and broke into a gallop to catch up to the fleeing Dale. So it was that at this pace they ran upon a group of thirty crystal spiders. The group quickly drew their weapons and ferociously attacked the bewildered creatures. Dale, McKray, and Sterling dispatched twenty, while Mathias killed nine more with his bow, and Amalia killed one.

"Is anyone injured?" asked Dale.

"No, we all appear to be unharmed," replied Sterling, looking at the others.

"Good, then let's finish this," replied Dale. "How far to the end?"

McKray closed his eyes, as if reaching through time and space with his mind. "We have already ridden two hours this morning and are about three hours from the end of the tunnel, if we keep this pace," said McKray.

"Then we better keep this pace."

"If we do, the horses will last an hour and a half before they drop out from beneath us," replied Sterling. "Then we will be on foot."

Dale, frustration showing in his movements, looked back to McKray. "What time would you say it is now?"

"It is not quite noon."

"Not quite noon, you had us sleep in?" yelled Dale.

"We needed the rest, we moved nearly twenty tons of stone yesterday."

"Ughh, we have to be out of here as soon as possible. Sterling, lead us at the fastest pace the horses will tolerate. McKray, tell me when we are three miles to the end of this infernal pass."

"Who died and made you king?" replied McKray, his own voice rising.

"McKray, I have to get out of here. Which way do we go?" Dale responded, controlling his voice a bit more.

McKray simply pointed behind Dale.

Sterling, wanting to defuse the current situation, turned toward the end of the pass and began riding at a pace he felt the horses could safely handle. Dale without a word followed.

"What has gotten into that brother of yours?" McKray asked Mathias as they hurried to follow Sterling and Dale.

"I don't know. I have never seen him like this. He never had trouble being underground before, in fact he kind of liked it," said Mathias. "He would tell me he wanted to learn to live like I did, using other senses to see the world around him, and he could only do that underground or blindfolded, and he hates things in front of his eyes."

The group continued, the hours slipping past.

Finally McKray called out, "We are nearly there, three more miles, and three hours until sunset."

Dale, hearing this, kicked his horse, urging it forward, racing past Sterling, riding now at dangerous speeds through the underground cavern. Luckily, the floor of this cavern was not marred by cracks, loose stones, or the usual imperfections found in nature.

McKray, riding behind, urged his own horse on as fast as he dared. He could sense the end of their journey in the dark nearing its end, which happened to be a solid stone door that only he knew how to open. Worried that Dale would ride his horse headfirst into the solid rock, he was just about to shout a warning when he heard Dale's horse whinnied loudly as it was reined in. He could see red sparks leaping from the stone floor some distance ahead of him as Dale's mount came to a sliding stop. Dale could be heard shouting a moment later.

"McKray, get up here quick, I need this door open now."

Chapter 13

The sun was hanging in the sky above the distant western mountains, causing Kragg's Valley to glimmer in golden brilliance as Dale emerged from Kragg's Pass.

"I still have some time," he said under his breath.

"Time for what?" asked McKray.

"If I hurry, I might still make it to the Bard on the North Road."

"Not on that horse, friend, and definitely not by going through the marsh."

"I have to get to them, I have to at least try," said Dale.

Sterling, Amalia, and Mathias had caught up by now and heard Dale's last word, *try*.

"What do you have to try?" asked Mathias.

McKray had heard something from the stable next to the dwarven throne room and had gone to investigate.

Dale watched the departing dwarf. "Mathias, I am sorry, but I have to go. Do you remember what Odin told us? We would all have new quests awaiting us when we reached the end of this journey." Mathias nodded his head. "My journey, at least for a time, takes me with the Bard. I have to try and catch them before it's too late. If I can, I will return. Until that time, Sterling will take my place as your brother and protector," said Dale.

"It would appear you were correct, Dale," said McKray, leading two large, beige-colored horses to him. "These horses were in the stables saddled and laden with food and bedding for a journey, but who is going with you?"

“I am,” stated Amalia. The men looked at each other questions in their eyes.

“What is the fastest way to the North Road?” asked Dale, interrupting the momentary silence.

“Follow the cliffs east, they will lead you onto a narrow ledge of rock that skirts the Marsh. It’s slow going, but after four miles or so, you will have to go through the marsh for maybe two hundred yards after that you hit the solid earth of the plains. From there it is a speedy thirty-five-mile trip to the North Road,” replied McKray.

Dale turned and hugged Mathias. “I’m sorry for the way I treated you earlier. Good luck, I know you will become a great king.” Turning, he took Sterling’s forearm in a grip of brotherhood. “Please keep him safe and well, I am counting on you to do what I cannot. McKray, it’s been life-altering. Do you release me from your service?” asked Dale.

“You are released. Farewell, may Odin’s blessing follow you,” said McKray as Dale mounted his horse and turned away.

“Farewell to each of you in your endeavors. I will return as quickly as I am able. Amalia, let’s be on our way,” said Dale.

Amalia, sitting astride her horse, looked back at the three men. A strange feeling coursed through her as she looked at Mathias. She could hear Odin’s words in her head about meeting someone else who would care for her.

“Farewell, I will return,” she stated awkwardly.

Moments later, she and Dale were out of sight.

“Don’t look so worried, the Bard will never let him enter the wood with them, he is not part of the company meant to do so. Plus, if they have reached the pass on the Great North Road as we stand and talk, they will be almost to Souvac before they stop for the night. They will have left Dale far behind. I imagine he will be back in three four days tops. Now come on, I have to show you something,” said McKray.

Mathias and Sterling followed McKray to the throne room of Kragg’s Golden Valley. “It appears we are meant to build our kingdom’s right away.”

Upon a mannequin standing at the right side of McKray's throne was a suit of armor silver with gold trim flashing in the light of McKray's lantern. Upon the armor, a note was fastened that read, "With the blessing of the God of the Living, go forth and build your kingdom, you will be known as the Silver King of the south." Upon the throne sat a suit of armor, all white with black-and-red trim. Attached to this was a note that read, "Take your rightful place king of the west." On the left side of the throne was another suit of armor, this of a reddish bronze hue. Attached to this was a note that read, "For the brother of the Silver King, guide and protect your liege."

McKray described in detail everything that they saw for Mathias.

"And if you understand the note on the red armor, Dale will be back to guide and protect you," said McKray. "However, we need something more, these are splendid suits of armor indeed, the finest I have ever seen constructed by dwarven hands, whoever made these was almost as skilled as me. I need help stoking up my forge, we will have swords and axes, daggers, belts, and shields to go with this splendid armor."

"He seems very giddy for someone of his advanced age—I mean wisdom," said Mathias, shifting his gaze to Sterling.

"That he does," replied Sterling, a noticeable hint of dejection in his voice.

"McKray will also need to make you a suit of armor, one that says I am the left hand of the Silver King," said Mathias, getting McKray's attention.

"Yes, of course, you just tell me the color you like. I can forge any color into metal," replied McKray.

"I suppose it should look very much like the armor that was made for Dale, you know for uniformity," said Sterling.

"Very well, let's get to it," said McKray, practically running from the throne room.

Sterling turned to follow, but Mathias stood where he was gazing at the suit of armor meant for him. Sterling opened his mouth to speak, but Mathias spoke first, "Go ahead, I will join you soon."

"Yes, Your Majesty," replied Sterling.

"You do not need to address me that way," said Mathias, half turning toward Sterling.

"Yes, I do, you are my king, and if I don't address you that way, who will?" stated Sterling.

"You're right, it will take some getting used to, but you are right," said Mathias with a smile. He turned back again to gaze sightlessly at the armor he would soon be wearing as king of the south. Sterling turned away to assist McKray with the forge.

Once the forge was lit and the fires were ready for metal, Sterling and Mathias sat back to watch McKray work. After several hours, Sterling and Mathias retired to the throne room and slept. Just before sunrise, McKray entered the throne room and woke his companions.

"Come and see what I have made," said the dwarf.

The two men followed McKray to his forge. Nearby on a table draped with black velvet lay four golden crowns, each with a different gemstone set in the middle of the brow.

"I thought you were going to make me new armor," said Sterling with a smile.

"I'll be getting to that next. What do you think of the crowns? One for each of the four kings," said McKray.

"They are magnificent, McKray," said Mathias also smiling. "But you can't even see them," said McKray gruffly.

Mathias picked up one of the crowns and felt it, running his fingers over the bold and intricate designs. He felt the green gem that was set in the middle of the crown, taking the time to really look at it with his hands. "As I said before, they are magnificent," replied Mathias.

Smiling, McKray moved back to his forge. "Now you'll get your armor," he said to Sterling. Sterling watched again in fascination as the dwarf worked forge and metal, shaping steel and precious metals into the beginnings of a suit of armor. Just after sunrise, in a moment of brief silence, when the ringing of hammer on metal and the hiss of red-hot steel being cooled was at a lull, Sterling heard a small tearing sound coming from the inside pocket of his tunic. Reaching inside, he removed the letter that had been given him before leaving Odin's house. Looking at it, he could see that the seal, which he had been unable to break, was now free.

"You should probably read that," said Mathias, his strange blind eyes turned toward Sterling.

Opening the letter completely, Sterling began to read.

> My brother Sterling, I call you this because we have become brothers. I saved your life, and you saved mine, we could be nothing else. If you are reading this, it means that the quest given to me by Odin is complete and my life has come to its close. You must now be the brother that Mathias counts on for support and protection as he becomes king of the south. I will always be indebted to you for this.
>
> My deepest gratitude,
> Dale

It was simple and complete. Sterling read it through several times just to be sure of what it said.

"How can this be?" he asked of no one in particular. "No, this cannot be. He just left a few hours ago, this has got to be some trick some perverse joke."

"What is it?" asked Mathias, a cold chill sweeping through his body.

"This note that I have carried with me, it was given to me by Dale. It was sealed. I have tried on occasion to open it for the last few days, but it was sealed," he was speaking quickly with an edge of madness to his voice.

McKray, hearing the others speaking, had stopped hammering and now heard the change in Sterling's voice. "What does it say, lad?"

Something about the calm tone McKray used brought Sterling back to himself. He looked at his old friend and reached his hand out to McKray. McKray took the note from him and watched as Sterling's arm fell limply to his side. McKray read the note at a glance. Then, stepping over to the still-seated Mathias, he put his hand on the boy's shoulder.

"I'm sorry, it appears that something has befallen Dale, something that he knew was coming, he is dead."

Mathias stiffened noticeably at these last words. He knew? Somehow, Dale knew he would die. There had been something different about Dale the entire trip since leaving Odin's house. This was why—he had known he was going to die, but that had not stopped him from continuing the mission that would be his end. With tears glistening in his eyes, he turned his face to the rising sun.

"Farewell, brother, may you soon be in the peace of the God of the Living."

"Farewell, Dale," came the combined voices of McKray and Sterling.

Mathias stood and walked toward the stable. Sterling began to follow a few moments later.

"Leave it alone, lad, he needs to be alone for a time," said McKray. Turning back to his forge he picked up his hammer and the metal he had been working. Soon the mixed sounds of hammer on steel and the deep resonant tones of McKray's voice began to blend into a heart-wrenching song of farewell.

*****

The Bard and his company reached the far side of the Kraggs as the sun was setting.

"Well, it seems we are a little later than Odin had wanted us to be, but we are here and well." As soon as the words left his mouth, Koyne turned to look back at Avalon, who rode at the rear of the column and directly behind him. In that moment, he saw the black creature detach itself from the cliff face, several feet above them.

He had just enough time to yell Avalon's name and turn his own horse into the path of the beast as it leaped from the wall. The weight and force of the creature hit Koyne and his unfortunate horse, fully knocking them into Avalon and her mount. Avalon was knocked from her horse; it ran away while Koyne disappeared beneath the mass of black fur of his attacker. Graham fired arrows into the beast, causing it to jump away in pain, leaving Koyne lying on the ground severely injured.

The creature—the last of Oaran's boarhounds sent here as a final precaution—now stood facing the Bard, Jace, and Graham. Avalon was getting back to her feet behind it. The creature angled itself slowly until it could see the injured man and woman in addition to those that posed a greater risk.

Graham continued to fire arrows at the beast; some of them hit while the beast dodged others. The Bard and Jace each drew their swords and charged. The beast lunged aside, and the men had no chance to strike. In the blink of an eye, the creature covered the distance between itself and Graham, slamming into Graham's horse and knocking him from the saddle. Before it could continue its attack, the Bard and Jace charged again; this time the men split slightly to cover if the beast made the same evasive move. The creature rose up onto its hind legs and leaped forward, rolling into a ball. Realizing the beast would go between them, the Bard switched his sword to his left hand. He and Jace swung their blades as if choreographed; unfortunately the beast unfolded its body at the same moment, slamming into the legs of the charging horses. The Bard and Jace were thrown to the ground. The beast shook its head and turned toward Avalon. She was the target after all.

By this time, she had regained her feet and drawn her own sword. The creature advanced toward her slowly, licking its lips with its long tongue, seeming to relish in the fear that emanated from this cowering girl. It was five feet away when it crouched like a cat hunting a mouse. Every muscle was tensing for the leap that would end this woman's life. Suddenly pain exploded through its side just behind its left foreleg. It jumped to the side and kicked with its back legs, which connected with something. Spinning around, it saw the man it had already killed struggling on the ground. Anger filled the creature as it lumbered toward the man set on killing him for good. It stood over the man, now opening its large mouth to bite the man's neck, when the forgotten scared woman appeared in his peripheral vision. In one stroke powered by love and desperation, Avalon brought her sword singing with vengeance through the air and severed the creatures head from its body. The beast reeled up and fell to its left side, driving Koyne's sword deeper into its heart.

Avalon fell to her knees at Koyne's side. "It's okay, you are going to be okay," she cried. Her three other companions arrived at her side in seconds.

Koyne looked up at her, waves of pain visible in his eyes. He tried to speak to her, to say something, but the pain was too great. The Bard, also now kneeling at his side, poured a small amount of liquid into Koyne's mouth. The pain appeared to ease slightly. Avalon, holding his hand, continued to cry and attempt to comfort him. As the pain eased slightly, Koyne finally was able to speak the words "Your love." His body convulsed once, and his eyes closed for the last time.

"No, no you can't leave me, I love you," cried Avalon, holding his hand and touching his face.

The Bard took her by the shoulders and firmly but gently helped her to her feet. Then he embraced her as she sobbed in misery into his shoulder. It was as if the world cried with her; the sunset in its deep purple hues were beautiful but seemed as full of sadness as Avalon.

Jace and Graham carried Koyne's body into the woods near the side of the road where they prepared him for burial as best they could. They then worked long into the night building a cairn over his body. Upon his chest they laid his sword which they had pulled from the creature; at his feet, they laid the head of the beast; and over him went the cloak from Odin. While they did this, the Bard had retrieved the horses, pulled the body of the beast away from the battle site, and set it ablaze. Avalon, mostly in shock, had laid down and fallen asleep, the fatigue of journey and deep sorrow catching up to her.

The night was halfway gone when they finished their work. The Bard gently woke Avalon and with a steadying hand led her to Koyne's cairn.

"We must leave this place soon. Before we go, I would like to say a few words… Here lies a man that started this journey as a boy. He believed he knew more than any single living person. He had darkness in his past, but brightness in his future. He was truly noble and brave, full of courage and love. It is with great respect that we entomb him here where we will later build a monument to his memory, so generations of people will learn of his sacrifice," the Bard ended his eulogy and stepped back.

Jace stepped forward. "I don't think I have words to describe what this loss means to me. We butted heads a time or two, but I have grown to respect you and care for you as if you were my own brother. I hope that I can live my life to the fullest like you lived yours. Farewell."

Graham stepped forward next while Avalon cried silently next to the Bard. "I hope you are truly at rest in the arms of the God of the Living. I don't know how we can succeed without you, maybe we will all be joined together faster than we expect. I am glad that you were able to find peace before the end of your life. I hope I can find the same peace as I become what I always wanted and feared, the king of Souvac. If I live that long, that is. Farewell, friend."

Avalon stepped forward. Warmth spread through her like a summer day as she began to speak. At first her voice cracked and her words came out between sobs, but as she continued, her strength and conviction grew. "Koyne, you gave your life for me, it seems like you have always given your life for me. I am sorry that we will not have the life that we dreamed of sharing, but I vow to you that I will forever be true to only you. You will not have died in vain. We will go to the knights of Souvac, and we will destroy them. We will complete this quest that you gave your life for. I will see my quest completed now and forever." As she spoke, the pain decreased, and she thought she heard a voice in her mind say, "Love does not die." She turned then, and after walking to her horse, she spoke, "We will finish this quest, to victory!"

The others drew their swords and raised them high in the air. "To victory!" they shouted in unison. Mounting their horses, they rode until the sun began to rise.

Souvac could be seen in the distance. Exhaustion had crept upon them, and they stopped to sleep in a grove of thick pine trees when still a few miles from Souvac. When they woke again, the sun was setting toward the western horizon. They decided to ride past the city going straight on to the edge of the King's Forest.

*****

Dale and Amalia reached the still-smoldering carcass of Oaran's tracking beast thirty minutes after the others left. Taking several minutes, they split up and studied the area to figure out what had occurred; that was when Amalia discovered Koyne's grave site.

"I am sorry, my friend, I tried to get here in time," said Dale, stepping up behind Amalia. "I did not want your death to happen as Odin told us it would." He spent over an hour carving something into the grave marker before lying down to sleep. He knew they were close and would catch up to the Bard and the others before they entered the forest. They had to if they were all going to succeed.

*****

The Bard looked to the setting sun. "It is nearly time to enter the forest."

They gathered together, picketing the horses, and discussed the final leg of their journey.

"When we go into the forest tonight, it is imperative that you keep yourselves completely covered in your cloaks. Avalon, this will be especially important for you. You must appear as though you are a man. The knights of Souvac will be expecting three men to come with me. They will stand in a line, Jerec first with Kell to his left and Oaran to Kell's left. Graham, you will stand before Jerec. Avalon, you will stand before Kell. Jace, you will stand before Oaran, and I will stand directly behind you," said the Bard.

"The knights and I will sing a chant that will bring our immortality from our bodies to be passed on to you three. While we sing the chant, you must all draw your daggers and prepare to strike. As soon as the chant ends, Jace, you will turn and stab me. While the knight's attention is focused on me, you two must strike. Jace, as soon as you bury your knife into my body, draw your sword and strike Oaran. Perhaps this will work, and the knights of Souvac will finally be defeated. If you are unable to kill Oaran, I fear he will be free to leave the forest while maintaining a portion of his awful power," finished the Bard.

"Shouldn't I strike Oaran first? Then there will be no chance for him to escape," said Jace.

"No, you must strike me first, it will cause some confusion and give everyone a better chance of succeeding. I know this will not be easy, but it is our only chance without Koyne," replied the Bard.

"Is there no way for us to win?" asked Graham.

"With the loss of Koyne, I don't know if we will defeat Oaran. It was by a blood relative that death was to be dealt—that is why it has taken me so long to complete this quest. Of course, little did I know that I was tracking a century's worth of family history by word of mouth and, in rare cases, written documents, not to mention the time spent traveling the world learning all I can about the Evil One and the strength of his curses and blessings," said the Bard.

Each man was looking at the ground, wondering is there any chance of success or are we going to our death this night. That was when Avalon spoke.

"We will have victory tonight. I don't know how I know this, but I do. We will survive while the knights perish. Keep your heads held high, we will overcome the evil."

The Bard smiled. "Avalon is right, get ready, we leave in one hour."

An hour later, four heavily cloaked people crept into the King's Forest. As they entered the trees, the branches seemed to reach for them; the sound of cold laughter sounded faintly in their ears. Several yards away, a dark figure crouched low to the ground and watched them enter the forbidding woods.

"The Bard is coming, and he is bringing three men as he promised," declared Oaran.

"That fool, always honest and good to his word, even when marching to his death," said Jerec.

"Death is what he seeks," replied Oaran.

"He has been free for a hundred years he deserves death, but soon we will finally be free. I can't wait to feel the full sun on my face as I cut down the worthless mongrels that live in Souvac," said Kell.

"Easy, brother, we aren't free yet, and I will tell you whom you will and won't kill, unless you have forgotten that I am your leader," snapped Jerec.

Kell glanced at Oaran, making quick eye contact that spoke volumes. "As you say, Jerec," he replied with a slight edge to his voice.

Jerec was too preoccupied with his own thoughts to notice the subtle change in Kell's voice.

Two hours later, the Bard stepped into the dark clearing. The knights stood just as he had anticipated.

"Let these men come forward and prepare for the riches and gifts that await their courage and bravery in coming here," said Jerec.

"I see you were able to find another volunteer to come with you. It is a shame that misfortune befell the young man who traveled with you all the way to Odin's house and back," said Oaran, a smile on his face. The Bard could feel the collective tension building in those that had come with him. "I do hope the young woman will find someone else to love."

At that last comment, Kell laughed. "A whore like her will always find someone else to love. Oaran gave me some entertainment when he explained the things he watched those two doing alone in the dark."

Avalon tensed further, her muscles begging her to strike this horrible man to the ground for his lies.

"If the God of the Living knew what they were doing, he would have struck them down himself, but then he doesn't really exist, does he?" said Kell, looking at the Bard. "If he did, he wouldn't have let us kill your dear wife and precious son," he said this with a mock frown.

"Enough, Kell, these men did not come here to hear you blabber but to receive a reward befitting a king," said Jerec, gesturing to the bleach-white bones of King Souvac sitting on his throne. "Once we finish a chant to bestow this treasure and our blessing of long life, you must simply accept our offer, then you will be the owners of that great treasure and the bearers of immortality." With that said, Jerec put his hands before him, as if cupping a bowl. The other knights made the same gesture.

"Stand before the knights as I instructed you," said the Bard.

Once his companions were in place, the Bard stood behind Jace and made the same hand gesture as the knights.

The chant began simultaneously, words in a language that had rarely been heard on the face of the earth. The sound of it rose and fell; the deep tone of the chanting men's voices seemed to be contained in the clearing, echoing off the trees instead of fleeing into the empty spaces of the forest. There was a dark power in those words, power that lured the listener into a false sense of peace. They created a desire to follow and accept whatever was about to happen. Graham struggled in himself, trying to focus and block out the words. Avalon felt the resolve to destroy Kell subside slightly. Jace was unaffected. All he could think about was the fate before him: he had to kill his great grandfather.

The chant ended slowly, the last sounds echoing back to the Bard's companions. Jace wasn't sure how long he had been standing there; it felt like ages. The thought that he had missed his chance flew into his mind, and then there was complete silence. This was the time. He had, as the Bard instructed, already drawn his dagger. In one fluid motion, he spun to face the Bard, and as he plunged his dagger into the Bard's chest, he said, "I accept the offer of the Bard." The Bard touched his glowing hands to Jace's chest and fell to the ground. The knights, surprised by this startling occurrence, dropped their guard.

Graham and Avalon struck with silent but powerful strokes. Jerec and Kell were ready for this. They each caught a hold of their attacker's arms to stop the momentum of the attack. Avalon's hood fell as she brought her head up. Kell looked into her eyes and let out an audible gasp.

"Avalon? Sister?" The words jumped from Kell's mouth, causing Jerec and Oaran to look over at him. Kell fell to his knees, pain ripping through his heart as he looked into Avalon's eyes. "I'm sorry for not being there for you. I'm sorry I failed you. Please forgive me," he said, tears glistening in his eyes.

Jerec continued to struggle against Graham's attack. "Kell, get off your knees and help me."

Kell looked at Avalon. She stood above him, her arms raised, the dagger poised to strike. She faltered as she saw the look in his eye. He bowed his head and waited for death.

"I forgive you," the words slipped from her mouth.

"Kell, help me now!" commanded Jerec.

Kell stood, drawing his sword. "I will help you, brother, the way I should have a century ago." Turning, he sliced at Jerec with his sword, leaving a large gash in Jerec's arm.

The wound weakened his hold, and Graham's dagger found its mark at the top of Jerec's armor, piercing down through his chest and heart.

Jace had spun back to attack Oaran, but his and Oaran's attention was caught by the events that unfolded between Kell and Jerec.

As Jerec lay on the ground, lifeblood ebbing from his body, Kell turned to face Oaran. "You're next."

Graham and Avalon, not sure what to do next, simply drew their swords and flanked Kell. Jace moved his body to block any attempt at escape by Oaran, who was moving toward Jace with sword drawn.

Oaran quickly lunged, attacking Jace with powerful, fluid strikes. Jace gave everything he had to defend against the attack, but his efforts were futile, and soon Oaran's blade tore through his chest. A wicked smile spread across Oaran's face until a black shape lunged from the shadows at the edge of the clearing, knocking Oaran back and dislodging the sword from Jace's body.

The black shape stood up and, drawing a sword, turned to face Oaran. The two beings circled each other. Oaran attacked first; his opponent matched his attacks with lightning-fast defensive parries. The two beings' swords continued in a hypnotic dance as each looked for a weakness in his opponent's defenses. Several minutes passed, and Oaran began to tire. At first the aggressor, he soon found himself on the defensive. His attacker's strikes were coming faster and faster as his own defensive strikes slowed. Pain suddenly exploded in Oaran's chest. His attacker's sword ripped through not only his defenses but his armor as well, the blade biting through his chest, puncturing his heart. He staggered back and for the first time saw the face of his heir—the eyes that were those of his beloved whom he betrayed.

Oaran fell to the ground. "But I saw you die, I killed you."

"Your creatures aren't as deadly as you hoped," said Koyne, shedding the black cloak that had concealed him. Oaran's eyes flickered and closed. Everyone stared at Koyne as he turned to face them.

Avalon ran forward, pulling Koyne into her arms. "How, how is this possible? We buried you," she said, but his focus was on the dense black form that had entered the clearing.

Jace had moved to the Bard's side and held his body close, feeling the heartbeat slowing.

All others in the clearing looked at the figure whose immense power seemed to command them to kneel. As each individual fell to their knees, Kish, the Evil One, spoke.

"Well done. The pathetic Bard found a way to kill two of the knights, but my favorite still lives. Kell, come to me, let me show you the glories that await you now that you are free."

Unable to disobey, he moved to stand before Kish. His eyes changed as if he were looking far away.

"Show me your loyalty. Kill this Avalon, and you will have all that I have shown you."

Kell turned toward Avalon. "I will not," he said through gritted teeth, as if forcing the words from his mouth.

"Then you die here and now," came the sinister reply. The Evil One raised his arm, a sword appearing in his hand, the blade burning with fire. As he began the downward stroke of death, a blinding light filled the clearing.

When those gathered could open their eyes, they saw Amalia standing before the Evil One, holding a medallion high above her.

"By the power of the God of the Living, I command you to depart."

To their amazement, the Evil One shrank back from Amalia. "I will deal with you shortly, woman," said the Evil One in disgust. "Jace, you have accepted the Bard's immortality, not even I can kill you. But the rest of you, I will make sure you suffer and die early deaths, especially you, speaker, don't get too comfortable with your victory, for it will be short-lived. Come, witch."

As the Evil One vanished from their sight, they could see a pale, sickly-looking woman with white hair. She wore tattered black robes that covered her emaciated frame. Holding her hand was a man of average height, well built, with dark hair. He was as pale as the woman and had an evil look in his eye.

"Don't worry, dear, your time is fast approaching," she said, pulling him after her. As soon as they were lost from sight, the remains of Jerec, Oaran, and the bones of the king turned to dust.

Once the evil party was gone, Amalia knelt at the Bard's side. Taking Odin's amulet in hand, she held it over the Bard's wound and prayed. The amulet began to glow, the wound closed, and seconds later his eyes opened.

"Why, why did you save me? I want to die, I was almost dead," said the Bard.

"If you were meant to die now, the God of the Living wouldn't have answered my prayer," replied Amalia.

"There will be plenty of time to die," said Jace, a smile spreading across his face.

Avalon stood before the still-kneeling Koyne and cupped his face in her hands. "How is this possible, we watched you die, we buried you."

"No, you buried Dale. I tried to get to you in time, but it was not possible. Odin told us, Dale and I, that this was the road that was set forth. We each had a role to play, and I had to survive if the evil of the knights of Souvac was to end," replied Koyne.

No longer able to keep silent, Graham asked, "How? I rode beside you, I spoke with you from Odin's until you were killed."

"Odin, he did something to us that last day before we left. He made Dale look like me and me look like Dale. He said it would go away at sunrise after Dale died," replied Koyne.

Kell lingered away from the group as they hugged and reveled in their victory.

After the elation of victory, and the fact that they were all living settled inside of the group, they turned to look at Kell.

"What do we do with him?" asked Graham, inclining his head toward Kell.

"A sound question indeed," replied the Bard. "You have proven yourself this day, as holding nobility and character obviously forged over the last century, Kell. I didn't believe it possible, especially given how you spoke when we arrived."

"It has been an act for many decades. I lost the desire for power and the thirst for blood as I watched my two counterparts sink into utter loathing and despair. I had a dream one night of a sun-filled day. I was speaking with my long-departed sister, Avalon. In the dream she told me to have courage and she would help provide a way for me to be free. As I focused on her words, I realized it was more than a dream. This was a memory, from before I became trapped in this hell of an existence. Since then I have prayed each night for deliverance to the God of the Living. It appears he has answered those prayers"

"But what do we do with him?" asked Graham again, cutting across Kell's words.

"He will come with me," stated Amalia. "He will have a new mission, one of service. You will serve me as I work to unite the free people as one. From this point on, Kell, you are in the service of the God of the Living even as I am."

"How do you know?" asked Jace.

"I am the speaker of the God of the Living," was her reply.

"The first in many, many years," replied the Bard, looking pointedly at Kell.

"I will not fail her as I failed before," replied Kell.

Stepping forward to the pile of treasure, the Bard picked up the crown that had, until moments before, rested on the skull of King Souvac. "Now we will commence the next step of this adventure. Come forward, Graham, and receive the crown of your forefathers."

Graham stepped forward and knelt before the Bard.

Placing the crown on Graham's head, the Bard spoke. "Rise, heir to the throne and rightful king of Souvac. Hail Graham, king of Souvac!" yelled the Bard.

"Hail Graham, king of Souvac," shouted the others in unison.

"Not Souvac," replied Graham. "The east kingdom of the four lands, or kingdom of the east, is what we will call it from now on. I want the taint of Souvac forever removed from these lands."

"Hail king of the east!" came the united reply.

They left the King's Forest then each with plans of a future. Two days later, they returned, all together for the last time, to the clearing where they had ended the threat of Souvac's knights. They collected the treasure in wagons and began preparations for a king to return.

Chapter 14

The company had little rest as the preparations for the return of a king to Souvac commenced. The day after recovering the treasure from the clearing, Avalon and Koyne departed to Kragg's Valley to call upon McKray, Sterling, and Mathias. Amalia, Kell, and Jace stayed in Souvac with the Bard and Graham, the soon-to-be, but unannounced rightful king.

There was a general buzz around the activities of these people, especially once the Bard revealed to the people, in rather public fashion, that Amalia was, in fact, the carrier of the medallion of the God of the Living, which meant she was the speaker.

It was also reported that the true king would return in great splendor and glory with treasures that once belonged to King Tean. He would take control of the affairs of the kingdom and rule justly; two other kings would arise out of obscurity to take their rightful place ruling their own kingdoms. Together with King Bareth of the north, these kings would create a seemingly new world for the people of the four lands, who had over the last hundred years lived mostly separate and untrusting of each other.

An abandoned cabin was cleaned, furnished, and given to Amalia from where she began teaching the words of the God of the Living. She had, since the fateful day that the knights of Souvac were destroyed, been able to clearly hear the God of the Living's voice, his directions to her a constant companion.

The Bard, Jace, and Graham had secretly taken the cart of treasure and secured it in the castle vaults to be used the day Graham would reclaim his family's throne. Orders were given for the castle to be cleaned and prepared for the return of the rightful king. The initial news of this returning king was not only looked down upon by the ruling council members, but attempts were made to squash the rumors. Until Amalia spoke with the power of the God of the Living, telling the people that a time of prosperity would accompany the king. Seeing the reactions of the people, the council members changed tactics. They knew that no king could be pronounced without the document that showed the original agreement between King Bowen and the nine lords who signed it. That document had not been seen since King Bowen left. With this information, the council believed they would be able to stop the rise of a false king while looking as if they wanted to welcome the supposed rightful king.

Talk of what would be continued until the entire town was working feverishly preparing a great festival for this historic event. In two weeks' time, the kingdom would once again feel as it had when King Tean ruled over a hundred years ago.

During this time of preparation, the Bard, Jace, and Graham traveled to a forested area on the southern outskirts of King Bareth's kingdom. Here they stood regarding the remains of the Bard's family cabin where he had enjoyed peace and happiness for a few years with his wife and son.

"Jace, I can stay with you awhile longer, recounting verbally my life experiences, you will also read all that I have experienced in my journals. I ask you to become the Bard of Souvac in my place, you will travel and tell the stories I was never able to rehearse to an audience. As you do so, you will have more adventures and experiences that you will also tell as you travel the lands."

"But you were the Bard of Souvac, and since Souvac and his knights are now gone for good, there is no need for anyone to be the Bard of Souvac any longer. You can take your previous name and live your life how you please," said Jace.

"No, there must always be the Bard of Souvac. He must stand as a witness and recordkeeper of these lands to keep evil from once again gaining a foothold and destroying the lives of innocent people. You will be that man, my time is ending, your time is beginning. I already look and feel like an old man. I live, but only for a short time more. You know this, you see it with your own eyes. When the rest of us have passed from this life, you will remain to keep the memories and lessons we have learned alive in the minds of the future kings and queens. In this way we can prevent many mistakes from being repeated, and the four lands can remain free."

Jace looked uncomfortable with the Bard's words.

"Jace, you are now immortal, my time is passing, I was dead, and my life returned because of the love of the God of the Living. However, I can feel the years I lived coursing through me, I will soon pass from this life. The additional time I have been granted is short, just enough to finish my work. You will live your life, and in time, when you feel you are ready, you can choose to pass this gift of immortality to another of your choosing, for it is a gift to you. Whether you choose one of your own bloodline or one you feel will respect the responsibility of this calling, you will have freedom that I never had to progress to the next life when the time comes."

The Bard then went to the back corner of the burnt home and walked thirty paces north. Here he knelt down and began digging at the edge of a seemingly large rock. After several minutes' effort, the Bard reached beneath the stone and with assistance lifted it from a well-hidden box. Inside were the journals containing all his experiences and stories he had learned and been a part of but had never been able to repeat. There were also several small chests of treasure.

"Use the treasure that I have gathered over the years to live well in your travels. I never did, because I felt I did not deserve such fine things. You, however, should enjoy the life you can have with this," said the Bard, indicating the treasure.

"I will do as I feel right."

Together he and the Bard loaded the journals and chests into the wagon they had brought with them. "Now we must go to Bareth's Castle. We will be accompanied, I think, by two more kings and our friends," said the Bard.

Jace looked east and could see five figures approaching, three on horseback and two on a wagon pulled by two horses.

"Be a good lad and ride down to meet our friends," the Bard said to Graham, who had been standing a bit away from him and

Jace. Needing no further instruction, he jumped astride his horse and rode quickly down to meet their friends.

After a brief meeting with handshakes, hugs, and several slaps on the back, the group of men, and one lady, turned up the Great North Road toward Bareth's castle. They arrived as the sun set. The smell of the White Sea was strong here, mixing with the pungent smell of the pine-covered mountains directly east of the castle. Mathias, Graham, and McKray were each wearing a golden crown on their heads; each had been made by McKray. The crowns were set with a different-colored jewel to represent the land of each king. Mathias wore a green emerald representing the south; McKray, a flaming red ruby for the west; and Graham, a blazing yellow sapphire for the east.

The group proceeded forward until they were stopped by the guards at the castle gate who stood a moment dumbfounded as Jace stepped forward.

"I am the Bard of Souvac. I come with the lost kings of the four lands to bid King Bareth greetings and present him with a gift and good tidings."

Once the shock of seeing a dwarf, as well as the presence of the Bard of Souvac (who had not been seen in the north in over thirty years) wore off, the companions were allowed entrance and escorted by the king's adviser to the great hall, where a runner had already arrived with the news of these strange visitors. A large group of men and women had already gathered in the hall as support to their beloved king.

Upon entering the hall, King Bareth, a large, broad-shouldered man with reddish brown hair and beard, stood to receive his guests.

"Welcome to my kingdom, friends, I apologize we do not have a meal set for your arrival, but we were unaware you were coming. I admit I have heard rumors over the last few days that the king of Souvac would be returning, the Bard of Souvac has been in the four lands with a group of adventurers, and a speaker of the God of the Living had returned. However, of anything else I must claim ignorance, and that is not something I care to do," he said with a wary gleam in his eye and an uneasy smile on his face.

For three hundred years, all kings of the north land were named after the first King Bareth and were somehow always aware of events transpiring in the four lands. For these recent and major events to occur without the current king's express knowledge had set him in an anxious mood.

"Worry not, good King Bareth," said Jace. "I am the Bard of Souvac, and I bring good tidings. The knights of Souvac are gone forever from these lands. You have heard truth concerning my travels, as well as the return of the speaker of the God of the Living. The king of Souvac has been dead for over one hundred years, but the king of the east is here, I present him to you now." Jace turned to Graham and held out his hand. "This is Graham, son of Bowen, son of Tean, son of Richard, rightful heir and blood king of the east. By his hand Jerec, captain of Souvac's knights, was killed."

Graham stepped forward and bowed his head to King Bareth. "It is my wish that you will travel in our company back to my kingdom and be present for my official crowning."

Bareth looked around at the group of men gathered before him. "You do me a great honor with your invitation, I would be pleased to attend with my royal guard of course," he replied, still wary that the men before him might be dishonest and mean him harm.

"It will be a grand festival, as we will also present the return of the king of the west and the king of the south," stated Jace. "For Mathias is to return to his rightful place as king of the south, as he is a blood descendent of King Garion, and McKray, dwarf lord son of King Kragg, will reestablish the kingdom of the west. We are entering a time of great peace and prosperity for the four lands. It seems fitting that all her kings are present."

With that said, McKray stepped forward, a square box made of red walnut in his hands. "We bring this gift to you," he said bowing.

King Bareth reached out his hand and touched the intricately carved and beautifully polished lid. Cautiously he opened the box; inside on velvet lay a crown exactly like those worn by the three kings before him; only it was adorned with a great white diamond.

"This gift we present to you as a crown of truce, a symbol of the great north kingdom to be worn and joined with the other three kingdoms of the four lands."

King Bareth, finally realizing the truth, reached into the box, lifted the crown from its resting place, and set it on his brow. As he did so, the great hall thundered to life with cheers and shouts of joy. A song began, and soon all in the hall were singing.

The kings return, the crowns are placed
Now our fears can be erased
The evil is gone
Good has won
Now our fears can be erased

The torn lands are again restored
Life can flourish here once more
The Living God has sent a soul
That speaks his message to us all
Life can flourish here once more

A dwarven king comes from the west
The legend lost with peace is blessed
The sightless king comes from the south
Speaking truth and peace of mouth
The bloodline king comes from the east
Once thought lost, he returns in peace
Mighty Bareth from the north
Joins the lost, all peace restored

The four lands once left in chaos
Will rise again amidst the grace
Of Living God and chosen kings
To be a symbol of great things
Dark and evil things will falter
As long as light and good remain

The kings return the crowns are placed
Now our fears can be erased
The torn lands are again restored
Life can flourish here once more
The kings return, the crowns are placed

As the song came to an end, Jace turned to his grandfather, who had been singing, "You know this song?"

"Yes, it is called the 'Song of Kings,' before the last speaker of the God of the Living was killed. He prophesied that which you heard in the song. Only the people here, in Bareth's kingdom, had heard the prophecy firsthand. They made this song so that hope would never be completely lost. Souvac did not want the prophecy spread throughout the four lands, but he also did not want Bareth's kingdom. As a solution, he simply had anyone killed that left Bareth's kingdom in order to stop the spread of the prophecy. It appears this tactic worked not only for the eighteen years of his reign but a hundred years later as well."

"How? Nobody has been regularly killing those from the north kingdom since Souvac's death. Have they?" asked Jace.

"But if you knew the prophecy, why didn't you tell others?" asked Graham.

"Quite honestly, it had been quite driven from my mind until this moment."

Just then King Bareth cut in, "I will accompany you on the morrow, with a grand company. Now let us feast and celebrate the fulfillment of prophecy and the peace of the four lands."

The gathered group cheered in celebration. The minstrels began playing more lively folk songs, and the people danced in merriment. Wine and food continued to be served as if it had no end.

"I thought you said there wasn't a meal prepared," stated McKray, looking at King Bareth.

"Truthfully, there is always plenty at my table to share for invited guests. Remember, I said, we did not have a meal set for your arrival. I did have a meal set for my court," responded the king, smiling broadly.

As the revelry continued, Graham had another question, "Who killed the last speaker?"

"We know it was one of the knights of Souvac," began Jace.

"Kell, to be precise," stated the Bard, cutting over Jace's words.

Jace turned sharply, "We left Amalia with the man that killed the last speaker?"

The rest of the group were also staring at the Bard, a look of horror in their eyes.

"No, we left her with her protector. Kell is a different man now. He has been forgiven by the God of the Living and called on to protect his speaker. The only danger Amalia is in, is…"

"Falling in love," said Mathias, cutting in on the Bard's words.

"But she was falling in love with you, Mathias," said Avalon.

"I am going to be king of the south, she is the speaker. My life will be spent reestablishing a kingdom in a fixed location. She must travel these four lands, maybe even the world, to reestablish a different kingdom. There is no way for our lives to be together."

"Wait, are you trying to tell me that she will fall in love with Kell?" asked Koyne.

"The truth is, I don't know, but often women fall in love with the man that makes them feel safe. Isn't that what happened between you and Avalon?" asked the Bard.

"Yeah, but we've known each other for ages," replied Koyne, looking at Avalon.

"And I fell in love with you because you have always made me feel safe. Even when we were children, I knew you would be there for me," stated Avalon.

Graham snickered, "I wish I had a pretty girl to make feel safe."

"All in good time, lad, all in good time," stated McKray, a distant look in his eyes. The rest of the group burst out laughing, much to his chagrin. "Ah shut up the lot of ya," he said before getting up and walking away.

Soon his booming voice could be heard as he spoke with King Bareth. The others continued their conversations until their meal was served. During the meal, King Bareth subtly looked at Koyne quite often, as if a secret conversation was taking place. Jace had noticed the looks and wondered what they meant.

That night word spread like wildfire throughout the kingdom of all that had transpired, the coming of the kings, the destruction of the knights of Souvac, and the return of a speaker of the God of the Living. Atop Bareth's castle, a great dragon sat smiling.

*****

Away in the east kingdom, Amalia sat in a hand-carved wooden chair. A lamp was burning on the table as she finished a verse of scripture that had come to her mind. The truth is revealed, a name is given, the God of the Living has returned. Amalia sat back in her chair and rubbed her eyes.

Kell watched her; he had not left her side since she claimed him as her protector. He thought back on his life, the mistakes, the evils he had been a part of. He thought of the last speaker, a middle-aged man with a kind face and warm smile. He thought of how he had secretly worked his way into the man's favor. He knew as well as anyone that that man was exactly who he claimed to be. He could remember the look in the speaker's eyes when Kell had stabbed him through the heart. It wasn't anger, shock, or even disbelief; it was pity. As he thought, he realized that was the beginning of the change that had been wrought in him.

Amalia's voice brought him out of his revelry. "What are you thinking about?"

"I was just remembering," he said. He knew he couldn't lie to her, but he was also unwilling to tell the truth yet.

"Kell, there is something that I need to know."

"Yes, my lady."

"You resisted the full power of the Evil One, how were you able to do that?"

"Over my life, I have seen much, what is most poignant is the nothing that is Kish. He fills your mind and heart with selfish desires that lead to complete emptiness. While in that small clearing, I found a spark of joy in my memories before Souvac. I held on to those, and after a time, I realized it was the God of the Living. I began praying to him constantly to find peace, forgiveness, and direction. I found it doesn't come all at once, but if we persevere, we will succeed. He knows us much better than we know ourselves, and in that moment, as I stood before Kish, I was granted another vision. It was you," he said, looking Amalia in the eyes.

Amalia looked away, a strange feeling entering her heart.

"What you feel is correct. Follow your feelings, child, they will lead you to your future," said a voice in her head that was not her own.

She looked back at Kell. "Why did you kill the last speaker of the God of the Living?"

"I hoped you wouldn't know about that," he said, looking at the floor. When she didn't respond, he continued, "His name was Boren, I was under orders from Souvac to kill him. I went to him under false pretense to get close to him and finally end his life. However, over time, I became his friend. When the day came for me to kill him, I wanted to run away from my oath, but I couldn't run away," he said, shaking his head. "I wasn't strong enough then. I was about to leave his home and let him live and return a failure to my king, but Boren stopped me. I was on my horse just starting to ride away when he stepped in front of me. I remember it as clearly as any memory I have ever had. He made me dismount from my horse and stand before him. He took ahold of my left wrist, his clear blue eyes looking into mine. He told me I had to do what was commanded of me. Therefore, I did what I was commanded to do. I drew my sword, stabbing him through the chest, killing an innocent man, my friend." The emotions so long held in check threatened to break free of Kell. His voice faltered, and tears began welling up in his eyes. He paused a moment to compose himself. Sniffing back his now slightly runny nose, he continued, "I believe Boren knew exactly who I was and why I had become his friend. He must have known where I would end up. I am sure he saw me here, in this lifetime, the protector of the new speaker."

A twinge of fear crept into Amalia's heart as Kell spoke, but as quickly as it came, it dissipated and was replaced with confidence. "I know you will be more loyal to this oath than you were to Souvac."

"I will, my lady," was his simple reply.

"What was Boren like? What did he do as speaker? Did he have a family?" came the flood of questions that Amalia had been holding back. "Please tell me all you can about him.

Kell smiled for the first time since Amalia had met him. The smile seemed to encompass his whole face. His eyes seemed to shine, and his mouth split in a broad opening, allowing his white teeth to be seen. "As I said, he was a good man, the best man I have ever known. He loved the outdoors. He could spend hours weeding his gardens. He loved wildlife but had strict feelings about no animals inside the cottage. I saw the way he treated people, always with kindness. He blessed people whenever they asked and held meetings to teach the people about the God of the Living." As he spoke, the regret Kell felt was painfully clear.

"What do you know about his family?"

"I did not know if he had a family. I sometimes saw him looking at a small painting he kept hidden in his room, but I did not know what it was for sure," he said, bowing his head in shame. Something about this last part of the conversation caused a change in Kell. "I wish to sleep now, please go to your quarters," he said a bit gruffly.

Amalia, recognizing his pain, stood and walked to her room. As soon as her door closed, Kell stood and left the cottage.

Two days later, with much fanfare, King Bareth arrived with his procession. The nine council members met him just outside the city; the inhabitants of the east kingdom crowded around them.

"Welcome, King Bareth, to what do we owe the great pleasure of your presence?" asked the oldest member of the council, Lord Darone.

"I come in the company of kings to witness the crowning of the heir to this kingdom's throne, and to make a peace accord for the four lands. A truly remarkable time is upon us," he said in reply.

"My dear King Bareth, I fear you may have come for naught. We, the council of this kingdom, have searched these many days, since hearing of an heir to the throne, for the original document signed by King Bowen and our own forebears," said Lord Darone, spreading his arm to indicate the other eight members of the council, "without success. I fear, without that document, we cannot in good conscience crown a king."

"Why not?" asked King Bareth tersely.

"My lord, the document itself states the way that we will know a true heir of King Bowen, as well as how the rule of law should continue," replied Lord Darone. The other council members nodded solemnly behind him.

At that point, Jace—who now looked so much like the Bard had before the curse was lifted from him that even the members of the quest had difficulty with his identity—stepped forward.

"Lord Darone, honorable lords of the council, I am the Bard of Souvac. You all know that I met with King Bowen the day he passed control of the kingdom into your forebear's hands."

They all nodded as there was no way to dispute this.

"Did you know that King Bowen went east and dwelt in the great seaport city of Tarshish?"

"We have heard rumors," said Lord Darone, answering for the others.

"Do you also know that there are two copies of the agreement made by the king and your forebears?"

"Yes, one was kept by King Bowen, the other was kept here at the castle, however neither document has been seen since Bowen left," replied Darone.

"King Bowen also kept the royal seal and a key that opens a secret vault in the castle that only the direct bloodline of the kings of this land knows about. Even Souvac himself knew nothing of this particular vault. Twenty years ago, as I sat with Bowen in his home and held his newborn son in my arms, he told me that he wanted to entrust into my care the document of which we have spoken. He would give his son the royal seal, the key to the secret vault, and the location of the vault." Reaching inside his tunic, he retrieved a leather tube from which he produced the document. "The other copy was secured in the secret vault. If it is brought forth, you will know the true king of this land, for only the heir of Bowen would have the knowledge and tools to retrieve it," said Jace loud enough for all to hear.

Graham stepped forward. "Lords of the council, I am Graham, son of Bowen, son of Tean, I have with me proof of my birthright. I present the royal seal," he said, holding up his right hand adorned with a magnificent golden ring.

Lord Darone approached him and looked at the ring. "This is indeed a royal seal, but how will we know if it was King Bowen's?"

"By comparing it to this," he said, holding up the second document that had been hidden in the castle vault.

Lord Darone gasped slightly as he looked at both documents and the seal. With no other alternative before him, he turned to the other eight council members. "Our king has returned."

At these words, King Bareth's musicians played a fanfare, and Jace yelled, "Long live Graham, king of the east!"

The shout was soon taken up by all gathered, and the growing procession continued to the castle. Graham climbed to the top of the steps with the companions from his journey, King Bareth, and his entourage. Here he turned to the gathered throngs of people.

"Will the nine members of the council join me?" he asked.

Lord Darone and the others pompously climbed the steps to stand beside Graham.

"You and your forebears have done a great service to the kingdom. I have a gift for you."

Kell on cue drove the same cart that was used by the knights of Souvac, from the side of the castle. Nine chests sat in the back.

"To each of you I present a chest of treasure, taken from the hoard that has sat at the feet of Souvac these hundred years, and I release you, with great thanks, from service to the kingdom."

A great cheer went up from the people gathered at the castle.

"But, my lord, won't you need councilors as you rule the kingdom? We would be honored to remain in your service," said Lord Darone.

"You are subjects of the king and are therefore always in my service, however you and the council have done enough for the kingdom in the absence of my father and myself. I will give others an opportunity to council with me on behalf of the kingdom. You are dismissed," he said with steely kindness.

The council members bowed, faces slightly flushed with anger as their power was taken from their hands before the whole of the kingdom. They walked down the stairs to the waiting carriage laden with treasure, trying their best to keep their composure. Kell climbed down, Lord Darone climbed aboard the driver's seat, and the other council members got in the back sitting on the chests. As they drove away, one of the citizens called out mockingly, "Don't spend all your gold in one place." A chorus of laughter from the citizens followed the departing council members.

"You'll want to keep your eye on those men, they could very easily cause you problems," stated King Bareth.

"Yes, they will be under royal scrutiny for a long time," replied Graham.

As the people calmed down, Graham spoke.

"Citizens of the Eastlands, for this kingdom is no longer that of Souvac, I ask you to revel in the new era that begins today. You see, with me, Bareth great king of the north, McKray dwarf king of the west, and Mathias heir of Garion king of the south, we are entering a new time of peace and prosperity. I know the grievances many of you bear. I have heard some of the complaints shared among you, so I ask that you choose from among you one man or woman of each industry that will be a spokesperson for you. Let them know your concerns, one week from today I will meet with them personally and together we will find the answers to your grievances." As he finished, the crowd cheered, a feeling of elation coursing through the gathered throng of people.

"Tonight I ask each inn and tavern owner to open your kitchens and ale barrels, feast and enjoy. Tomorrow I will compensate your costs," said Graham. Again, a cheer rose, and the phrase "Long live the king" was shouted repeatedly.

The gathered host slowly dispersed while Graham and his guests entered the castle. A host of servants tended to the king and his guests. The next several days were spent discussing boundaries for each kingdom, treaties of trade, monetary compensation, and other political subjects. On the seventh morning since Graham's return, King Bareth, satisfied with the outcomes of this diplomatic meeting, left.

Amalia and Kell, who were granted freedom and protection in all lands, began teaching the words of the God of the Living. Mathias, eager to put his own kingdom back together, left with Sterling for the Southlands. Jace, the now recognized Bard of Souvac, promised to meet up with them soon.

The original Bard of Souvac, who had aged tremendously over the last several days, watched every council that occurred that day between Graham and the chosen citizens. He could see in his mind Bowen meeting with the nine lords and passing the right to rule onto them.

"Things have come full circle," he said to no one in particular.

"You have completed everything you wanted to do, Grandfather. What's next?" asked Jace from where he stood behind his grandfather.

"I will leave the four lands. I need you to watch over Graham and the others. It is up to you to help protect them all. Tell my stories and make them your own," said the Bard, looking Jace in the eye.

Late that night, the Bard quietly crept to Jace's room and left a note on the table just inside the door. "I love you, my son, I am grateful for the chance I had to know you," he whispered. He continued through the empty halls to the south tower, and there at the bottom of the steps stood Graham.

"Your Highness," said the Bard.

"I knew you would leave this way, the same as you always have," said Graham.

"Whatever do you mean?" asked the Bard, a look of innocence on his aged face.

"I learned all I could about you from my father, and anyone else that has seen you come and go. When you leave, it is always to the south. I imagine it has something to do with your first home being in the south," replied Graham.

"You are much more resourceful than even I gave you credit for, young man. Yes, I always leave heading south so I can go home."

"Have you ever been back to your village?"

"No, I don't think I will ever go back, my journey is nearly at its end, just one more leg to go."

"You cannot go alone."

"Most of my life I have been alone, it is nothing new, however I will have company on this journey. He awaits me at the top of the tower."

"The top of the tower?" asked Graham. The Bard merely smiled in response. "It has been a pleasure, sir," said Graham, extending his hand.

"The pleasure has been mine." Taking Graham's hand in his, he said the last words any mortal heard from the Bard. "Be wise, young king, I go to my rest." Turning, he slowly ascended the steps to the top of the tower. There, a great dragon lay curled on the roof.

"Have you said your goodbyes?" asked the dragon in its deep voice.

"Yes, I'm ready," responded the Bard as he climbed into the saddle on the dragon's neck.

The dragon leaped into the air, spreading its magnificent wings. It flew south for a time before turning northwest toward the White Mountains. The Bard closed his eyes and fell asleep; as the minutes passed, his heart slowed. The dragon increased speed and soon was landing at Odin's hall. As he landed, the Bard's heart came to a stop.

Teran and two elves came to the dragon's side and gently lifted the Bard from the saddle. As they carried the Bard's body into the hall, the dragon shimmered and change. Soon Odin, God of the Living, stood where the dragon once was.

"We have placed him on a table in the gardens," said Teran.

"Bring her to the gardens," was all Odin said.

A short time later, the Bard was opening his eyes. He brought his hands to his face, rubbing away sleep. As he rubbed his eyes, he realized his hands were smooth. Pulling his hands away, he was surprised as he looked at his young hands. Then, looking to his right, his eyes filled with tears of joy as they met the face of his beloved wife.

*****

Jace woke the next morning and found the Bard's letter. After tearfully reading it, he went to find Graham, who was in a small private dining area.

"Graham, good morning, I fear I must be leaving today, but fear not, I will return from time to time."

"I was never afraid of you not returning. I only fear you will do so without announcing it," Graham said smiling. "Where will you go next?"

"I will travel the land, see how our friends are faring in their own endeavors. I hadn't planned to leave so soon, but I feel it is time to go."

"Jace, you have been my friend throughout this journey, you believed in me when others did not. You will always be welcome here. This is the second time I have said farewell to the Bard of Souvac," said Graham as he took Jace's hand.

Jace smiled. "I will see you when you least expect it."

"Here is a key to the door at the base of the southern tower, you are always welcome." Jace took the key and walked away. He arrived at Haven's inn several minutes later, where he found Koyne and Avalon.

"My friends, I have come to say farewell," he said.

"Bard, it has been a pleasure to know you and the rest of your family," said Koyne pointedly while raising an eyebrow. "Because of you, Avalon and I can be together. You gave us both freedom from our past. We will be married in six months when Amalia returns, it would be an honor to have you at the ceremony," he said, taking the Bard's hand in a strong handshake.

"The honor and pleasure are mine," replied the Bard.

Avalon came forward embraced him and kissed him on the cheek. "Don't be a stranger."

"I will see you again soon."

The new Bard of Souvac left then, heading south. He had something he needed to do for his grandfather. He drove a wagon that Graham had given him. It was laden with food, the chests his grandfather had given him, as well as the journals and stories of his past adventures. After many days, he arrived in the vale where his grandfather had lived; there were so few people living here now. He went to the home of his ancestors and found it empty. As he explored the dilapidated farmhouse, a man rode up on a horse. He wore bright-green breeches and a red shirt of high quality. His dark hair was long and well groomed, hanging to his shoulders. His deep brown eyes were full of suspicion. His hand rested on the handle of his short sword.

"Evening, stranger, are you looking to settle here?" the man called.

The Bard stepped through the doorway. "Yes, I am planning to settle here in the house of my ancestors."

"Well, if you want this place, you will have to buy it from me," he spoke with an air of arrogance. "My family bought this deed eighty years ago when the owners passed away," the man said. "I don't know that you will be able to afford it though," he continued as he looked at the Bard's travel-worn appearance. "You see, the kings have all returned, and this land is now very valuable as a resource to the kingdom."

"This house, the buildings, and the land appear to be in poor condition. Have you completely neglected it in your time as steward?" asked the Bard. "With it in this condition, it could be considered worthless, much like yourself."

"Now look here, sir, this farm has always looked this bad. The people we bought it from were old and useless, they are the ones that let it become what you see."

The Bard had to work to hold his anger in check at this point. "So your family has owned this for eighty years and have done nothing with it? I believe that makes you and your family useless."

The man paused controlling his own anger, his grip tightening on his sword handle. "As things are, I am willing to sell it at a fair price, take it or leave. I am done living in this lifeless hamlet."

"Is that so, and where is a fine young gentleman like yourself going?"

"I am moving to Green Tower, where Garion once dwelt as king. The word is the last remaining descendant of Garion has returned. He is in treaty with King Bareth of the north, a king who is returned to rule in Souvac, and a great dwarf king that is establishing a kingdom in the west."

"That is true, the king of the south that will dwell in Green Tower is Mathias, great-great-grandson of Garion," replied the Bard.

"How do you know that?" asked the man.

"It is easy, I traveled with him, for I am the Bard of Souvac," he declared.

Upon hearing this, the man's hand released the sword, and his mouth dropped slightly. "You are the Bard of Souvac?" he asked pointing slightly. "But I heard the knights were finally destroyed and the four lands were free of that curse."

"You heard true, but my life has not ended. I will always be," replied the Bard. He tossed a fair-sized pouch to the young man. "Here is gold enough for the farm, you will bring me the deed tomorrow."

The young man opened the pouch and peered inside, an involuntary gasp escaping his mouth. "I am a bit embarrassed, the cost for this ground is slightly greater than what you have provided," said the man, a glint of greed in his eye.

The Bard seemed to swell, growing in size. "I have given more than fair compensation for this farm, if you try to deceive me further, I will show you all my power and wrath."

The man shrank in fear, and his horse whinnied nervously. "Oh yes, it appears I had misjudged the weight of this purse, I shall return tomorrow with the deed."

"See that you do, and remember, it was because of me the knights of Souvac were destroyed," said the Bard loudly to the retreating man. Feeling confident that the man was sufficiently scared, he began cleaning his home and moving his possessions into the house. A few hours later, as the sun began to set, the Bard opened one of the many books he had carried with him from Bareth's kingdom.

Herein lies another tale from the Bard of Souvac.

They looked at me as if I had no business in their tavern. This was my first time sailing across the endless sea. The dark skin of the people here was disconcerting at first, but as I began talking and telling my story, these people began to change the way they treated me.

Epilogue

Lord Kish, the Evil One, had spent the last two weeks watching the actions of the Bard and his petty followers from the darkness of his underground lair. He sat in his obsidian throne, looking at the Oracle that hung on the grey stone wall in front of him. As he focused his attention on these miserable mortals, his interest was increasingly pulled to the hated speaker of the God of the living and her protector, Kell.

Kell, the traitor, who had been one of the wicked knights of Souvac, had resisted the command to kill his own sister's descendant, Avalon. Then just as he was about to kill the traitor, she, the speaker, had appeared wielding the cursed medallion of Odin, blinding him, the Evil One, with light, causing him to retreat to his dark lair. He had sworn then and there, in his wrath, to destroy them all.

This was the promise that the witch's son heard and, in an effort to endear himself to Kish, offered to fulfill. At first, Kish was ready to allow this revenge, but caution had stayed his approving word. Now, as he watched the Bard pass from his sight and the others continue their trivial lives, his dark thoughts reeled with excitement.

"Whelp," he called out. He had always called the witch's son this. Mostly, due to the fact that she had made the decision to have him without Kish's permission, thinking he would approve of her offspring.

The whelp came running into his master's presence. "You called, my lord?" He asked, dropping to his knee.

Kish seemed to swell in height and power his black cloak, hiding his features. "Of course, I did, you imbecile, that is why you came scurrying the way you did. I have made a decision. I want you to bring pain to the speaker," said Kish.

"I will go now, my lord."

"I did not tell you to go now. This must take time and planning. Jerec, that worthless mongrel utilized a very good way of hurting a person. He understood that physical pain ends too quickly. No, I want you to go for the heart, the soul. Currently, she possesses the medallion of my brother, Odin. As long as she holds it, I won't be able to touch her. I want you to study her, learn everything you can about her, and then we will destroy her and the traitor, Kell. She will build churches and gain followers for my brother. This, you will quietly oppose, but do not bring too much attention to your actions."

"But, lord, this could take years."

Kish turned his full attention to the whelp. "Did you just question my orders?" The question was dripping with venom. Kish began to swell with rage, ready to unleash his power on this worthless being.

"My lord, please forgive him. He is still young. He meant no disrespect. He will do anything you ask of him," said the witch, stepping from a dark shadow to place herself between her son and the wrath of her master.

"Very well. You have your mission, whelp, but I caution you, do not fail me," he said, anger and loathing flowing through this last statement.

With little urging from the witch, the whelp quickly departed. "Thank you, master. He will not fail you," stated the witch as she followed her son from Kish's chambers.

Why do I still put up with her? thought Kish as the witch stumbled away.

In the silence, he turned his attention back to the ever-changing images that danced across the surface of the water held in the Oracle hanging on the stone wall before him. He did not have the sight of his brother, Odin; he could not see into the hearts and minds of the beings of this world. He had stolen this relic from the ancient elves before destroying them completely. It allowed him to focus on anyone or anything in the world. That is how he knew the Bard had died, for he passed from Kish's sight.

Focusing, he quickly found the false Bard of Souvac sleeping in a cottage in the south kingdom, having fallen asleep reading his grandfather's stories. Suddenly, a bright light filled the cavern, chasing away every shadow and burning Kish's thoughts. Turning his thoughts far from the Bard, he yelled in anger. "Ahh, I will see you once again chased from these lands brother!"

*****

"Why does he call me whelp?"

"Do not worry, Coran, he believes all mortal beings are below him. It is possible to win his approval, and you will do just that. When you succeed in the mission he gave you," replied the witch.

Coran nodded his head. "How do I succeed in this thing he has asked?"

"My dear boy, it is easy." The witch's eyes changed as if she were remembering a far distant past, a look of pain creasing her pale brow. Taking a deep breath, she continued speaking as her body began to tremble. "You learn everything you can about her, get her to trust you completely, and finally destroy her with that trust," these last words were said through gritted teeth as if they were painful to utter.

"Where do I begin?"

"With the people that know her best, her family. They live in the west kingdom."

"Before I go to the west, I must create distress in the east kingdom to the blood of the man that destroyed my father."

"My dear son, you make me so proud."

About the Author

Tony Bishop was born in Payson, Utah. He grew up working on a farm and as a tree trimmer. After spending two years in Japan, he returned to Payson where he met his wife. They have been married for twenty years.

Tony has worked as a licensed massage therapist and as a physical therapist assistant over the last several years. In these roles he has met many people who have inspired him to seek his life's goals.

One of these goals has been to share the stories that have always been in his head and in his heart. Tony first gained a love of writing in the fourth grade. This has continued throughout his life, and now he shares with the world his first novel *The Bard of Souvac*. Please enjoy the adventure.

CPSIA information can be obtained
at www.ICGtesting.com
Printed in the USA
JSHW030928120521
14618JS00001B/23

9 781646 702978